The Mist Will Lift

by

Ruth Sauder

THE MIST WILL LIFT

Library of Congress Number: 2001130205
International Standard Book Number: 1-930353-27-8

Printed 2001 by
Masthof Press
219 Mill Road
Morgantown, PA 19543-9701

Preface

Here is the girl's story you were requesting. I had started writing it before *Hidden Man of the Heart* and *Not Worthy To Be Compared* (sequel) were published in 2000, but I just could not finish it.

After the first two books were published, I began receiving requests for a girl's story and I returned to finishing this manuscript. In fact, my niece after reading it said that it was better than the first two books.

Again, this story is entirely fictitious. As long as one person is spiritually strengthened by reading *The Mist Will Lift*, this book will be worth the effort. I so much enjoy the people who have contacted me as a result of the first books. I feel unworthy of their praise especially when I think that these three books almost did not get published.

- Ruth Sauder
January 2001

Chapter One

Humming to herself, sixteen-year-old Clara got out the cookbook and propped her arms on the countertop. Leaning over the book as she scanned recipes, she said to herself, "No, we don't have coconut." She turned another few pages and glanced at a recipe thinking, *These sound like good cookies*, but she decided they were too much bother. She wanted to bake them now, not wait till they chilled overnight.

Then her eyes caught sight of Aunt Ada Arlene's chocolate cookie recipe that was pasted in the book. She would try those. She knew there was a pack of chocolate chips in the pantry.

She got out the mixing bowl and measured the butter. As she hurried to and fro from the pantry to the kitchen, Clara saw that Mom was glancing up from the sewing machine where she was working on the mending pile. It seemed every time Clara looked, Mother was watching her.

Mother turned back to her mending, but Clara noticed she didn't continue sewing. She stared out the window as if deeply thinking.

As Clara whirled the egg beater, she was thinking of the time they were at the quilting at Aunt Ada Arlene's house and the good cookies they had. She had asked for the recipe, which cousin Etta Grace found for her, and Clara copied it.

When Clara lifted the egg beater out of the bowl, she almost jumped when she saw Mother standing at the other side of the table. Clara hadn't heard her come over from the sewing machine.

"I'm making Ada Arlene's chocolate chip cookies," Clara said, as she mixed in the sugar.

Mother watched in silence, then slowly, barely above a whisper, she said, "Clara, you have to comb your hair down."

Clara, who was licking her finger, looked up surprised.

"We have told you before that you cannot wave your hair like that."

"Wave my hair?" Clara repeated questioningly. "Cousin Etta Grace and Lucinda wouldn't even call these waves. Suppose I'd comb my hair like Beth Ann?"

"Yes, I've noticed that ever since Etta Grace and Lucinda were here the other weekend, you are getting more careless with your hair," Mother agreed. Clara tried to keep a straight face when Mother referred to her "getting careless" with her hair. The truth was, since her cousins were here and she saw how much time they spent setting their hair, Clara had paid a little more attention to her hair and helped the waves form better.

"Did you hear me?" Mother reminded her. "Go and comb your hair in place."

"Oh, you mean now?" Clara asked as she wiped her hands with the dishrag. She went over to the washbowl, pulled out a few bobby pins, ran the comb through her hair, and slipped the bobby pins back in. "That looks better," Mother said, praising her.

Clara continued mixing the dough, and then she started baking the cookies. Her hands worked mechanically, but her thoughts wandered, pondering things she often wondered about.

Her cousins on Dad's side, the Brubakers, were quite a contrast to the Reiffs on Mother's side.

Whenever Clara questioned her mother as to why she can't have so and so when her brothers' and sisters' children may, Mother never said, because you know Dad doesn't like it, or it is against the church rules. In fact, Dad hardly ever even mentioned anything about them disobeying. He seemed not to notice. Why was Mother so different from her family? Mother always responded with a reference to a certain verse in the Bible in I Peter 3, where it says, "whose adorning let it not be that outward adorning of plaiting hair, and of wearing of gold, or of putting on of apparel; but let it be the hidden man of the heart, in that which is not corruptible, even the ornament of a meek and quiet spirit, which is in the sight of God of great price."

Clara tried to picture Mother as a young girl, comparing her to her sisters, Clara's aunts, but she shook her head. Dad's family, who mostly lived in this same community, seemed to match so well to Mother. And Alice and Laura, the cousins nearest Clara's age on Father's side, made her feel as if she belonged to them. She had no such desire to play with her hair when she compared herself with the Brubaker cousins. But there were only a few near her age. Most of the Brubaker cousins near her age were boys. But then, Dad's family wasn't as large as Mother's family either.

As Clara turned out another pan of cookies, she shifted her gaze over in the direction of the sewing machine. Mother had a pair of Dad's overalls laid before her. In her hand, she held material from which to cut out a patch to mend the overalls, but her hands were idle. She was staring at the utility cart that stood across the kitchen from the sewing machine and where the daily mail landed on the first shelf. The second shelf held the Bible and a few hymn books, the ones used in church and at singings.

The bottom shelf was empty now, as that was where the school lunch kettles went after her four sisters cleaned them out after school. In the morning, after the lunches were packed, they were also placed there.

When her sisters—Norma, Mildred, Sylvia, and Loretta—were in school, Clara and her mother were often alone in the house between meal times. This was the first year twenty-year-old Cleon, her only brother, was regularly at home during the day. He had worked as a hired boy for a few years and also helped for a few years at the butcher shop where Dad also worked part time, since their small farm didn't provide enough labor to keep someone busy full time. Now, since Dad was having back trouble, Cleon was helping Dad with the farming, and more people were bringing their horses for Cleon to shoe. For a few years, Cleon had been shoeing his own horse, and also started shoeing horses for the neighbors. But, now, it wasn't just for neighbors anymore. In fact, he considered setting a few days aside as horse-shoeing days, but then it would likely be on

3

one of those days that the hay was ready to bale. He also started fixing bicycles for people. Lately he bought some at an auction and fixed them up to sell.

Clara wondered if Cleon was getting ready to take over the farm. Then she thought of Rachel Leinbach, the tall, dark-complected girl who was so neat that you could almost call her charming. Cleon had been dating her for more than a year already. She was friendly, but Clara sensed that Mother didn't seem so happy about the pains she went to in making herself so neat. Clara's thoughts continued to wander. *Would Cleon take over the farm some day? Where would we go then? Would they build a house? Wasn't it about time to start?*

As Clara took the last pan of cookies out of the oven, she thought of her older sister, Virginia, who was married. She was ten years older than Clara, so she didn't seem so much like a sister. Clara remembered when Caleb Hoover started coming to their home on Sunday evenings to see Virginia, who was quiet like Dad. (Actually, Caleb was even quieter than Virginia.) When the younger ones went into the parlor to visit with them, Caleb hardly ever spoke to them, but he seemed to enjoy listening. For as little as Virginia spoke to Caleb, Clara was surprised he kept on coming. She remembered she used to ask Mother what Caleb wanted and Mother would say, "To visit with Virginia." However, Clara never did hear much visiting.

Then came the day when Caleb and Virginia were married and moved fourteen miles away to the edge of the settlement. Thus, it was always an event when she came home. Virginia seemed a little more talkative now than when she lived at home. Maybe she got a little homesick since Caleb didn't say much, and during the first years they had no children. A lump came to her throat as Clara remembered how Caleb was ordained as minister before they were married two years, and the struggle he had standing before the congregation and speaking.

It seemed there had to be a mistake somewhere. But with time, Caleb had won the victory in the struggle. He was now able to stand and let the Spirit bring forth a touching sermon, although it still appeared to take every effort to rise and face the congregation. Maybe

4

that was why the sermons seemed so valuable, knowing the effort he put into each one.

At times, Clara had heard Mother and Father talking, so she knew Caleb was seeing a mental health physician when he was first ordained. Clara remembered the times she was in Virginia and Caleb's home helping with the work. She would see Caleb enter his bedroom with the Bible, close the door, and hours later he would come out and go about his daily work. They had a fifteen-year-old boy helping with the farm work, in order to give Caleb time for his church duties.

Clara's heart filled with joy as she remembered how a son, Paul Henry, was born to Caleb and Virginia. His birth seemed to brighten their home.

Clara saw her mother was still in deep thought. She was tempted to question her, but since the forenoon was far spent, she knew she should be cleaning the upstairs before dinner. Sometime, when they had time, while working together, Clara would ask Mother some things, or what she was thinking.

Chapter Two

There was a chill in the air, and the breeze chased the fallen leaves which had been raked the other day. It was typical November weather. Clara pinned up the last of her hair and looked out the window at the barren cornfields. Only stubbles remained where high stalks had been hiding all the scenery. Now she could see over the neighborhood again. For a moment, she looked at the buildings in the distance, across the meadow at the edge of neighbor Irvin's fields. The gray stone house was well-worn with years, with smaller buildings scattered around. The sight of the house almost dampened some of the strength and life that flowed through her ambitious sixteen-year-old body.

Mother came up from the cellar carrying a bowl of pears and, raising her eyebrows in surprise, asked, "Didn't you leave yet?"

"I'm leaving now," Clara replied as she slipped on her wraps. "But shouldn't I help you with the pears?"

"No. What I don't get done today can wait till tomorrow. Tell Beckie you can't help her tomorrow, but maybe Friday or Saturday," Mother replied.

Coming out the door and feeling the fresh autumn air boosted Clara's energy, and she briskly walked out the field lane across the meadow and through Irvin's field. This was the same path that Frankie's children had come down last evening when Mosie and Annie had come to bring a note asking if Clara could come help clean house tomorrow.

It was a familiar message over the years. Clara enjoyed cleaning house at home, helping Mother, but at Frankie's, she never knew if she would get the room done that day.

6

Last week she had gone over with plans to clean one of the boys' bedrooms. She got no further than gathering up and shaking out the rugs. Then she helped Lukie with his clothes. Next she washed out some diapers, since washday had been postponed for a day. Finally an injured rooster had to be butchered. Since the water was hot anyway, they decided to butcher two more roosters. By then Frankie had to go to the feed mill and Mother Beckie went along to pick up some much needed groceries at the store. Clara stayed to babysit Reubie, Katie, and Mandie. Lukie went along to the store.

Clara could still see Mother Beckie hurrying around, searching for her handbag, getting Lukie ready and quickly tending Mandie. Before she left, Beckie said to Clara, "If you get a chance, sweep the boys' green room out good, and get the spider webs in the corner. Shake out the bureau scarves, and put the clothing in the drawers. If you don't get it all done, it's all right. Take care of the children first."

Clara smiled to herself as she mused over the fact that Beckie and Frankie's children's names all ended with "ie." One day Clara saw "Amanda" written on a prescription and realized it was for baby Mandie, who was taken to the doctor for a cold she had had for over a week.

Clara wondered if Mandie would some day grow up to be Amanda. But then she thought of the older boys. Sammie, the oldest, was taller than his parents—almost six feet tall—but his mother still called him Sammie. Mother was often heard saying, "Sammie will fix it when he comes home." Whenever something didn't work, she trustingly would say, "Maybe Sammie can fix it."

Clara hardly got to see Sammie much anymore, since Sammie had recently begun working at Busy Bear's Produce greenhouse and orchard. He was always gone early in the morning and seldom was back by suppertime. Clara suspected he ate supper when he came home, because every time Clara helped over suppertime, Beckie kept the leftovers saying, "Sammie will be hungry when he gets home."

The people had feared that the Snyder boys wouldn't get much of a chance to learn management, since Frankie's work didn't always prosper. But Clara's parents said things were better since the children could work. One building on the farm was a chicken house where there were a good number of chickens. They sold the eggs to the huckster, but Clara found out that a few times some of the eggs were rejected. With feed strewn around and unbedded nests, one could see the school children tended the chickens with little supervision.

And then there were the calves tied here and there in the barn, with hay bales scattered around that the calves had pulled apart.

It wasn't much of a farm with only the two fields and a pasture where the horse was staked in, since the fence needed repair. But Frankie had many sick people to see. He seldom missed seeing one, and Beckie often went along. If she didn't go along, she sent food.

During the months from January until mid-April, Frankie helped his brother file people's income taxes. If only figures could repair buildings and fences, the Snyder farm would be a different scene.

Johnnie, the boy next to Sammie, was out of school, too. He wasn't as tall as Sammie, but it was obvious that he desired to be something more than one of Frankie Snyder's boys.

So busy were her thoughts that Clara hardly noticed she had arrived at Frankie's place and she was startled out of her thoughts when Beckie greeted her with, "It's so nice today. I'm afraid we'll soon be getting the November rains, so I thought we could rake the yard today instead of cleaning house." Clara looked up to see Beckie coming out of the washhouse.

"Is it all right with you?" Beckie asked.

"A-h yes, it's quite all right," Clara said, coming to her senses, asking, "Where is the rake?"

"It should be in the wood shed or by the back porch," Beckie added.

Clara's search in both places proved fruitless. Reubie, who was playing near the woodpile, asked in his childish inquisitive way, "What are you looking for?"

"Oh, the rake, to rake the yard," she answered, wondering why she wasted her breath to tell him. But he had sounded so concerned.

Reubie got up and brushed his hands on his pant legs and said, "Over here it is." Clara followed him around the house when he stopped suddenly by the tree. As she looked around, Reubie pointed under the washline where the rake was standing. Clara looked at it and then at Reubie.

Reubie said, "The bed sheets were hanging on the ground, so Mom put the rake under the line to hold them up. But it didn't help much."

Clara got the rake and went to the corner of the yard where she began raking in earnest, her thoughts wandering. After awhile, without realizing it, she stopped raking. Resting her arms on the rake, she stared ahead, thinking to herself. *If Johnnie desired to do better than his parents, why didn't he clean up the place, put things in order, and tighten up the washline for his mother? Why didn't he have the bicycles, rakes, and things in their places?*

Glancing up toward the fence in the yard, Clara saw, in disarray, a bicycle, a pail, a broken lawnmower, and two baskets. She couldn't see what was beyond that. There would be many better ways Johnnie could show his maturity than by the worldly way he combed his hair and by wearing such a small hat with the sides turned up.

Clara heard a truck go by and, looking up, she saw it was Neffs' truck. The Neffs were big cash croppers who lived along the other road. Johnnie worked for them and she saw him riding in the truck, which was loaded with straw. Of course, Johnnie had no hat on now. It seemed Sammie could care more about his clothes and improve his looks by being neater, too. His shirt was often a little loose and his pants not freshly pressed.

Then, there was Bennie. He was in his last year of school. It was hard to know what his ideas of life were. He was still honest and rather innocent and child-like. It seemed he didn't realize he was growing up. Eleven-year-old Lucy, the oldest girl, was very timid. She smiled easily, but spared her words and seemed so tender in contrast to Mother Beckie's outspoken nature.

Clara was so busy raking she was surprised when Beckie called, "Clara." Throwing her rake down and heading for the house, she supposed Beckie wanted her to make dinner.

9

Reaching the house, she thought, *Oh, no, the horse is hitched. I guess they're going away and I'm to babysit.*

Beckie met her at the porch. She was pulling on her wraps, saying, "Frankie wants to go to town, so I guess I will go along and drop in at Alvin and Lena's to see how she is coming along. Since I thought you might be ready for a rest, you can make dinner and watch the children." Beckie smiled encouragingly at the break she was giving Clara, not knowing that Clara would have taken great satisfaction in finishing the raking before taking a break.

After Clara had the kitchen straightened up and dinner on the stove, she went into the living room to tidy things up. She was preparing to clean house in case the children didn't demand her attention and Frankies returned late. Clara straightened up the bookcase and, finding some unfolded wash on a chair, decided she would fold that. When she put the wash in the children's rooms, she found a pair of muddy shoes that needed to be cleaned. In the dresser where the rags and handkerchiefs were kept, all the drawers were partly opened, with Mandie's and Katie's clothing hanging out. Hearing Mandie cry, Clara found her in the kitchen, wrapped in a blanket, under a chair. By now it was high time to make dinner for the hungry children.

That evening as Clara was walking home, she felt a bit weary. She had hoped to do a little cleaning in the afternoon, but when Frankies came home, they just tossed their wraps in the living room. Also, the groceries they had bought were strewn over the countertop, the chair, and floor. The supper dishes were still in the sink where the children had piled them. As Clara prepared to wash the dishes, Beckie said they could do it. Instead, she gave Clara Mosie's Sunday shirt that had a button missing and one of Annie's dresses, which needed a seam sewn. Two-year-old Katie broke a dish as she was putting it in the sink. Beckie was looking for an address and asked Clara to put the Sunday wash, which was on the banister and stairs, upstairs in the wardrobe in the hall. Hanging the shirts on hangers, Clara noticed that they had not been ironed. No wonder Sammie's clothing never looked neat.

Later in the afternoon, Clara had been assigned to rake leaves again. When she came into the kitchen, the schoolchildren were home and the kitchen was enough to dampen anyone's ambition.

Lucie was reading the mail; Katie and Reubie were cutting up newspapers; Lukie was crying; and Mandie had discovered some of the lunches on the wood box and was throwing everything on the floor. Ah well, Clara was going home.

Chapter Three

Clara got ready to go to bed, but then walked over to the dresser and looked in the mirror and sighed. The girl who looked back at her had a rosy complexion and arms that had strength and ambition. Her hair was not combed as carefully as it had been this morning.

Was it just this morning that she had been upset before she left for Frankies? It had been a long day. Momentarily she went over the conversation between her and Mother about how she combed her hair. She didn't think it was much different than usual, but Mom had ordered her to re-comb it, and she had talked back. She loved Mother and felt bad that it had happened, but her hair didn't look worse than other girls' hair did. She put her hand up and touched her medium brown hair. Pulling out her hairpins, she let her hair down and combed it. She turned it up the way it formed naturally. The girl in the mirror who smiled back at her looked so becoming. *Why do I have hair that waves if I may not set the waves?* she thought. *Mother must know this looks nicer.*

It had been a bad start to the day, and she had found herself short-tempered all day. It didn't make matters better when they made noodles at Frankies and the children wanted to help so much. Beckie had intended to help until she remembered she needed to check if the chickens had enough feed. Clara guessed the schoolchildren didn't get it done before they left.

And then she had to fix a latch and Clara gathered that Beckie had also put fresh straw in the nests. In the afternoon Beckie was helping Frankie put plastic on some of the windows in the chicken house, and Clara had a rough time keeping the children entertained.

Lukie and Katie were picking on each other and all the noise woke up Mandie.

When Clara came home, fourteen-year-old Norma was baking cookies for lunches. She was stirring up a few different kinds, and the worktable was cluttered. The wash Mildred had brought in was lying all around. Clara, preparing to make supper, scolded Norma and Mildred. Mother, who was nearby sewing, reminded her that if she was a little kinder and helped her sisters more, things would go better.

Once again, Clara got a desire to work elsewhere. There were too many girls in the kitchen, but she knew it was a vain thought as long as Norma was still in school. At least Mom allowed her to have her own room, even though it was a small room. She used to share a bed with Norma.

The other three sisters shared a room that used to have a double and a single bed, but now Clara used the single bed in the small room. Mildred and Norma were in one room, while Loretta and Sylvia shared the other room.

To forget about her difficult day, Clara turned her thoughts to the future. Tomorrow she would be allowed to sew her new dress. Oh yes, and she had to make dinner for the men since Mother was going to a quilting with her cousins—a rare occurrence.

In a few weeks it would be January. Her heart rejoiced, knowing that February was a short month, and in March she would be seventeen—old enough to join the young folks. Finally, she would belong to a group. These years between being a school girl and too young to join the young folks were difficult years. Yet, Clara remembered that Mother had warned her that her problems might increase when she gets to this age. How could they? It sounded like the girls who were old enough to be with the young folks were having fun. Her cousin Alice, who was close to her, and Alice's friend Elsie had been close friends during most of their school years.

Tomorrow she would try to be more obedient in combing her hair. Maybe things would go better.

At first, the house seemed strangely quiet as Clara started sewing, her mind once again wandering. In the afternoon, Dad sat at his desk going over his accounts, getting ready to file income tax for the end of the year. Now and then, he opened a drawer or got a book from the filing cabinet. Other than that, the house was silent except for the whir of the sewing machine. As she sewed, Clara was deep in her daydreams, hardly aware that she wasn't alone in the house. She jumped when Dad started talking to her. Dad grinned when he saw how startled she was. He asked her if Mother knew she was making a dress, and she assured him that Mother had assigned her this job. He then wondered if she was using the usual decent pattern. She gasped. "Of course, Father. Mom helped me cut it out the other day."

Clara was slightly insulted that Dad was starting to mistrust her. *Mom must have been telling him how she disliked the way I combed my hair*, Clara thought as she continued sewing. She wasn't sure what to expect as Dad sat nearby with the *Budget* on his lap. He apparently wasn't reading it because he asked her if she had any ideas as to where she would want to work when she was able to work away from home more.

Looking amused, he asked, "Do you want to continue helping other families here and there, instead of just working at Frankies?" He seemed to be saying that some families were easier to work for.

Clara took a deep breath and stared ahead. Finally, she said, "To tell the truth, I haven't really been thinking much about where I'd work. Some of my cousins and friends work at Shady Lane Greenhouse, and it sounds interesting, but still I'm not overly excited about working with plants. Maybe I can learn though. I was hoping I wouldn't always have to work for Frankies," Clara finished, rather forcefully. She took the skirt of the new dress on her lap and started pinning in the pleats, the measuring tape at her side. Dad remained silent. As an afterthought, Clara said, "I've always been rather interested in Uncle Benjamin's bulk food store. The few times I was there, I helped with weighing and labeling. It's something I enjoy and Aunt Hettie seems to be a kind, motherly woman, even if she has mostly boys working for her who would rather play in the soil than get their hands in flour and sugar. They also seem to have an aversion to dried fruits like prunes, Hettie says." Clara finished with a chuckle.

14

Then she added, "But it's quite a distance over there." While Clara was measuring the waist, taking pins out and redoing them, she was still thinking of Uncle Benjamin and Aunt Hettie who lived in the next district in a place they were renting. Hopefully, some day their boys would be a good help. But about six years ago Benjamin was in an accident when the horses ran off. As a result, he was not as strong as he had been, and he was slightly crippled. In time, they were offered a small place near her brother's where they opened the bulk food store—now a thriving business. Since most of their children were boys, they found working in the store almost as bad as doing dishes—except they did like to try a sample while they weighed the food.

A smile played on Clara's lips as she remembered the few times she was there and watched the boys weighing things. They made it so amusing. At times, Uncle Benjamin called them down if things were getting out of control. Hettie was a woman who kept things sunny. Little Katherine, arriving after so many boys, was almost to be pitied, but she was full of pep and got along well with the boys.

Dad interrupted Clara's thoughts, asking, "What are you thinking that caused you to smile to yourself?"

"Oh, I was just thinking of Ben's energetic family with all those boys, but Hettie turns everything to sunshine. And Katherine— she'll have to learn to stand her ground against all those teasing brothers."

Dad tapped his shoes on the linoleum floor. What was he thinking?

Clearing his throat, he rubbed his fingers over the chair arm and, with uncertainty, said, "So you find it hard to comb your hair as decently as we expect of you?" Clara felt her cheeks get warm. She hated it that her parents thought she was disobedient. She just wanted to be like the other young girls. Many thoughts raced through her mind and her throat felt dry. Dad hardly ever talked of such matters. Clara got up from her chair, got a fresh drink of water, and sat down on the rocker. Suddenly she felt very tired. Dad was patiently waiting.

Finally, Clara spoke saying, "I don't think I comb my hair any differently than most of the girls my age do, and certainly not the way my cousins do!"

"**All** your cousins?" Dad answered kindly.

"For sure the Reiff cousins," Clara continued in a small voice. The clock seemed to tick loudly in the silence of the kitchen. Clara felt bad; she didn't mean to be wild or disobedient to her parents. She felt tears pressing. Dad didn't look stern; he looked kind.

Finally, with all the strength she could muster, Clara spoke without looking up. "I often wondered why Mother is so different in her ways than her sisters are. I have never heard you talking to her about that. You don't seem to think I wave my hair too much." Clara held her breath. *Had she actually finally said what she had wondered about so long?* She was almost shivering as she looked up to see if Dad was angry at her. He had his head bowed down and was cleaning his fingernails. Did she see a tear glisten?

Very kindly he answered slowly, "I guess Mother doesn't want her daughters to learn what she had to learn." Looking up, he saw that Clara was listening intently—waiting, wondering.

Dad wiped his nose; then he said, "This is between me and you. I only share it with you because it might help you see your mother's reason for her beliefs. She means well. You are growing up on a different level than your cousins on Mother's side of the family. And likely you wonder if Mother was always so modest, or if I'm the one giving her strict orders."

Clara drank in every word. She hoped Dad would talk faster. There was a pause and then, as if trying to collect his thoughts, he spoke with a catch in his voice.

"When I was about twenty years old, I was working for Abe Shirk. When Abe and his wife had a baby, they hired a girl to help. Abe's wife didn't recover very quickly, so the hired girl stayed longer. All I knew about this girl was that her name was Etta Louise Reiff, a distant niece of Abe's wife. She seemed young, but she was just starting to go with the young folks. She wore her hair and dressed fashionably. She wasn't loud or forward like many others were. I really didn't bother about her, but she was kind and the children liked her.

One time I stayed for the weekend and she needed a way to the singing. She asked if she could ride with me. When I told her the buggy wasn't washed, she asked if I wasn't going. I said I was and if it was good enough for her, she could ride along.

"I still remember the charming way she came out the walk as I wondered what she would think about my old dirty buggy. A spoke I had replaced in the wheel had never been painted, and the inside of the buggy wasn't cleaned recently either. Seeing the tools I had forgotten to get out after helping a neighbor dismantle a shed the week before, I quickly took them out. I didn't bother myself about her as we drove in silence until she seemed awed by something that got her attention. Two frisky goats were frolicking around and there were chickens leisurely stirring in the dirt, looking for food. Our neighbors had a big chicken house with the chickens in cages, and I was thinking about how much freedom these other chickens had. I still didn't know what had gotten her attention until she mentioned the yard on the other side of the road. There was an array of beautiful flower beds throughout the yard. These beds and the shrubbery were raked and mulched. I, too, thought it was a picture of beauty for those passing by.

"I also knew that the woman who lived there was so obsessed with keeping things tidy that her husband couldn't relax when he came in, and the children were easily upset. I had once worked there off and on, and I learned to wipe cobwebs from my head before I went in the house. I, also, had to set my shoes on paper on Saturday evening when I came in. I didn't intend to tell all this to the girl, yet I thought maybe I should. Since she was so young, I didn't waste my breath.

"When Abe and his wife no longer needed Etta Louise, she went out of my life, but I didn't go out of her life. I had no idea she was admiring me, and she was somewhat insulted that I was such a goodie goodie, too stuck up to associate with people.

"Etta discussed all this with a friend who was kind enough to be honest without being rude. She reminded Etta that she knew me well enough to know that I was not stuck up or proud, but that likely I wasn't looking for a companion dressed so fashionably. This same friend then asked Etta Louise if she wasn't looking for a friend who had a sparkling, decorated buggy and who wore a small hat on top of his hair. She told Etta Louise that if she was looking for a common boy, she'd have to live in such a way that the common ones would notice her.

"Well, it was the beginning of a battle for Mom. She started searching the Scriptures and found many clues. Slowly she started changing her dress and style. She joined church, but her family was alarmed and thought she was going too deep. In spite of a few good friends who respected and understood her, she at times was a little confused, and it was disturbing to her mind. She went through a great deal of turmoil. Her home life was confusing, but she found she enjoyed being with the young folks.

"She was better accepted now and found herself with a new circle of friends. She enjoyed these new friends more, and I was no longer her priority. In fact, a boy from her district showed an interest in her.

"Then one day, some out-of-state visitors came to our community. A few of us guys took them down country the next day to visit, and some of the young folks traveled along with us throughout the day.

"At the place where we ate supper, we had an enjoyable time as a small group gathered together. After visiting awhile, we walked a way off from the buildings down to the waterfalls in the woods. With a few of us lingering at the falls watching a twig being tossed about, the others started walking back to the buildings. One of the girls, whom I had noticed before, was still leaning on the rail fence, voicing her thoughts. 'It's on a rocky course. It almost went with the stream, but it was guided aside.' She watched as the water eventually tossed the twig to a safe place, avoiding the main stream over the falls.

"I looked at the girl a moment, but she didn't notice me. She seemed to be in deep thought as we started walking away. She looked back a few times and, in doing so, she stumbled over a tree root. I grabbed her and kept her from falling, but she was embarrassed. By now, the others were further ahead. I asked her if I should know her, since something about her smile looked familiar. Looking at me for a moment, she said, 'I'm Etta Louise.'

18

"I doubted her and said, 'Etta Louise? Not the one who worked for Abe Shirk's?'

"She assured me by saying, 'Yes that was me.'

"Looking at her questionably, I said, 'You were also led from going along with the current stream?'

"She said it had been worth it, but it was a battle. 'The currents of the water tugged and pulled. It kept trying to wash me along. I was watching that twig to see if it would get away and not be washed along. If we take our stand, the current won't wash us along; it's when we start gliding.'

"I couldn't see any likeness to Etta Louise except when she smiled. I asked her if she had a way to go home and was told she had walked across the fields. I then asked her if I could give her a ride home. Looking a bit flustered, she said, 'It doesn't matter.' By the time we got home, I felt as if I knew her better. I asked her if she would be interested in getting better acquainted. She told me it was my choice.

"Quite a while later, I discovered I was the beginning of her struggle. She had found enough peace following her struggles that she forgot the one who had persuaded her. She was startled at how God reached down and directed us together. And she knew if she had not changed her views, I wouldn't have noticed her. That is why she is so concerned that her daughters live so that only decent boys will notice them and be interested in them."

Clara had been drinking in the words. Then she meekly asked, "Is that why she never says we can't dress or wear our hair the way the church doesn't allow?"

It took Dad a few moments to catch up with her thoughts.

He nodded. "Yes, it goes deeper than the church *Ordnung*, and she has proved that she didn't change her life in order to win a partner, which was an accusation of her family. So, Mother means well. She is not just strict and demanding. At times I've felt that we could give things a better chance since most all young people go through a time when they want to follow the fashions until they mature. Mother says the longer the seed is growing, the deeper the roots, so respect your mother. She is a good mother."

Dad got up, pulled on his wraps, and went outside, but Clara lost interest in sewing her dress. She found herself just staring ahead, trying to recall what Dad had just said. She wished it had been written down so she could read it again, because she couldn't remember everything.

She was thinking about it so much that a few times that evening she almost started talking about the conversation she had with Dad.

The next day, Clara awoke at three o'clock in the morning, feeling very wide awake. What was bothering her? Was it only a dream? She thought she was at home and Sammie had come to pick her up to go to a singing. He had been standing beside the buggy waiting. The buggy was in much need of being washed, and one light was dangling. Sammie's clothes were in their usual shape. From the way his pants hung, it looked like he had lost weight. Either there were no creases pressed or they had faded already. She wondered if that really was his Sunday hat.

Her own shoes were freshly polished, and as she stepped down on the porch step, her royal blue dress sparkled as the pleats shifted. When she closed the storm door, she saw her reflection, the freshly combed pair patted in place. Her bonnet didn't hide all the waves. Her eyes sparkled with pleasure as she was looking forward to the evening events. She was a little amused, as she never went away with Sammie. And his team didn't look as haggard as it did in her dream. She was almost embarrassed by the reflection she had seen of herself in her dream. Well, at least it was just a dream.

These thoughts kept her awake until it was time to get up.

Chapter Four

The mild breeze that floated in the window where Clara had propped it open surely didn't feel much like a February breeze. It felt more like a soft, spring breeze.

Clara had finally finished picking up all the things from the floor of the small boys' bedroom: socks, clothes, hangers, paper, string, boxes. It was hard to know where to put everything, like the box with a few stones in she found on the window, or the pheasant feathers that lay on the chair. And this cardboard thing! Clara inspected it. She was about to toss it in the trash, but decided it may resemble cattle pens; she had better be careful with them. As she moved the beds and bureau, she found dust settled behind them, and swept the cobwebs and dirt together from all corners of the room.

Lukie and Katie were playing with handkerchiefs in the girls' room. They had pulled the drawer open and were taking them out, amusing themselves by hiding and stacking them elsewhere. *It will be worth having to gather them all up again and refold them for all the time they're being entertained by them*, Clara thought.

Beckie had gone to town to take Mosie to the dentist, taking Mandie and Reubie along. Clara quickly dashed downstairs and filled a pail with warm water, adding some pine oil. She hurried upstairs and started washing off baseboards behind bureaus, dressers, and beds, and also the backs of the furniture, making the room and house smell clean and fresh.

Somehow Clara felt she needed to hurry. The sounds coming from the other room alerted her to the fact that the children weren't happily playing anymore. She threw the rag in the pail and went into the other room. They weren't only playing with handkerchiefs anymore. Clara scurried around, pushed an assortment of shoes and books against the wall from the middle of the room, and put the covers back on the bed, It looked like a whirlwind had gone through. She didn't find all the handkerchiefs, but she picked some up here and there, hoping to later put them back in the drawer.

Oh, no! Where did the children get all these paper scraps and crayons? They must have been through more drawers. As Clara passed the window, she saw Beckie was coming home already. No wonder the children weren't satisfied anymore; they must be hungry.

Clara took the children downstairs, stoked the fire, set the soup on the stove, and started setting the table. Mosie came in, dragging along a crying Mandie. Clara rescued and comforted her, and Mandie, eyes glistening with tears, gave Clara one of her innocent smiles.

While they were eating dinner, Beckie got excited and said, "You know, Clara, it's so mild and sunny today—just the kind of day we need to get the windows washed on the outside." Then she added questioningly, "You aren't done with the room upstairs, are you?"

"No, I just started with the water," Clara informed Beckie.

From near the top of the stepladder, Clara looked at the sparkling window she had just cleaned. Then, as she stared unknowingly across the countryside, seeing the glorious, deep blue sky stretched across the heavens, Clara also recalled what Beckie had said when she went upstairs after dinner. She commented on the clean room and its clean smell, telling Clara that she and Lucy would put the room back in order when Lucy came home from school. Clara reminded Beckie that she had not finished washing the woodwork, and had not started washing up the floor, but Beckie said they could do that some other time when it isn't so nice outside.

Clara knew it had been her sixth sense that had warned her to hurry and get things a bit cleaned. Although she hadn't realized it at the time, that was what had driven her—that Beckie would think of something more urgent to do and leave the room unfinished.

Clara's thoughts went back to the day in January when Dad had talked to her. The question turned in her mind again. Where would I like to work? Maybe not always for Frankies. At least I could make things good enough for Beckie. But it would be so satisfying if we could finish jobs, or find the things we need to do the jobs. A mused smile crossed her face as she turned back and washed the next window. Reubie was on the inside, smiling back; he thought she had chuckled at him.

She was recalling the ordeal of getting the stepladder to wash the windows. She looked in the washhouse where it sometimes was, but it wasn't there. She discovered the washwater hadn't been drained out of the washing machine from the last washing, so she did that. When she asked Beckie where the stepladder was, she suggested it might be in the cellar, since Sammie had been fixing something down there, but she didn't find it. She did find a broken canning jar at the bottom of the stairs which must have been dropped by one of the children when the carried the empty jars down.

Finally, Clara found the ladder in the shed beside the barn, but by now she had almost forgotten what she was looking for. She found the water trough was empty in the pen where a few horses were. The horses were licking at the trough, neighing, so she found a pail and carried water over from the hydrant outside the barn, since she wasn't sure how to operate the spigot at the water trough. It looked like she would need a tool to open it. Then one of the calves was tangled up in the ropes. She finally managed to loosen the rope, untangle it, and fasten it again.

She had tried not to let the heap of corn cobs that lay on the ground in front of the corn crib bother her. The wheelbarrow had tipped over on its side with some corn still in it. Hopefully the school boys would see after that when they came home to do their chores. There would be so many things the school boys could do if someone would help get them started. But, likely they would have to gather and clean the eggs.

Late in the afternoon as Clara walked across the fields on her homeward way, her sore muscles and tired arms and back kept reminding her of the tasks she had done. After she had finished washing the windows and the schoolchildren had come home, she helped the children stack the firewood in the shed from the trees the men had cut down earlier in the backyard. She had raked up all the tiny twigs, sawdust, and bark pieces.

As she arrived home and entered the porch, she was wondering if she was in time for supper. It was later than she usually came home, but she was determined to finish the jobs, for who knew when she'd get another chance to finish them.

Opening the door and expecting to see the family at the supper table, or maybe leaving the table, she was surprised to see her eight-year-old sister Loretta playing with little Paul Henry, and her fourteen-year-old sister Norma working on some embroidery, while munching on popcorn.

Clara stopped in her tracks in the doorway exclaiming, "Well—what?"

Norma looked up at her and said mockingly, "You act like you don't know us. You can close the door, then look at us."

Clara wordlessly stepped in, closed the door, and saw the school lunches standing on the counter, lids open, jars and thermoses still standing in or around the lunches—a job that was supposed to be done as soon as the children came home from school.

She finally asked, "Is something wrong? No supper around, and why is Paul Henry here this time of the day? Where is Virginia and Mother and everyone?"

"Everyone is at the sale at Mrs. Fredricks. We thought maybe you'd come home early, or maybe you went right from Frankies. Virginia left the baby here. We had gone over to the sale for a while, but the baby was tired of it, and they were selling dishes piece by piece. I got so bored, so Loretta and I came home again." Then she added, "Over here is cheese and bread. We made ourselves fried cheese sandwiches."

Clara was thinking out loud, "I didn't remember about the sale. I didn't even notice the cars. I could have seen the sale while walking home from Frankies if I would have looked while walking up over the fields. What time did it start?"

"I don't know," Norma answered. "We were in school, but Mom said Calebs were here for dinner."

Clara took the jars and the thermoses out of the lunch boxes and returned them to the serving cart where they belonged. She then prepared a cheese sandwich, put it in the pan, and began straightening the cluttered-up sink. When the sandwich was done, she poured a glass of cider—a quick supper. She picked up Paul Henry who was crawling under the table, becoming dissatisfied.

"My, he is getting heavy and getting to be a big boy. Sure makes him look different with his hair growing so much. With his little teeth that are more noticeable now, he looks more and more like Caleb," Clara marveled.

While they were entertaining Paul Henry, brother Cleon came in the door. Taking a glance over the relaxed atmosphere he asked doubtfully, "Did anyone milk the cows?"

Clara looked at him hopelessly and replied, "I didn't know the chores weren't done. I guess it's about time."

Cleon bargained with her, saying, "I'll do the feeding if you milk Brownie and Flossie. Virginia is on her way over to fetch the baby. Mom and Dad are staying till it's over—maybe another forty-five minutes.

"Okay." Clara yawned as she stretched her stiff muscles. "I guess I can still milk, but I'm getting stiff from all the work I did at Frankies today: washing windows, housecleaning, stacking wood, and raking yard."

Clara grabbed a sweater and hood and picked up the milk pails in the cellar. She didn't know how she felt. It seemed she saw a twinkle in Cleon's eyes that she couldn't figure out. It was something like the look he had when he was ready to go see Rachel.

As Clara milked Brownie—the old faithful gentle family cow—she leaned against her big body, thinking about the sale.

Years ago they had been quite closely acquainted with Mrs. Fredrick. She lived alone and was always glad for company, sometimes needing little errands done. In fact, that's where she got her name, as her name is Clara, too, but they mostly called her Mrs.

Fredrick. Clara often wondered what her parents would have named her if she hadn't been named after Mrs. Fredrick.

Over the last few years, some of Mrs. Fredrick's nieces or grandchildren had lived with her. They didn't seem too friendly, like they didn't want to be bothered with company. They stood waiting as if wondering what the visitors wanted. Often they weren't there; they had gone away and taken Mrs. Fredrick along. But these last couple of years, the house hadn't been occupied. Mrs. Fredrick's things appeared to be inside, but Mrs. Fredrick had been in an old people's home for close to two years after breaking her hip and being in the hospital. After that they didn't see her much anymore.

Clara recalled memories of going to Mrs. Fredrick's house. She could almost taste the after-dinner mints in rainbow colors that she always had on hand to give to them. She pictured the furniture that was always there. What had prompted Mom to go to the sale? Maybe canning jars, which always seemed to be in short supply. Or maybe another dresser. Since Clara had a room by herself, it would be handy to have another dresser, as the one in the girls' room wasn't very suitable. Sylvia was always irked about it.

Clara hung the one milk pail on a hook out of the cats' reach, then sat down beside Flossie. Flossie was a little nervous. Clara hadn't milked her often, but the cow soon relaxed and trusted her, so Clara milked in ease and continued reminiscing about going to Mrs. Fredrick's house. She thought about the hutch that was in the side room where Mrs. Fredrick had her dishes displayed. On the shelf where the top and bottom part met, she always had photographs of her sons and grandchildren, and more worldly treasures like fancy trays with jewelry that Clara and her sisters had spied on many a time. But in the drawer on the right side were the old children's books with many interesting pictures in them.

"What have you been thinking, as fast and quietly as you are milking?" Cleon asked, disturbing her thoughts. He smiled when he saw he had scared her.

"I was thinking of when we were younger and we often stopped at Mrs. Fredrick's house. I hadn't remembered about the sale today. It must have been an interesting sale. Even Mom was interested in going. Has she gotten anything?" Then she added, "Likely canning jars?"

Cleon scratched his head. "They had some boxes sitting around them. Can't remember if it was canning jars. I would sooner say maybe cooking utensils."

"I was thinking about the hutch in the side room. That always fascinated us—the fancy dishes displayed, the photos arranged on it, the trays of jewelry, and the drawer that held the books that we looked at. And the antique Viewmaster in the next drawer."

Cleon nodded his head and commented, "That Viewmaster was a hot item today among the antique dealers." Then he added, "Were you tempted to have the hutch for your parlor?"

"Cleon!" she cried, much like in their school years when Cleon did things to aggravate her.

"We dragged something out of the house," Cleon recalled.

Clara looked at him and asked, "Who did?"

"Dad asked me to get a few guys to carry some cupboard-like thing out of the house. I'm going to take the wagon down to fetch the things," he replied. Cleon took a few steps, then hesitated. Clara squeezed the last milk out from Flossie. As she got up, she saw the a sparkle in Cleon's eyes.

Finally, Clara asked, "Was Rachel there? You seem so deep in thought as if something is keeping you from knowing what you are doing."

Cleon smiled sheepishly and admitted, "Yes, Sis, Rachel was there. But she left already."

"Was she buying furniture?" Then she added excitedly, "Did she buy that cupboard thing that you carried out?"

"No," Cleon answered. "She didn't buy that, but she did buy a bedroom suite."

Clara smiled knowingly. Then she mischievously asked, "But what does it help if she buys a bedroom suite if she has no house to put it in?" Cleon gave her a quick look, but saw that she was teasing.

Cleon thought quietly for a moment, then chose his words carefully saying, "Of course she'll have a house for her furniture. Dad can't handle the farm anymore with his back trouble and only

27

girls to help him. Are you sure it's not **you** who doesn't have a house to live in when Rachel and I move in here?"

Clara was taken aback. Cleon never before shared such serious thoughts with her. She asked further, "Well, why don't you get started building a house in the lower field where we'd have a nice view of the creek winding through?"

"Well, for one thing," Cleon started, "this farmette is small enough without taking a big corner out of the field."

Clara wished Cleon would go further in discussing the future. She so often thought these things over and never had the nerve to discuss them with anyone. She picked up the other milk pail and started walking through the feed alley. When she got to the door at the forbay and set one pail of milk down, she saw Cleon was there. He had taken a short cut through the horse stable and was lingering in the forbay. He looked somewhat like a guilty boy who would feel better if he'd share his misbehavior.

Grinning at Clara, Cleon said, "No, Sis, don't get worried. Rachel and I won't chase my parents and sisters out of their home. Dad now owns Mrs. Fredrick's house."

Clara set down the milk pail and gasped. "Are you serious?"

"Don't I seem so? I thought you told me that I was deep in thought, not knowing what I was doing."

Clara wanted to ask so many questions. Cleon saw her struggle and replied, "Just go on living. It will go a few months before we get possession, and even then, we will have a lot of things to do to get the house like we want it. Repairs have not been kept up, so get ready for a busy schedule. At least, we don't have to build a house. Dad and I waited a long time to find out the results of this sale."

Then Cleon disappeared into the barn. Clara slowly started for the cellar where the milk was strained. She thought, *No wonder Rachel and Calebs and Mother went to the sale.* Suddenly, Clara had a great desire to see how the house really looked on the inside. There was so much to think about.

Chapter Five

The soft breezes were gently blowing and spring was waking up. The yard was pulling on her green dress, shedding her dull brown one from the winter. Trees were responding—dressed in buds—and a new crop of leaves were beckoning.

As Clara brushed more varnish remover briskly over the wood, the birds were chattering in the trees on each side of the washhouse making rich melody, sounding out that they were ever so grateful that winter had loosened its grip, rejoicing over their survival, and praising the warm breezes.

Clara's ears were almost deaf to all that spring was proclaiming as she brushed on more paint remover and watched the old varnish blister up. Then, taking a scraper over the area she had soaked before, she removed years of varnish and scuff marks off the old hutch.

She had misgivings about refinishing the hutch, fearing it would get spotty. She was also reluctant to scrape off the many years of memories from the aged sturdy hutch—memories which had grown for years when visiting Mrs. Fredrick. It was scarred and scuffed, and had signs of several coats of varnish, but it had looked right with the other things in the house. Her sister, Virginia, however, had urged her to refinish it and bring out the natural grain. It appeared that at one time it was painted, and when the paint was stripped, it was varnished again.

Cousin Alice and her friend Elsie had also talked her into getting all the varnish off. Alice had even come over and helped one afternoon. They had done half of the one side all the way to the grain to see how it would turn out. Alice marveled at the original grain underneath after they had cleaned it off and taken turpentine over it to get the dull streaks out.

Alice exclaimed, trying to impress her, "Just think how this will shine when you put varnish on. This will be quite a piece once the whole thing is refinished." Alice was in awe, as if she couldn't grasp how it would appear when the whole job was done.

Clara could almost get the vision through Alice's eyes, but she couldn't explain how it made her feel. It almost seemed like she was destroying the old familiar hutch of many year's acquaintance from visiting at Mrs. Fredrick's house and this would be a new one, replacing the old. But since she had started, she had to continue now. It couldn't be left like this.

As she went to fetch more rags from the washhouse, she saw Mom was still in the garden, planting more peas and some beans. Clara had pulled the row marker through for her before working on the hutch. Mom had assured her that she could do the planting herself.

Clara continued putting on more remover, trying to get some stubborn streaks out—streaks which seemed reluctant to come off after holding on for so many years. She thought back to the day this hutch came to their house. Clara hadn't been fond of the old buffet that was in their parlor and had envied some of the hutches that some of her friends and cousins had in their parlors. But she hadn't even tried to reason with Mom.

The evening after the sale, after the younger girls had gone upstairs, Mom told Clara that one of Mrs. Fredrick's children had come over one day and asked them if they were planning to come to the sale. They said they were planning to be there. Then, when Dad went over to see the house the Saturday before the sale, the children had talked to him and told him that Mrs. Fredrick had mentioned in her will that Noah and Etta Louise Brubaker were to choose some worthy item they desired to have, and it should be theirs in honor of naming Clara after Mrs. Fredrick.

During the sale, the children talked to them again, asking them what they preferred. They wanted to know, as they were going to sell everything over auction and the children were going to buy back whatever they wanted. It was Virginia who had urged Mom to get the hutch. Mom didn't think they wanted such an expensive item, but the Fredrick children convinced her to take it.

Since it was Mom's request, the family felt it may just as well go to them as to the antique dealers. After it went for almost eight hundred dollars, Mom tried to pay some of the cost, but the children said it was what the will said—a worthy item.

For once, Clara appreciated her name. It was a name that was only heard occasionally, and it seemed to be a difficult name for the children to pronounce.

As Clara walked into the shed next to the barn to get more remover, she paused and lifted her eyes over the countryside and across the meadow and field. Spotting their neighbor Frankie's house, she thought of the many memories and frustrations of trying to work there, never getting done what she was planning to do. It was always sort of a drag when Mom promised Beckie that Clara could help again. But now, since spring work had begun, there was also much work to be done at Mrs. Fredrick's house. Mom told Beckie they had no one who could help them until school was out. After that, maybe Norma could help them. She was older than Frankie's Lucy, who was only about twelve; Sister Norma would be fifteen this summer.

It did make her sad to think of not helping out at Frankies, even if she wasn't very fond of it there, because she would still miss them. And she did have some misgivings about Norma helping there. Oh well, maybe they wouldn't ask.

As Clara, with fresh energy, scraped off more old varnish, she recalled she didn't quite lose contact with the Frankie Snyder family, since she was slowly learning to know a member of the family whom she had rarely seen while working there.

With the coming of spring, Clara's seventeenth birthday had also arrived and she was now going to the young folks gatherings. Sometimes she could go with her brother Cleon. But usually she had to find a way home, since Cleon took Rachel home. Beckie offered her a ride with Sammie, so before Sammie left each gathering, he asked her if she had a way home or he left her know if he had another passenger.

31

Clara recalled the first time she traveled with Sammie. She thought he would probably complain or apologize about the way things were at home, maybe about Johnnie being disrespectful, or things never being organized, or that they can't have things like other people have. When she thought about his team not being done up as most of the other young boys, and his clothing not getting pressed and better care, she thought he likely felt inferior.

But the times Clara rode with Sammie, she found him not to be overly talkative. When he did talk, it was something that his little brother Reubie had done, or something that little sister Katie had said, or maybe something Dannie had come up with. (He sounded like a little nine-year-old boy who had a great interest in trying to invent something.) It sounded like Sammie looked forward to coming home to his family after his day's work at Busy Bear's greenhouse and orchard. At times, he talked about certain workers at the greenhouse. At times he mentioned something that the ministers had quoted in church. Clara gathered that he got more out of the church services than she usually did.

Sammie often referred to Lloyd and Shannon. She learned that Lloyd was a little older than Sammie and was from the upper part of the district. But since the one minister's name was also Lloyd, Clara was at times thinking of the wrong Lloyd when things didn't make sense. At times he had an amusing event to relate that involved a boy called Nevin. Nevin was one who could get most anyone to chuckle without even trying. Another boy he talked about was Shannon. It sounded like Sammie had many friends and that he respected his family.

If he ever talked about girls, it was about Fay Ellen or Lois Jane, and things that disgusted him. Fay Ellen's name was heard a lot among the girls. She did have very good looks and hair most girls would desire. Clara often envied her, but Sammie never talked about her hair or about her beauty. She seemed to always be happy and outgoing, but it sounded as if maybe she wasn't as popular as she desired to be—not as popular in other peoples' minds as she thought she was. Clara always imagined that people envied Fay Ellen. Clara wasn't sure what Lois Jane had in common with Fay Ellen, since it seemed they didn't blend too well. They both seemed to have the same nature—or maybe one made the other worse. She heard much more about them through the girls. Sammie didn't say much. Clara was looking forward to getting to know the young folks better.

Chapter Six

The warm summer sun was traveling slowly across the big blue sky on its way toward the west. It was only a little over half-way, thus being right overhead. Cattle grazed in the meadow, choosing to eat grass that was beneath the trees in the shade where the air was a little cooler. Flowers waved in the breezes, smiling back at the sun. The grass was beginning to thirst for more moisture with the sun bringing so much warmth all week. Gardens were holding up their fruit; the hull peas hung in bunches. A few more sunny days and their pods would reach maturity.

Strawberry patches were giving up their fruit already as people searched through the plants, robbing the red juicy berries. The sun beat down merrily, turning green-tipped berries to red, while men and women left their work lay and rested on the Sabbath.

Two sparrows sat on the yard fence singing a lustrous tune, then chirping at the girls to give ear to their song. The sparrows looked at each other and then perched in the other direction, where horses stood munching grass in the meadow, offering their song to them. The girls were much too engrossed in their conversation to hear their melody.

Clara took another handful of popcorn from the bowl and refilled her glass with lemonade. She had gone home with Elsie from church. The two of them had a simple warmed up lunch, as Elsie's parents were away for dinner.

The girls talked awhile, then each dozed off. Now they moved out into the yard.

Elsie exclaimed, "Another week has gone by, and I still haven't seen your new house—"

"New house?" Clara interrupted in mock seriousness.

"Well then, Mrs. Fredrick's house. As you have been talking about all you're fixing and adding on, I have been picturing it. But tell me, how is the house laid out? Maybe I can make a blueprint in my mind."

Clara took a deep breath, asking, "You mean how it was or how it is now?"

"Well, just describe it," Elsie requested as she stroked the kitten that came purring at her feet.

"Well, you come into an enclosed porch. One door leads to the kitchen; the other door leads into one part of the living room. The living room was sort of divided. The men closed up the one part and made a *Kommer* for Mom and Dad's bedroom, so that door isn't used. On down . . ."

"Sorry to interrupt, but did Mrs. Fredrick sleep upstairs?"

Clara tried to remember. "Oh, let me see, she did for a long time, but as she got older she had a bed in the living room. They had a part curtained off. Now let's see, where was I?"

"On the enclosed porch, showing me where the door goes," Elsie reminded her.

"Oh, yes, and on down the enclosed porch, another door leads to an over-sized garage, part of which they have been making into a wash house."

"Where did she wash?" Elsie quickly asked.

"Wait, I will get there," Clara said as she got a fresh breath. "In the kitchen, we painted a sunny yellow over the dull gray boards. There were old-fashioned narrow boards in the kitchen. The sink is a collection of white metal sinks and cabinets hooked together that serve the purpose but not the eyes too well." Clara looked for a moment at Elsie, who looked sort of baffled and asked, "What's wrong?"

Elsie looked at her soberly, but sort of mischievously, saying, "I was just wondering how we came in the kitchen?"

"While we were looking at the washhouse, we came into the kitchen," Clara quickly explained. And without missing a beat, she continued, "We put the sewing room next to the kitchen, and turned one part of the big hall into a pantry, closing up the open stairway.

35

The other part of the hall leads to the big bathroom with a laundry. The men remodeled a part of the laundry into part of the kitchen, leading to the corner where it goes down into the basement. You go down four steps onto a landing, then down another four or five steps. The upstairs has two big rooms and part of a room where the stairs come up. I guess we girls will all sleep in one room for the time being. We want to do some remodeling later, making one room smaller and another room bigger," Clara said as she finished drinking the lemonade.

Elsie asked, "Is there no parlor or sitting room?"

"Ah, yes—on the south side there is an enclosed porch which we will use as a sitting room when we have company. It's like a sun porch, but on the west side along the hedge, as you come to the basement, it's level. You enter a little hall to the right, which leads to a few smaller rooms—one for the furnace, one for the coal, and one for canned things. To the left there is a room with a few large windows and a fireplace. It looks as if it could have been used for a kitchen at one time. I think Mrs. Fredrick just used it for storage. Mother said that if I work hard, we can fix it up for my parlor."

"A parlor with a fireplace in the basement?" Elsie whistled romantically. The dog came out from under the bushes to see what was up.

"We'll see. Maybe we'll build a parlor someday," Clara said, not able to match Elsie's delight at the thought of a basement parlor.

A few buggies passed by on the road. The girls looked at each other and hurried to the house. It was time to be on the way to Abner Leid's home, a mile or so down the road, where the young folks were invited for supper and a singing.

Clara hurriedly pulled out her hairpins, taking a comb through her hair, while Elsie was upstairs changing her clothes.

For a moment Clara stood looking at her image in the mirror. She patted her hair, pressing at the wave and smiling at her accomplishment. Maybe she shouldn't let it so loose, but she just wanted to look like the other girls. She was about to take out the bobby pins and redo it more carefully, as Mom would say, but Elsie came down the stairs, humming to herself, her hair styled as usual—the hair on top of her head smoothed all the way down over her ears—making her look quite attractive. Clara had never dared to try combing her hair that way. It was a style that had just been discovered. Clara quickly pinned up her hair and smiled back at her reflection in the mirror.

Clara walked to Abner's home with Elsie. There were quite a few teams there already, and more were coming up the road. Sammie would be there, so Clara would have a way home.

It was a beautiful evening. The evening skies and summer breezes made it almost too beautiful to go into the house and sing.

After supper was served, a group of boys gathered in the yard, enjoying a game of croquet, while others were pitching quoits. Some girls stood watching; others were just standing around visiting.

Clara went for a walk with Elsie and cousin Alice, and when they returned, they joined the other girls in the yard near where the boys were playing croquet.

Clara became aware that Fay Ellen was giving Anna a hard time about something. Anna looked a little flustered and Fay Ellen was enjoying every moment, her eyes sparkling as she laughed. Fay Ellen's hair always looked so nice. No wonder she was always so happy.

Fay Ellen chimed again, "Well, didn't you come with Sammie?"

A few of her buddies—Edith and Karen—exclaimed, "She would say no if she didn't!"

Then Fay Ellen asked, "Did you wash his buggy first?"

Lois Jane stood over by the tree hearing every word; then she mockingly said, "Let's wash it right now." Clara looked around wondering if Sammie was close by.

Clara saw Sammie with Shannon by the windmill getting a drink.

Sammie must have heard Fay Ellen start to say, "Let's also . . .," when a girl from the end of the circle addressed Fay Ellen, saying, "I will let Sammie know that if you are walking like Anna was and he comes by, not to pick you up. You are much too good to drive with him." There came a total silence over the group.

Fay Ellen nudged Edith and said, "Let's get out of here." Lois Jane looked around, wanting to add something to the conversation, but no one seemed interested.

A group of boys came from the barn to the windmill. Suddenly there was a lot of activity. Russel came running over to the game, his shirt quite wet from an apparent water battle.

One of the girls exclaimed, "Russel! Your shirt!"

Russel chuckled and said in English, "I never was so wet."

Nevin, turning around startled, said, "What did you say?"

"You are newly wed?" A hearty chuckle went over the crowd.

"And with whom?" Lois Jane, who was in the midst of the group, asked.

"Well, not with you," Fay Ellen shot back. Apparently she hadn't left the group after all.

The boys finished the game and went out to their teams to fetch their songbooks.

Clara was feeling a little strange. She had always somewhat envied Fay Ellen, who was so charming and able to talk to everyone. But now she was beginning to wonder if words flowed so easily from our lips, would we regret some of them? She noticed quite a few of the young folks looked embarrassed or with disapproval.

Now, the voices rose and fell in unity as the youth were circled around in the kitchen, singing. Somehow Clara had missed getting next to Alice or Elsie. As she lifted her eyes over the group she saw Sammie was sitting beside Lloyd on the chairs behind the table. For a moment, Clara's attention was focused on Fay Ellen throwing a tightly-wadded gum paper over to the boys' side. A few boys looked up and Fay Ellen pointed at Karen. Karen nudged her.

Dennis winked at Karen who glanced up, looking very sober. A few of the boys got a giggling fit. Fay Ellen looked down and held the songbook in front of her face, talking to Karen. Dennis and Larry rolled their eyes while the two girls talked away.

After the singing died down, groups of boys were going out the door while others continued to talk. Clara was getting a drink and, as she walked away, she met Sammie and Shannon in the hall.

"Are you going to ride along home?" Sammie asked.

"I guess if you have room," Clara replied.

Sammie nodded. "Give me another half hour. I'll let you know then," he replied as they disappeared into the sitting room.

As Clara was waiting for Sammie to drive up, she remembered how, early in the evening, the girls had mocked Sammie's buggy in his hearing. She had never before heard the young folks mock him. She had feared they might, but Sammie always seemed so happy and appeared to have a lot of friends. Clara had hoped Sammie had forgotten about what he heard them say. What could they talk about?

Moments later, as Clara climbed in the buggy and Saylor dashed out the lane, Sammie turned around to watch the horse acting up behind them.

"That's Peter's horse," Sammie said, as he pulled one rein sharply. "Come on, Saylor, next we'll end up in the ditch looking back at Peter's horse." Sammie slowed Saylor down and was turning more of the buggy lights on as they were approaching the road. Instead, some lights went off. After more clicking, the lights all came on. Sammie didn't have that many lights, and why wouldn't he know where the switches were?

Clara asked, "Is this your buggy?"

"No, it isn't," Sammie mused. "I'm doing chores at Waylans this weekend while they are in Canada. He wanted a feeder so I took a one along over for the calves. I went in the spring wagon and decided to come from there and use his buggy instead of going home to fetch mine. He's getting rid of this since they have two children and need a carriage." Then Sammie chuckled, "I was hoping Fay Ellen and the others would wash it."

"You were?" Clara asked in shocked disbelief and surprise.

"Yes, I was, because Waylan's wife is a sister to Lois Jane."

"Who was the girl who quieted Fay Ellen down?" Clara asked.

"Did someone?" Sammie asked.

"Yes, a rather tall girl who hasn't much to say. She was wearing a dark green dress."

"Did she wear glasses?" he asked.

"Oh, yes, I believe she did."

39

"Probably it was Caroline. I can't remember the color of her dress, but there should be more girls like her. She has a way of humiliating those who are so forward in a way that they don't rebel and talk back. I wondered why things quieted down so soon. What did she say?"

Clara tried to remember. "Oh, something about what she was going to tell you if she ever saw Fay Ellen walking. She said she'd tell you not to pick her up since she is too good to drive with you."

Sammie chuckled and said, "Oh yes, that is what started it up, as they were after Anna. I was on my way over here when I caught up with Anna. She was walking from her grandparents' house all the way to Abner's house."

Soon Sammie was talking about the young folks he met from Ohio who had stopped in at Busy Bear's Produce, and then he asked how they were coming along in remodeling Mrs. Fredrick's house. He seemed interested in the room in the basement, wondering what the original purpose was for this room. He was interested in finding out the history and facts of things.

After Sammie dropped Clara off at her house and she was up in her room, she saw her image in the mirror. She experienced feelings too hard to describe. As she lay in bed, she began sorting through her thoughts, hearing the clock announce every half hour that passed.

In earlier years, Clara had often sized up Sammie by the way he chose to dress, and the fact that his buggy did not sparkle as much as most buggies did, but she had never heard others mock him. Why had the girls mocked him in his presence in front of so many people? Why would Fay Ellen, who always seemed so friendly to everyone and so charming, mock Sammie? *Does pride kill kindness? Does she feel so superior?* Before she started going to the singings with Sammie, she had felt the same way, but since learning to know him, she found him to be an interesting and cheerful person.

Clara thought of her mother's many admonitions. *Is that what she fears, that if I dress as I desire and comb my hair fashionably, I will start mocking others?*

Suddenly it seemed vain and useless to comb her hair in a more stylish way. It surely wouldn't impress Sammie and she felt strange—not sure who she wanted to impress.

Her thoughts went to Caroline. Sammie spoke respectfully of her. It seemed as if she came from a more talented family than Sammie did, but Clara really didn't know Caroline's family very well. She always looked neat. Why did she respect Sammie so much?

Clara had at times desired to be like Fay Ellen, but tonight she felt ashamed of her and the girls she called chums. *Well, I have to sleep. Tomorrow will be Monday and there will be washing to do, strawberries to pick, and work to be done at the other house. I'll have to figure things out some other time.*

Chapter Seven

A cool autumn breeze floated in the window as Clara stood on a chair, putting up the green blind at the cleanly washed window. Clara pushed the upper window further up, since the blind was flapping. It felt good to have a fresh breeze filling up this basement room, Clara thought, as she reminisced over the past weeks when it had been so dusty. Since the old plaster had seemed to draw more moisture, the men tore it all out. What a dirty mess! She had wished the men hadn't attempted it, but the wallboard now made it look like a room again. They had decided that paneling would make the room too dark, so last week she had helped Mother paper the walls of this room which was to be her parlor.

The small fresh lavender blossoms among the green stems on the white background made the room almost breathtaking, totally changing its appearance. Now, as she cleaned the woodwork and put up the green blinds, the room looked even more appealing. As Clara watched, another gust of wind came and whirled the leaves around in the corner outside the house.

Clara stood for a moment looking out the window. Her sister Loretta was playing with Paul Henry, who was happily trying to chase after the leaves that swirled around and hurried to other places. Norma had been at sister Virginia's place for the week, helping her with the washing, and had brought Paul Henry along home for the weekend so Mother could take him along to church. Caleb, being the minister, couldn't very well take such a young child along. Virginia was still staying at home from church to take care of Hannah Mae, their new baby.

Clara stepped down from the chair and looked again along the south wall at the hutch which Cleon had helped move in last evening. For a moment she glanced at the board floor that they had sanded and varnished, which they discovered under the linoleum. It really was almost like a new parlor.

Loretta and Mildred came in asking if she was ready to move the sofa in. For a moment Clara contemplated where she wanted to place the sofa. Did she want it at the wall where the door was? Or would it look better along the north wall where she wouldn't face it when entering the room?

"Or," Loretta asked impatiently, "can we take Paul Henry for a walk down to the bridge?"

"I want you to help me move in the rug that Cleons gave first."

As she spread the rug in the center of the room, Clara stood for a moment to see the effect it made on the room. She hadn't initially planned to have a rug in the parlor. Cleon and Rachel had this rug for their living room, but got a new one that matched their room better, so they had no use for their old one. Clara wasn't enthused about a green rug with darker green borders. She had visions of a light brown or tan rug in the parlor. Of course, Mom had agreed on the rug Cleon offered, since she knew Clara was envious of people with rugs in their parlor. *But this green one? It won't look any better after we move in the brown sofa and wooden chairs.* The hutch already stood there matching the refinished floor.

The door opened, interrupting Clara's thoughts. Her sisters were so eager to move the sofa and the rest of the things in. But it was Mosie Snyder (Frankie's boy) who started talking. Clara hadn't seen who had come in.

Clara hadn't seen Frankie's children for a while, except in church. Mosie had a note. What could he want? She wasn't working for them anymore. When she was needed at home and school wasn't out yet, Nora, another neighbor girl, had started helping Frankie and Beckie.

Clara unfolded the note and read, "The young folks are going to Wilmer Leinbach's house to dig and pick up their crop of potatoes early this evening. We assume you will want to go along. Now, instead of the earlier plans, I'll be there at about five."

Clara caught her breath and re-read the note. It must be about three o'clock already. She had looked forward to being with the family these few short days. She had come home from Uncle Benjamin's and Aunt Hettie's place on Thursday for Cleon and Rachel's wedding and helped Cleon and Rachel move in. It had been over a month since Clara's parents and sisters moved into Mrs. Fredrick's house. She smiled as she remembered the time when she was riding with Sammie, and she had mentioned Mrs. Fredrick's house. He had said, "You don't look much like a Fredrick to me," so she was trying to say and think "our house."

It took the men a long time to finish remodeling the parlor, since they were also fixing some things in Cleon's house.

Clara had planned to go with Sammie to the singing on Sunday evening and from there back to Uncle Benjamin's house, but now this party. The party interested Clara enough, but that meant losing time at home. *Could I come back after the potato digging?* She would see what Mother said.

No more going with Cleon, but at least she didn't always have to be asking Sammie if she could ride along since he offered to take her.

It never occurred to Clara that the young folks could help Wilmer Leinbachs. First, Wilmer's son had a badly broken leg and a long hospital stay. Then Wilmer himself had an appendectomy and a few setbacks from that since he didn't take enough time to recuperate. Also, their baby was so tiny and having a hard start and the three-year-old, who was retarded, demanded a lot of attention.

Mosie had long since disappeared out the door. Guess he wasn't looking for an answer, but she went out to see if he was still there. She found him with Loretta, who was down at the bridge with Paul Henry.

She gave the note back and said, "Give it to Sammie." She had written, "Yes, I'll go along, thanks."

The battle was on again, as Clara stood in front of the mirror combing her hair before leaving for the potato-digging party. Over

44

the months she had become convinced she wasn't going to try to be attractive like Fay Ellen and the others, because, at times, she had been ashamed of them. And, if all boys were like Sammie, she thought they wouldn't notice anyhow, since Sammie never mentioned anything about how some girls comb their hair.

But, at Cleon's wedding she had seen many Reiff cousins again. She re-did her hair several times, finally feeling satisfied. She felt a little uneasy as she put on her bonnet, since she normally didn't put on her bonnet until she was ready to go out the door. She would rather not be seen by her mother right now. Something made her turn back. She took off her bonnet and started taking off her covering. Deciding to redo her hair a little, she remembered the undesirable feeling the disobedience brought the other times.

Soon Loretta called upstairs, "Clara, quick, hurry up. Aren't you ready? Sammie is coming." Tying her covering again, she tried to push her hair down as best she could, put on her bonnet, grabbed her sweater, fled downstairs, and picked up her luggage. She saw Saylor coming in the lane.

As she stepped in the buggy, she sensed that Sammie was almost staring at her. She looked up questioningly when he didn't tell Saylor to go.

With an amused grin on his face, Sammie said, "I was just wondering if you remembered that we're going to dig and pick up potatoes. You look sort of dressed up." Clara glanced at him as he picked up the reins and saw that he didn't have his best clothing on. She hadn't stopped to think. She never was at such an outing before, and Mother didn't say anything. Well, it didn't matter; her clothes were washable.

They rode in silence. It seemed precious to be going with Sammie again, as it brought back memories of when she first started going to singings. She said, "It seems like this spring when I first started going to singings."

Sammie roused from his thoughts and looked at her and said, "Yes, it has been awhile since you were in this area and able to go along. How are things at Uncle Benjamin's? Are you adjusting to the job?"

"I liked my job from the beginning. I had been there a little sometimes before and really enjoyed helping in the bulk food store, so I looked forward to working there. But it isn't a joyful thought that I was needed," she answered.

"Isn't Benjamin any better?" Sammie asked, concerned.

Clara took a deep breath and replied, "Some days he seems better. They have been trying a different doctor again. It's rather unusual that something is flaring up now when the accident happened years ago."

After a few moments, Sammie said, "Don't you miss us here at the east end? We miss you." He clicked to the horse to hurry him over the road before the next car came too near. There was a catch in his voice.

Clara paused a moment and admitted, "I sort of miss not being at home with the family. It was so pleasant to be home for a few days, I thought I would stay until Sunday evening."

"You can still. I'll take you home again if you wish. Then we'll go again on Sunday evening," Sammie offered.

"Mother said I may as well go on to Benjamin's, since we are in the area."

Clara thought Sammie was going to say something. With a sigh, he tried again. "Well, I often . . ." he started, taking a deep breath. He finished, the words pouring out, ". . . wish things could have continued, with you helping Mother with the work. I never realized how one person could make such a difference. Since Nora is helping at home, there has been disrespect shown towards us. I guess Nora doesn't enjoy helping at home. She is very friendly with Edith, and Edith seems to be getting along well with the girls who get a little loud and do not show as much respect for others. I have been going with the young folks for a few years now, and we haven't been targeted like we have been lately." His last few words were barely above a whisper and it sounded as if he was swallowing tears.

So Sammie had noticed that the girls were making fun of his team and family. Clara felt rather unworthy that he was praising her and for his respect while she worked there, as she, too, was often

46

disgusted and mocked their unorganized home in her mind. And she had looked down on Sammie for not dressing better. But she hadn't shared it with the others at home as she knew Mother and Father would put an end to her disrespect. And she had not brought it up with Elsie and Alice, since they wouldn't understand. Clara hadn't realized that it was since Nora started working there that Nora had been feeding the mockery, as she hadn't heard much of Nora in a group.

Clara remembered how she thought Sammie likely felt looked down upon when she first started going with the young folks. But then she was surprised to learn that he was so satisfied in life and so well accepted and that he respected his parents.

Speaking aloud, Clara said, "But you have a lot of good friends."

"I know, and I'm learning to appreciate them more."

Suddenly they turned in a lane. Clara had been wondering why they didn't go up State Route 56.

"Is this the way to where Wilmer's live?" she asked, doubt in every word.

"No, I'm stopping here to pick up my good friend Merle Garman."

As they drove in, a buggy stood out by the fence, and a horse was harnessed and tied by the barnyard fence. A blond-haired boy, wearing glasses, came toward them.

"What's up?" Sammie asked. The boy smiled so easily and his expression spilled mercy and kindness.

Merle invited, "Why don't you unhitch Saylor and let him rest; we'll take my team the rest of the way."

"So, you are staying for the winter?" Sammie asked.

"Yes, there's a lot of work to do till we get this barn ready for cows."

In a few minutes they had Saylor unhitched and the other team hitched. Merle did the driving. Sammie quickly introduced Merle to Clara, telling her he was a brother to Earl who lived there.

While they were at Wilmer's house, Clara was busy picking up potatoes in the field, but she was unable to keep up with the ones working in the row beside her and was falling behind. Suddenly from behind her, a person came stooping along, picking up potatoes much faster than she was able to and gathered the ones in front of her. He smiled so easy and a few of his light curls hung loose on his forehead. He said, "This must be the good worker. I heard about the good work you did at Frankies. We need more such people. Never give up your good example."

It must have been Merle; he had such light curly hair. Soon he was going further up the row, leaving only a few for her. Clara was soon able to catch up with the girls who were working in the row next to her. Merle had jumped over three rows to where no one was picking at the time, swiftly picking up as he went.

Reviewing what Merle had said, Clara thought Sammie must have talked about her to him. *Do boys talk about girls?* She thought it was just girls who talked about boys and that boys talked about tractors and cows and going hunting.

Merle came from another district. Sammie was giving her more credit than she deserved. Her cheeks burned when she thought of all the times she had looked down on Sammie and his home life. In Clara's heart a strange feeling was growing—a new respect for Sammie and his family.

It was while she was trying to fall asleep at Uncle Benjamin's that a thought kept rising. *Why, if Merle had his team here, didn't he drive to the potato picking? Oh, yes, Sammie hadn't known that Merle had his team here. But Merle could have just rode along. We didn't have far to go anymore. It seems strange that they had bothered to rehitch.*

Clara was trying to put the pieces together. Sammie had seemed a bit depressed earlier in the evening. It was the first time she heard him complain about—no, he wasn't complaining about his home life; he seemed depressed that his family was being mocked. And he pointed out that it stemmed from Nora, the hired girl—that she was spreading the information. *He must have told Merle because Merle praised me for the good work I had done at Frankies.*

Suddenly, wide awake again, a new thought entered Clara's mind. *Had Merle offered to hitch his team because the young folks made a mockery of Sammie's team?* Although Nora herself wasn't heard mocking Sammie in public, maybe she did help Fay Ellen and the others to be aware of things. Clara remembered about a month ago when Nora made a remark that Clara knew was referring to Beckie, and Nora had opened the subject for Clara to relate her own experiences.

Clara knew very well what Nora was talking about when she said, "I was going to sweep the upstairs, and I couldn't find the broom." She glanced at Clara, who could share volumes, and continued, "When Beckie looked for the broom in the hallway and saw the pumpkins, she remembered it was a good time to bake pumpkin pies."

Clara just listened, pitying Nora when Edith said, "Didn't you then discover you had to fetch eggs first?"

Edith held the sentence while Karen added, "And the egg baskets all had tomatoes in them." Soon they were all laughing. Clara had been too stricken to talk. At first she was afraid she would talk and help along, since here was someone who understood. But then she was shocked to hear they were making things worse, because they didn't use their egg baskets for other things.

What happened to the dreams she had a year ago, looking forward to going with the young folks? Now the happenings were keeping her awake. Didn't Mother say that maybe going with the young folks would increase the problems of life rather than solving them all?

Chapter Eight

The March breeze stirred softly, and there were plants and green growth everywhere. Everything felt the mild air as the grass was shedding its fading brown winter garment for specks of green dress. Many tiny shoots were pushing growth. The winter had not been long—not nearly as long as last winter when Clara was counting the days till March would come and she would be seventeen. Where had the year gone?

"Clara, I'm talking to you," Alice said. "What have you been thinking about?" Clara looked up at Elsie and Alice, who stood idly watching her.

The three had been walking down the road after eating dinner with the rest of the young folks at Ivan Musser's house.

"I was just thinking. I can't believe this is March already. I don't know where the past year went," Clara replied.

"Just think of all that took place since then," Alice said, starting to count on her fingers. "Number one, you were still living on the farm."

"Number two, Cleon wasn't married yet," Elsie chimed in, "and Alice wasn't going with Peter yet."

Alice slapped Elsie playfully and blushed, then continued, "It isn't polite to interrupt. I wasn't done yet. You fixed up your parlor. You started working for Uncle Benjamin."

"Let's go up this field lane," Elsie cut in. "Then we don't have to turn out for cars so often."

The three girls walked leisurely along the field lane leading to the fields beyond till they came to a cluster of trees. Finding a fallen tree to sit on, they rested before resuming their walk.

"Oh yes," Alice said, turning to Clara, "what I had asked you when we were coming down the road was, Are you still at Uncle Benjamin's since the baby is older now?"

"Oh yes," Clara answered. "I have been done with the baby job awhile already.

"Benjamin is better again, isn't he?" Elsie interrupted

"Yes, he is nearly as well as he was before, but since my sisters are older, my mother doesn't need my help as much. And Benjamin's oldest boy, Charles, who is fifteen going on sixteen, is not very enthused about weighing bulk foods. There are always people needing hired boys, so Charles is hired out. I find the work interesting and will be staying for the time being. We were really busy during the Christmas season. January and February were slow months for business, but it's getting busier again. Now, I'm waiting to hear what Alice has to say about Peter. It seems we hear nothing much," Clara added.

"I'm glad it's not a month ago," Alice admitted.

"Are you saying that after the first few months, it isn't very interesting?" Elsie asked.

"You just have no idea, girls," Alice confided.

"Well, tell us," Clara said, "so we know what not to do."

"And who were you expecting to take you home?" Elsie asked Clara. "Were you expecting to hear from Peter?"

"You know I wasn't," Alice answered with a look in her eyes Clara didn't understand.

Alice continued as if thinking aloud. "About a month ago, I was just starting to know him well enough to look forward to and enjoy the visits, but then he was so reserved a few evenings that I couldn't relax very well. I kept holding my breath, thinking he would soon say he wasn't coming back."

"You mean you can feel for Karen?" Elsie asked.

Alice nodded and said, "Merle was still new in the community. I guess Karen caught his interest even though it took the breath out of everyone for a few moments. It did seem to mature Karen somewhat, but before maturing enough that people noticed it, they broke up. I pitied both of them."

Clara picked up a twig from the ground thoughtfully and confided, "Sammie said it was about more than Merle could bear to quit her."

"Yes, I heard through Peter that Merle isn't the same boy he was before," Alice added, "but I'm glad he chooses Shannon and Sammie as his friends." Sadly, she added, "Karen seems to have lost the maturity she had gained."

Clara looked up and slowly said, "I don't know about Karen, but I have come to the place where I'm ready to start a new life. It was so hard at first. I just couldn't give up last year like you did, Alice. I had so many struggles. I still have some doubts, but I'm willing to learn and hopefully I'll grow yet."

Elsie looked at her with feeling. "I have been wanting to talk with you, since I've been going through the same struggle."

"Well, it will only be a few more months till the church seeks the names of those who desire to be in instruction class." Alice had gone through instruction class last summer and had asked them about it, but Clara remembered the raging battle she still had been fighting then. Learning to know Sammie had somehow helped her awaken to new thoughts that led to a desire for a new life.

Clara thought of the deeper bond she had with Mother since she combed her hair more decent and not just because Mother demanded it.

Alice had risen from the fallen tree and declared it was time to head back to Ivan's before they lose their rides to the supper at Harold's place.

From church, Lucy, one of the other girls, had also driven with Sammie and Clara to Ivan's. Sammie said they could go along to Harolds in the afternoon if they desired to. But Lucy caught a ride with her cousin, so it was only Clara who stepped on when Sammie drove up with his team. Most of the other teams had left already, so they didn't hear any disrespectful things being said.

Sammie, however, seemed rather preoccupied. At last he ventured to speak, saying, "Going in this direction must seem to you like going home."

"It does rather. It's not often that the young folks' gathering is so near to Uncle Benjamin's house."

"Does it feel almost like home to you by now?" Sammie questioned.

"In a way, yes, but it still stirs me to go home to the family. Maybe it helps me to appreciate my family more." Clara was thinking of the joy she felt coming home to her mother, dad, and sisters. It still felt empty, not having Cleon there. When she thought of home she often thought of the basement parlor—the room she had worked on so hard—and its contents, like the hutch that she refinished. Then there were things she didn't like to think of, like the fact that Norma was growing up and following some of her own traits. Clara wondered if she had actually plaited her hair as much as Norma tried to. Norma felt Mother was always picking on her and didn't like her as much as the other girls. Without thinking, Clara sighed. Sammie, his eyes gazing ahead, looked up at her when she sighed. She smiled weakly as she saw concern on his face.

Sammie wiped his hand nervously over his face and apologized, saying, "I guess I am poor company today. I have been thinking too much. Maybe you have heard?" he asked looking at her.

Clara just looked at Sammie blankly, not able to read his thoughts. "You mean about Shannon?" she asked lightheartedly.

"No, that's not so new to me. Shannon had confided in me that he was seriously thinking of dating Anna. So I had time to get used to the idea before he started dating. But I surely miss him since he is not with us as often anymore."

When Sammie didn't continue speaking, Clara asked, "Then what have you heard, if I may ask?"

He scratched his brow and asked, "Then you haven't heard that our family is moving?"

Clara stared at Sammie and questioned, "Moving? Where? To another settlement?"

Looking at Clara briefly, Sammie weighed his words. "My uncle's neighbor in the Spring Hill area has offered my dad a job in his hardware store. The job involves a lot of paperwork and Dad has taken the offer."

Clara was trying to grasp what she heard. "Do—do you mean you are m—moving?" she stammered, the words not coming out right.

Sammie drove on in silence as if he hadn't heard her question. But Clara sensed he wasn't done talking yet; he was weighing words. They had reached a hill in the road, and Saylor shifted to walking.

Sammie sat back and relaxed as he slowly spoke, "It all was so confusing at first. Mother didn't like the idea from the beginning, but then Johnnie got all enthused about joining a carpenter crew in the area where some of my cousins are working. There are mostly Mennonites on the crew. That seemed to change the picture for Mother, seeing Johnnie taking an interest in a decent job. And Bennie has been offered a job as a hired boy on a farm. Since there are more young couples there, they don't have as many young boys."

It was hard to grasp. Never in Clara's wildest imaginations did she think of Frankie and Beckie moving elsewhere.

"Are you sure you are not kidding?" she asked, still somewhat doubting.

"Me kidding?" he asked rather lightheartedly. "If I'm dreaming, I'm not done yet. There is a part that Mother doesn't like." He finished with a more serious tone. Clara looked at him to continue.

"When I told my boss at work, he wasn't very happy, since I've been helping with the produce and at the greenhouse for a long time. He talked to me awhile. The next day he asked if I would stay and continue my job if I had a place to live? I said I would need to think it over and talk with my parents. I finally told him it would depend on what the living arrangements would be.

"The next time I talked to my boss, he had a few options. He said he had talked to John Hoover and that I could with them. I wasn't too enthused about that since they have a number of small children who aren't a big help yet. With my hours, Mrs. Hoover would have to save supper and I would hate to ask that of a busy woman.

"Shannon came up with the idea of checking with Eli Fox. They have a few rooms they added when their aunt lived there. After my boss talked with them, they agreed I could stay there. They were using the extra rooms for storage since it wasn't big enough to rent out to a family. It has a small kitchen and a bedroom, but it's enough, and just a little over two miles from my job. Mother isn't too happy or relaxed about it since I've rarely cooked a meal. I'm sure she'll give Mrs. Eli Fox many instructions.

"And Mother is trying to quickly teach me to do some cooking. It sounds confusing—you cook potatoes to make them soft and eggs to make them hard," he chuckled.

"Couldn't you have stayed in the house with whoever is going to live there?" Clara asked, suddenly interested. "Anyhow, who will live there?"

"Well, you know Alvin Groff owns it. He didn't say who is moving in. He wants to do some remodeling and fixing up so I guess no one will move in right away."

"When are your parents moving? Soon?"

"Yes, they plan to move in about a month." By now Sammie and Clara were driving in Harold's lane. "Do you have a way to go to Benjamin's tonight?" Sammie asked.

"Yes, I can always depend on Elva Mae and her brother when I'm in this area."

Chapter Nine

Mechanically, Clara's fingers moved swiftly as she weighed the box of bulk raisins in five-pound and ten-pound bags. She had not planned to weigh the raisins now, since she was still trying to catch up with the Jello, but Uncle Benjamin had a few customers who wanted raisins, and there were only one- and two-pound bags on the shelf. As she weighed some larger amounts, she decided she may as well weigh the rest of the box in larger amounts for the shelf. Glancing at the countertop, she saw the container with tapioca. Yes, she had to weigh that, too. She had meant to do that in the morning, but when a delivery came in, she had to rearrange things in the warehouse.

"Are these ready for the shelf?" Roy asked, coming in from the main part of the store.

"Almost. I need to put on a few more labels."

Roy stacked the labeled ones on a cart and took them out to the store. Clara washed her hands and got the assortment of bags to begin weighing the Jello. She'd start with the cherry.

As Clara put the twisters on the Jello bags and set them in a row on the countertop, she thought of Sammie and a few weeks ago when she had traveled with him to Paul Eberlys for dinner. Miriam had planned to ride with him, but her plans changed. She had asked that a girl go with him when he pulled up at church, and the girls appointed Clara. A smile played on her lips when she remembered how he said he had made Jello, and it just didn't set, so he drank it. Clara asked if he had the water boiling before he poured it into the Jello. He said he had. She wondered how much water and how much Jello he had used. He couldn't remember, but he had followed the

56

directions. He left it sit on the table to cool a bit, then put it in the refrigerator. When it still didn't get firm, he drank it. Clara gathered he had it in the refrigerator for only a little over an hour and a half. She asked if it was set by the next meal, but he said what he didn't drink, he put in his lunch, which he left setting on the countertop, and drank it at work.

From what Sammie said, Mrs. Eli Fox must make some meals for him, since he mentioned the variety of things that were in his refrigerator.

It didn't seem real that Frankie and Beckie and their family were no longer living in the house close to home, but it was true. The house was still empty. Groffs were doing some remodeling.

Clara and her sisters had been eagerly looking forward to the new occupants, wondering who would move into the house. Maybe it would be someone with young folks. But it sounded like a young couple was planning to move in in August, another month away.

When Clara pictured Sammie, she became aware that the picture she had of him had changed from her former ones. She reminisced of how she had always tended to criticize him in her mind because his clothes weren't neatly ironed and his buggy wasn't tidy— things that wouldn't have cost anything to improve. She now became aware that it didn't bother her so much anymore. His friendly attitude rose above that. Had she changed so much, or had he also changed?

For a moment Clara dwelled on the thought that Fay Ellen wasn't in the community anymore since she was dating Danny from West View. She moved there, and very little was heard from her friends since it seemed they had lost their leader, but she didn't think that made all the difference. Just on Sunday she had noticed Sammie's clean blue shirt. It looked so fresh and . . . well, it made Sammie look so . . . She didn't know how to describe it. She doubted that it was a new shirt. In fact, she had seen him wearing it before, but it was so carefully ironed. And weren't his shoes freshly polished? Was it really Sammie? Had he gained weight? Or were those new dress pants that he wore?

From what Sammie said, Clara could tell he didn't take much more time working on keeping his clothes in order, since they were busy from early morning till late at night with the produce and taking care of the orchard. Even if the greenhouse wasn't busy right now, it sounded as if they stretched the days, trying to add more hours to them.

Clara thought of Eli Foxes. Their daughter Eunice was with the young folks and two of the girls were out of school; however, they had more girls still in school. She wondered if the girls might be shining and pressing Sammie's clothing, still not sure if he really was dressed better, or if she was seeing him through different eyes.

When Clara thought of Sammie's friendly smile that cheered one's soul, she also thought of Merle. Since Shannon had a steady girl, Sammie was often with Merle and Lloyd.

Pausing a moment, Clara reached for the stickers to put on the Jello bags. She almost trembled as she relived the moment a few weeks ago when she had arrived at Adam Zeiset's house. She came up the steps and met Merle on the porch. He had smiled and said "Clara" so warmly. It was as if the young folks were one big close-knit family. She couldn't remember that Merle said more than her name, but his smile seemed to spread. Or was it the friendly look in his eyes that made it appear he was smiling? She had returned a feeble smile and hurried on. But the memory of his pleasant smile and kind eyes, his light curls partly spilling on his forehead, kept returning to her.

Roy entered, partly awakening her out of her dream world. The bell rang at the meat case. Or was it the alarm? Was she dreaming? No, the bell rang again. She was at Uncle Benjamin's store. As she turned around, Roy was dragging the oatmeal bag toward her. Looking at him questioningly, she almost stepped on the bag.

"Dad said we need more oatmeal on the shelf. A customer took five pounds, since there were no smaller bags out," he answered her questioning look.

In a daze, Clara met the woman who had rung the bell. This woman talked on and on, asking many questions. Clara didn't need to know how many people were coming or how far they were traveling. What did she really need to know? Oh, now she understood. The lady wanted to know what kind of cheese she should use in her casserole so it didn't get stringy.

As Clara went back to the table where she had been working, she was trying to remember where she had left off. Roy stood by the table and looked at her almost pitifully. She wasn't sure what caused his expression.

Finally, he said, "I asked Dad if I could put the Jello on the shelf. He came to see if it was packaged, but found they needed other labels." Roy looked at her questioningly.

Clara repeated, "Other labels? Did I put the wrong price on?" Picking up a bag of Jello, she read the sticker which said "two pounds of raisins."

"Raisins?" Clara said. "I guess I'd better put on other labels."

Roy looked at Clara is if all the troubles in the world lay on this matter. She smiled at his concern, as if he thought she would try and tear off the labels, which would likely tear the bag. Finding the correct roll of stickers, with swift movements she wrote the correct amount on and pasted the new label over the wrong one. It didn't take long, and Roy's troubled brow eased as he piled the packages in a cart to wheel them over to the shelf. A minute ago he was so troubled, but soon he was relieved. This problem could be easily solved. And to think the Bible says in Matthew 18:3: "Except ye be converted and become as little children, ye shall not enter into the kingdom of Heaven."

Clara thought of the last instruction meeting the class had attended to prepare to join church. They were admonished to trust. They were preparing to give their lives to God and when they got baptized, it was not the end; it was the beginning. Salvation was explained in terms of how Jesus went before and opened the way for us. If we knocked, the door shall be opened to us—if we ask, we shall receive. We were told to be aware of where we were knocking and what we were asking for. We were compared to little trees. In our first growth, maybe we would not bear fruit right away, but with greening and budding, and showing that we have the new life, the fruit would come forth as we grow.

It all looked so overwhelming. The ministers knew the Word so well and lived good lives and it sounded as if even they often failed. Clara wondered where? She felt like the expression that Roy had on his face.

Clara thought, *How can we? Could I have faith like Roy had when he saw there was power and knowledge beyond his that could work out things? Can I have that faith and believe that if I trust and follow all that God reveals through the ministers, any problem can be solved?*

Clara was trying to grasp the meaning and power of grace. It took so little to ease Roy's mind. And through instructional meetings, we get guidance, comfort, and strength. We learn that God will lead us. Could she trust? How would she know what God's will is? For a moment she remembered the thoughts she had been dwelling on before the bell rang, bringing her back to reality. She vowed to herself that she must pray more and trust that God will lead her in the way He has planned for her life. She had heard in church that we are here for a purpose, not by chance. We all have a purpose to fulfill.

When she thought of people having a purpose, for a moment Clara thought of Merle. Originally from another community, he first helped his brother build a dairy barn. Now he was helping other people with building projects. Is his purpose here? Then she automatically pictured Sammie. His parents moved out of the community and things worked out for him to remain here. Does God have a purpose for him in this area? What is my purpose in life?" How long will I work for Uncle Benjamin? If all their boys start working as hired boys as they grow up, they will need help in the store for many years.

In the evening after the store hours were over, Clara was weighing bulk items for almost two more hours. She hadn't planned to work so long, but she kept seeing more things that were low in stock. As she came in, she met Uncle Benjamin and Aunt Hettie in the yard enjoying the cool summer evening breeze.

Hettie asked her, "Did you have a visitor, that you stayed so long?"

"Oh, no, I just got carried away weighing things in case we have a busy day tomorrow."

The older boys were playing catch. The younger ones were just throwing the balls and running after them. Clara was glad Hettie had time to relax, as she had been busy canning string beans, trying to get the boys to help clean and cut the beans. Clara was too busy in the store to help with the beans.

Sitting on a lawn chair for a moment, Clara watched the boys play. Yawning, she realized when she finally sat down that she was very tired. Benjamin was telling Hettie about a customer whom he hadn't seen for many years.

Since Hettie was usually in the store quite a bit, she asked about an order that was due to arrive. Maybe Benjamin wasn't so strong, but he was a needed and loved man. Benjamin and Hettie seemed to be very close. It must have been a disappointment when Benjamin got hurt and had to give up farming. Clara wondered if she could have accepted such a change in life if it would have been her lot. She never heard Benjamin and Hettie complain about their misfortune.

After yawning again, Clara said she was going to bed before she falls asleep. She felt humbled when she realized that Benjamin would probably tell Hettie about the raisin labels on the Jello, or maybe Roy had already told her. But Hettie would smile and wonder what was on my mind. Clara knew Benjamin would not mention the mistake in the children's presence. The children never told things against her, saying Mom or Dad said so and so about you. It seemed they had a way of teaching their children respect.

When she was upstairs, she sat on her bed for a moment thinking. She had seen the boys outside washing their feet, getting ready for bed; then the chatter moved in the kitchen. Soon Clara heard one voice—Uncle Benjamin was telling them a Bible story before they went to bed.

They were a happy family. Clara thought of Peter and Alice. Clara could sense that Alice was becoming more fond of Peter as time passed. Their love was growing. Alice had no special thought of Peter before. How could she accept him? Would a girl say yes to any boy that asked her, thinking he was led from God or he wouldn't have asked?

These thoughts led her to think of Merle and Karen. It was a wonder Merle didn't leave the community and go home if he was so torn apart over the ordeal. People said he wasn't quite the same after that as he was before.

Another thought flooded through her mind afresh. It was when she met Merle unexpectedly on the porch and he had greeted her so heartily. His deep tone had sounded as if he wanted to talk, and the look in his eyes struck her deeply, leaving her speechless. It was just the same as the time when he helped her catch up in potato picking when he praised her. He is so . . . There were no words. It seemed almost like the look in Alice's eyes when she spoke of Peter, or when they met.

Clara calmed down when she thought of Sammie. He was so humble, a friend to all. And his smile, his expression. Well, it stirred her to share thoughts. He didn't leave her awestruck, maybe because she knew him better than Merle. It was time to pray, but her heart was so full. She finally prayed for a guiding light on her path. That was her purpose, not my will but Thine be done.

Chapter Ten

Clara lay on the sofa staring at the ceiling in the basement parlor, reminiscing over the last few days. She felt grateful that she was allowed to be home for half the week. She enjoyed working for Uncle Benjamin, but there was always so much to do in the store. And Benjamin had offered to get other help for awhile so she could have off to attend the last class meeting, the preparatory service, and baptism. On the following Sunday, there would be footwashing and communion.

Now it was late Sunday afternoon. On Tuesday Clara's parents would take her back to Uncle Benjamin's house. She hoped she could always keep that awed feeling that had come from the many admonitions they had heard over the past three days. They had been admonished to "Seek ye first the kingdom of God and his righteousness; and all these things shall be added unto you," from the sixth chapter of Matthew. They were also encouraged and praised because they had made a good start and had made a vow with God to deny the world and take up the cross.

The bishop spoke so fervently as he asked them to give their hand, and he raised them up from their knees "to a new life and a new beginning. "The Lord strengthen you to live your new life. Know the truth and the truth shall make you free."

They were told that making this vow was not the end. It was only the beginning. They were on proving ground. Satan wasn't ashamed to tempt Jesus after He was baptized, and he wouldn't be ashamed to tempt them. The class was told they would be tried in order to prove if their faith is of hay and stubble that will burn with the heat of the afflictions and temptations, or if it is of gold, which gets stronger and purer when sorely tried with the heat of the day.

Right now the things that at times had troubled Clara or tempted her seemed of no worthy account. They were warned and admonished of so many heavier, mightier things, like soldiers are instructed to go out into battle:

> *Onward, Christian soldiers.*
> *Marching as to war,*
> *With the cross of Jesus*
> *Going on before.*

And what were the words of the song the visiting minister had quoted on Saturday? Clara went upstairs to her bookshelf and found *The Church and Sunday School Hymnal*. Finding the page, she read:

> *Am I a soldier of the cross,*
> *A follower of the lamb?*
> *And shall I fear to own His cause,*
> *Or blush to speak His name?*
>
> *Must I be carried to the skies*
> *On flow'ry beds of ease,*
> *While others fought to win the prize,*
> *And sail through bloody seas?*
>
> *Are there no foes for me to face?*
> *Must I not stem the flood?*
> *Is this vile world a friend to grace,*
> *To help me on to God?*
>
> *Sure I must fight if I would reign;*
> *Increase my courage Lord;*
> *I'll bear the toil, endure the pain,*
> *Supported by Thy Word.*

And when the battle is over, we shall wear a crown. Yes, when the battle is over, then we shall wear a crown. The crown is not given in the beginning, nor halfway through, but after we have held out, at the end of our good fight.

For a fleeting moment Clara thought of the last few years. She thought that was when she had done the fighting to give up her will to lay down the desire of adorning her hair the way she desired. But that was just the beginning of her deciding to be a soldier. What battles still lay ahead?

Clara saw that Cleon and Rachel had walked over and joined Mom and Dad out in the yard, so Clara went out and joined them. Mildred and Sylvia were coming in the kitchen to make popcorn and lemonade. They all joined in visiting while they sat around munching popcorn and sipping lemonade.

Later, Rachel and Mom had gone around to the back of the house to check on some late-blooming flowers. Cleon and Dad were exchanging farm and butcher-shop news. Clara yawned. Today there would be no gathering for the young folks, as they had partaken of the sacred communion. The young folks stayed home to reread and grasp the sacred vows.

Clara found her thoughts also turning to the young folks. In the past few months, she became aware that Merle wasn't at the gatherings anymore. Apparently he had finished his jobs and went back home. It almost seemed she could still see his easy smile, his kind eyes, and his light curls dangling on his forehead. But it was Sammie's smile that she glimpsed when she looked over the sea of faces. There were no curls dangling on his forehead, but his friendly appearance and humility went deeper than curls.

Clara had somewhat lost contact with Sammie since, having not been at home for a while over the weekend, she couldn't go to church or to gatherings with him. But all that seemed of no worthy account now. They were so richly admonished in their new life to give all to Christ and let Him lead. If they did this and sought first after the kingdom of God, God would direct their lives.

Returning to the kitchen, Clara's thoughts went back to a month ago when cousin Lucinda had a quilting for the cousins. How

Clara had enjoyed the day, meeting the cousins she seldom got to see. She felt the old urge stirring when she saw how some of the cousins had so beautifully plaited their hair in perfect waves and carefully pleated their coverings to fit every wave just right. She thought she had laid that desire down, conquered it, but she felt the desire stirring. It faded though with Saturday's sermon. If only she could always remember her true value and not give in to vain temptations. She wanted to be a soldier of the cross who fought with all her might. She had heard that Satan would try to get a hold wherever she relaxed her convictions a little. But Satan could not get a hold of one who stood firmly. He was always on the lookout to find where doubt, discontentment, and worldly temptations weakened one's hold, but he could get a hold only if she eased up. It was important to stand fast, for this was no child's play.

Chapter Eleven

Clara was humming to herself as she pushed the molasses pails aside to sweep thoroughly. The month of December had been so busy at the bulk-food store that they had neglected to do the cleaning as thoroughly as they should have. Now that she had started cleaning, it seemed she would never finish. She kept seeing neglected corners. *And these empty boxes surely don't belong here,* she said to herself as she picked them up and went out to the warehouse with them.

Seeing the bag of doughnut mix standing beside the door, Clara thought Uncle Benjamin had apparently not weighed that yet. Even though the holidays were over and business had been slack, customers were starting to buy products related to doughnut making.

Thinking Uncle Benjamin would be out again, Clara wasn't sure what to do. Should she continue cleaning or should she weigh the doughnut mix? She saw more shelves that needed dusting and many neglected corners.

When the door opened, Aunt Hettie came in with Landis and Paul bounding in after her. "Were you almost done?" Hettie asked, then added, "I guess you'll soon want to get ready."

Clara looked up for a moment. Hettie must have been able to read her thoughts, as she said, "I know there's never any getting done in here, but just leave the rest. There will be time next week. Maybe I can get a few things done this afternoon, but we should eat soon, so you can go."

Clara hadn't realized it was so near noon already. As soon as dinner was over, Clara went upstairs to get ready. She had meant to help do the dishes, since Hettie had just stacked them in order to go out to the store. As soon as Clara came downstairs, Elva Mae drove in. Elva Mae said she would take the team and then her brother would come with a neighbor in the evening and drive the buggy home.

As Clara and Elva Mae arrived at Cleason Weaver's house, more girls were arriving. Some were already seated at the quilts, as they were invited to help quilt and stay for supper. There would be a singing in the evening.

How Clara enjoyed the afternoon! But with two quilts, she just couldn't hear all the conversations. Sometimes she heard enough of a subject from the other group to make her eager to know the rest of the story. With people talking on either side of her, she couldn't hear everything.

In the afternoon, when they took a break from quilting, cookies and drinks were served. Alice got Clara's attention and beckoned her to follow her into the bedroom where they could be alone.

"Have you talked with Elsie?" Alice asked, sounding eager and curious.

Clara, trying to remember said, "I think I talked with her a little while I sat beside her at the quilt. I asked her about the spring dresses she was making. Have you made yours already? I've cut mine out, but it seems I just don't have time for sewing."

"I have to tell you. Brother Elmer said that cousin Levi asked Elsie for a date last week, but she didn't accept him."

"Levi?" Clara repeated, letting the echo bounce off the wall.

"I wonder why she wouldn't accept him, now that he finally asked someone. I thought quite a few girls were noticing him. It must be that she wasn't one of them who were waiting to see what he would do. I wonder how Levi took that."

"I don't know, but I thought Elsie wasn't quite herself. She seems extra quiet today. Elmer said Levi told him he didn't receive his answer for over a week."

As the day wore on and the last stitches were made on one of the quilts, they took it out of the frame. Many of the girls helped to take the pins out and stash the frame away. Even though some of the girls were preparing supper, there still wasn't enough room for all of them to sit at the remaining quilt. That was when Clara met Elsie in a corner of the kitchen.

Elsie wearily said, "I wish I had a way to go home."

"Way to go home?" Clara repeated. "You sound like the twenty-two-year-olds who are getting tired of being with the young folks. Come, let's go upstairs." Retrieving their sweaters from the pile on the bed downstairs, Elsie and Clara fled upstairs, seeking a room for privacy.

"Let's hear about it," Clara urged Elsie. "Alice just told me today. Not many people know about if, do they?"

"I'm afraid a few too many people know," she sighed.

"I didn't hear anybody else talk about it," Clara said, "so why would you want to go home?"

"Clara, you just don't understand. I knew if Levi asked a girl, he was serious, but I never expected him to ask me. I still wonder if it was a mistake," Elsie sighed wearily.

"But why didn't you accept him, even if you don't know him so well? It would have been a good chance to get acquainted. What more could you want than Levi?" Clara asked in all sincerity.

Elsie sighed again. "Don't ask me. I haven't slept good ever since I got the letter."

"Did he send you a letter?" Clara asked.

"No, his cousin Bertha (who lives next door to him) did; but I was to send my answer to Levi."

"But what girl would refuse Levi?" Clara asked in wonderment.

"Would you accept any boy who asked you?" Elsie said, becoming weary of the questions.

"Not Levi. He is my cousin," Clara replied truthfully.

"But I haven't been dwelling on Levi. Ah, well, I just didn't know what was best."

"You could always have given him a try. Didn't it make you eager, just grasping the fact that he thought you were special?" Clara asked with excitement in her voice.

"It wasn't that easy," Elsie replied, adding, "maybe someday you will understand. I'm hoping Levi isn't here tonight. I don't know how to act."

"But you haven't told me yet why you didn't want to learn to know him better." Clara pressed her further.

As they got deeper into the subject, Clara gathered that Elsie was admiring another boy and didn't feel it was honorable to accept Levi while she had special feelings for someone else. But Clara couldn't get any clues as to whom it might be.

Now and then Clara and Elsie heard buggies coming in the driveway and more voices downstairs, but they were mostly engrossed in deep conversation. They guessed they had missed supper, but they didn't care.

Suddenly the singing of "How firm a foundation, Ye saints of the Lord," floated up to them. Composing themselves, Clara and Elsie quietly made their way downstairs. Since the singing had already started, they wanted to be in kitchen before the boys filed in. When they opened the stairway door and took their places behind the table, quite a few of the girls looked up, some with a puzzled look, as if they were thinking, *Oh, so they didn't go home after all.*

Just as they were seated, the boys filed out from the sitting room, filling up the places at the table that the girls had left for them. Some stood in a row behind the chairs, while others moved their chairs closer together. As Clara looked up to see if the boys would all find room, she happened to meet Sammie's glance. His smile widened in recognition. For a moment, she felt her face get warm, hoping the blush wasn't visible. As the boys continued coming out and pushing chairs together, Clara saw cousin Levi standing behind the table. At that moment, he looked around behind him, found a chair in the corner, and wiggled over to it. Peter moved over to make room for the last two boys who came.

As Clara looked around, her heart stood still. She took a deep breath as she recognized the blond curls which lay neatly in the swirl of hair that was tossed back. Harvey, Elva Mae's brother, motioned for him to crowd on the bench beside him at the table.

Shaking his head, the young man gave Harvey a smile which lightened up his pleasant features. He rubbed his hands nervously over his forehead as if to hide behind it. Lloyd took the place beside Harvey.

Clara pulled her gaze away before Merle could look up. She wanted to look again, but she knew without taking another glance that it was Merle. She thought he had left the settlement. *And why did it matter if he was here?* she asked herself. *Was there a girl here that he was interested in? Oh well, his brother lives here. Was it maybe Merle whom Elsie was admiring that she couldn't accept Levi?* She looked over at Elsie, who, with the others, was singing:

> *What a friend we have in Jesus,*
> *All our sins and griefs to bear;*
> *What a privilege to carry*
> *Everything to God in prayer!*

For a moment Clara lifted her eyes and saw a few boys leaning forward talking to each other, which gave her a view of Levi who blew his nose and blinked his eyes while the voices rang out.

> *Oh, what peace we often forfeit,*
> *Oh, what needless pain we bear.*
> *All because we do not carry*
> *Everything to God in prayer.*

Clara's heart was smitten to see cousin Levi wasn't singing, since he was a good singer. Then she realized that she wasn't singing either. Only a few hours earlier she was looking forward so much to the evening singing. Now her heart felt so troubled.

Clara looked in Sammie's direction just as he announced, "Page 91." There was a rustling of pages, and then the voices blended as the volume rang out,

> *How many times discouraged,*
> *We sink beside the way.*

About us all is darkness,
We hardly dare to pray . . .

Sammie looked up sincerely as he joined in with the singing, which seemed to come from his heart. He looked so submissive.

Clara tore her gaze away and glanced in Merle's direction. She was always a little unprepared for his striking appearance. He was singing, but he wasn't looking in his book. He seemed to be looking out the window. Seeing Merle had quickened her heartbeat, but the appearance of Sammie always struck deeply, too. She would try to forget and enjoy the singing.

Chapter Twelve

Clara paused before taking the rest of the wash off the line. She gazed at the sun, which was lingering in the west, delaying the end of another spring day.

Soft breezes played around the bushes. Clara took a deep breath as she noticed all the twigs pushing buds, preparing to unfold. The grass seemed so green. When had all this happened? Clara surmised that it had taken place bit by bit, unnoticed in the past days as she hurried to and from the bulk food store—opening it to get ready for another day, and keeping the house running. How she had missed Aunt Hettie these last days.

Clara looked back at the washline and pulled out the shirt sleeve that was doubled up inside the shirt. But it was already dry. The air was so mild today, spring breezes playing joyfully, caught the wash and dried it even if it wasn't properly hung. Clara pulled a stocking loose from where it had twisted around an apron string, which Nevin hadn't noticed when he hung it up this morning. Though Clara had gotten the wash ready, Nevin had hung it to the best of his ability. He said he would do the wash rather than work in the store; however, Clara helped Nevin when she could slip out of the store.

Aunt Hettie had gone to the hospital with a neighbor to bring Uncle Benjamin home. Benjamin wasn't feeling well during the last few weeks. Finally, the doctor suggested he go to the hospital; however, there wasn't much the doctors could do. It appeared his previous injuries were taking a toll on his body. From what Clara overheard, the infections were spreading—something Hettie had been aware of for awhile. Uncle Benjamin tried hard to go on for his family.

As Clara picked up the washbasket and started toward the house, she saw a team driving in at the store. Anna Lois, the older girl, had already left. She had recently started helping out in the store since Hettie couldn't help as much. Clara entered the side door of the store just as Shannon came around the third aisle.

"Oh, so you are still here," Shannon greeted her. "I was afraid the store would be closed already."

Looking at the clock, Clara said, "We will be closing in a half hour."

Shannon didn't seem very interested in shopping. "Let's see, you weren't at David's on Sunday evening, were you? Maybe you were home for the weekend and didn't want to bother to travel that far. We had a good time. It was mild so we decided to eat down by the river."

"No," Clara replied. "I stayed here at Uncle Benjamin's since he wasn't feeling well. He was in the hospital from Saturday until this forenoon, so I was here with the children while Aunt Hettie traveled back and forth to and from the hospital."

Shannon's face fell as he said, "Not Benjamin again. Seems he has had his share of struggles. Is he better? You say he's home?"

"Yes, he came home. Aunt Hettie didn't explain much to me, but I gather that the reason he came home is not because he is so much better, but because the doctors can't do more there than what can be done at home."

"You mean this is still the result of his previous injuries?"

"It seems nothing can be done to keep the infection from recurring." Clara could read the unspoken sympathy in his expression.

"I surely wish them well if the Lord so wills," Shannon commented as he buried his hand in his pocket, adding, "God moves in mysterious ways, his wonders to perform."

Clara nodded and asked, "Is there a singing for this weekend?"

Coming back to life, Shannon said, "Not really, but we are having the young folks at our place for Sunday dinner. Then, for those interested in joining, we plan to go around to sing for the elderly, the widows, and others."

74

Looking around the store, Shannon said, "Mom needs ten pounds of cheese, 10X sugar, and . . . ah. . . um, seems there was something else. I didn't give her time to make a list. What could it be?" he asked, looking at Clara hopefully.

"Maybe noodles?"

"No, Mom made them the other day," he said. "I'll look around. Maybe I'll see something and remember," he suggested, turning around while Clara got the things he did remember.

"Here it is," Shannon said from the last aisle. Bringing a few boxes of cupcake papers to the counter, he admitted he would never have remembered them if he hadn't seen them.

As Shannon paid for his purchases, he started talking about their Sunday afternoon outing, eating by the river and having races and games like they used to have at school picnics. It sounded like good old-fashioned fun.

Shannon picked up his groceries and set them by the door. "There's one more thing I need, but I don't have money to pay for it. Maybe you could lend it to me," he said, rubbing his hands together like an eager little boy, looking a bit mischievous.

Clara looked at him as he put his hat on his head. Shannon continued, "Would you be interested in entertaining some company on Sunday evening?"

"Me?" she asked, perplexed, then added, "Whom?" She was wondering it company was coming from another district and needed a place to stay. Suddenly she grasped the meaning and felt her face get hot. As Clara's heart was hammering within her, Shannon seemed to be enjoying the anxiety he was causing.

Sammie's humble smile floated through her mind. For a moment, she wildly thought of Shannon's steady, Anna, who had a brother Fred.

When Shannon almost whispered, "Merle sent me," Clara gasped and felt the strength go out of her, feeling she could crumble any minute. She wished she were alone. Remembering Merle's easy smile and his pleasant face with his light curls dangling on his forehead set her mind spinning. Carrying the work load of the store alone for awhile and the stress of knowing Benjamin wasn't well had put pressure on her, and now such a sudden turn. Maybe she was dreaming.

Shannon chuckled and reminded her, "I'm listening."

Clara, dumbfounded, looked at him and stammered, "Are you . . . I mean. . . d-do you need an answer tonight?"

Picking up his groceries, Shannon shrugged his shoulders saying, "I thought you would have an answer for me. Would it help to have time to think it over more?"

At length, Clara answered, "I can't answer since I don't know."

Shannon looked at her and smiled, still amused, as he made his way toward the door. Turning, he said, "Well, tell me on Sunday or before. No one else needs to know." Then he was off.

In a daze, Clara watched after him. Propping her head in her hands, she sighed. She had noticed that Merle was regularly attending the gatherings again. And there was something about him that stood out. She didn't know him real well, but she imagined that he stirred more than one girl's heart. She couldn't grasp that he asked for her friendship. The thought of watching him drive in the lane on a Sunday evening and spending a few hours visiting stirred up her emotions. She shivered nervously. They could learn to know each other. He would become a real person rather than a figure in her imagination.

As always, the picture of Sammie's humble smile came and destroyed the picture. Clara would have lots of things to discuss with Sammie, but she hardly got to talk with him anymore. Then a voice within reminded her, *But Sammie hasn't asked you for your company.* What had she asked Elsie? "What keeps you from accepting Levi?" And Elsie had replied, "Would you accept any boy who asked you?" But Merle wasn't just any boy.

Suddenly Clara remembered she had to give Shannon an answer so he could tell Merle. Merle was expecting an answer. Her heart was starting to throb as she continued thinking about the question.

Suddenly Nevin came in the door saying, "Are you still out here? Mom thought maybe something was wrong."

76

"Yes, I'll be coming," she said as she closed up the store and followed him.

Clara saw the full washbasket standing in the kitchen, but Hettie said, "We'll fold the wash tomorrow." Sitting on a chair, Clara thoughts continued to churn. She didn't even remember that it was time to help the little ones with their nightgowns until she saw Hettie helping them.

When the children were in bed, Hettie turned to Clara, asking, "Is there something you should tell me?"

Clara rose out of her stupor for a moment and said, "I have a headache. I will go to bed. Maybe that will help."

Slipping upstairs, Clara flopped on her bed. She had a great urge to talk to Elsie, but she couldn't. No, she couldn't tell anyone why she couldn't accept Merle and learn to know him better. But how could she turn Merle down? The more she thought, the more confused she felt. And how she dreaded Sunday!

Remembering the power of prayer, Clara got down on her knees, but her mind strayed too much. She didn't have to answer today, but Sunday was only four days away. Maybe tomorrow things would be clearer. She found out tomorrow wouldn't come so soon. She kept tossing. Every time she convinced herself she would accept Merle, she dwelled on the thought of his coming to visit on Sunday evening, and tried to think of things they could talk about. But it always turned out to be Sammie she was talking to about his job, etc. Then a voice reminded her, *But Sammie didn't ask you.*

Clara met the next day in a daze, going through the motions of opening the store, greeting Anna Lois, and weighing various products. When a customer came in, Anna Lois looked expectantly at Clara. When Clara didn't stop what she was doing, Anna Lois said, "I'll ring it up for you."

Anna Lois returned after the customer left and said with concern, "Are you tired today? I guess you have more on your shoulders since Benjamin isn't well." Then she added, "I wish I didn't have a dental appointment this afternoon."

Clara looked up remembering, "Oh, yes, you have off this afternoon. Well, maybe if I have more to do I can wake up. I feel as if I'm only half awake."

"Maybe you should tell Hettie," Anna Lois replied as she turned to check out another customer.

Hettie didn't need to be told. When they finished dinner, she told Clara, "Now go and take a nap; I'll do the dishes. Nevin is out at the store."

Hearing Ben James cry awoke Clara an hour later. Getting up, she came to her senses, picked up Ben James and changed him.

Uncle Benjamin, who was resting on the recliner, said, "You can take the baby and Katherine along out to the store where Hettie's working."

The customers were few and far between in the afternoon. Clara enjoyed working with Aunt Hettie as they weighed things. Five-year-old Katherine was so motherly to her little brother, Ben James. In the storeroom, where two one-hundred pound bags of flour lay, one on top of the other, the children were playing house, pretending the flour bags were their table. Hettie gave them pretzels and marsh-mallows and they continued playing while Clara and Hettie contin-ued weighing bulk food items.

As Hettie unfolded the top part of the sunflower seed bag and began dipping seeds out to fill smaller bags, she chuckled and said, "This morning and noon, when you looked so weary, I was reminded of how I felt for a few days many years ago when I was in a turmoil, and there was no one to unburden to."

Clara looked at her. "You mean when you were with the young folks?"

Hettie had a faraway look in her eyes. Clara became very much interested and asked, "Then what did you do?"

Hettie smiled as she put the bags on the scale. One by one, she put a few more seeds in some of them.

When Hettie didn't continue, Clara couldn't imagine cheer-ful Hettie, who always made the sun shine, ever being in a deep turmoil.

Hettie looked up and asked, "Do you mean in choosing a partner? In knowing which one?"

Clara nodded and asked, "Isn't that what you were starting to say?" Clara stood waiting, forgetting she had tapioca bags before her waiting to be twist-tied and labeled. Ben James was getting unreasonable and Katherine was upset trying to manage him with her play. Hettie gave Ben James his pacifier and nestled him down with his blanket in the corner where he took naps in the store. Katherine started playing with her dolls which certainly cooperated better than her brothers had cooperated.

Hettie came back to life and continued her thoughts. "Maybe I'd better tell you how I got into my turmoil before I tell you how I handled it. Among the young folks there was a boy known as Clarence who always struck my fancy. I never had a clue if he knew I existed. Well, yes, I knew he knew I was around. He was a friendly fellow, but he never seemed to hold one girl more precious than another. I suppose many a girl longed after him.

"The time came when I was invited to a wedding in another district—the district where Uncle Ivans lived. My mother had been wanting me to help out at Uncle Ivans, and she thought this would be a good chance, so I planned to go by bus. Ivan would pick me up or send someone. Mother lost no time in sending them a letter with the message. They would answer if it didn't fit into their plans. My parents were invited to that district on the Sunday after the wedding, so I could come home with them.

"I was a little leery about going on the bus alone, but I didn't have to change buses, and there was just one layover on the way. I still remember that as we were nearing the small station where we were expected to arrive, there was another bus pulling away. The station was a small place—a restaurant with a little lobby where we could get tickets and wait for the bus. As I got off the bus, I looked around to see if I could see someone waiting for me. There were people going in and out of the restaurant.

"As I was about to enter the building, I saw a young Mennonite man walking along the side of the building. It wasn't Ivan, but I thought maybe they had sent someone. Just at that

79

moment, the man turned and looked at me. Seeing my anxious expression, he paused.

"I walked over and stammered, 'Did you, or I mean did Ivan send you?'

"He got such a puzzled look on his face and politely answered, 'I don't know what Ivan you are talking about. I just brought my friend, Jacob, down to meet the bus that just left. He is on the way to Wisconsin. Did you just arrive on another bus?'

"I told him I did and I thought Uncle Ivan Kulp or a driver would be here to pick me up. He made himself helpful and checked to see if anyone was in the restaurant, but no one seemed to be around.

"Then he said, 'I'm going back that way; I can take you along to Ivan's house.' I really didn't know what else to do, so I accepted his offer. He introduced himself as Benjamin Brubaker. In the conversation we had on the way to Ivan's, I gathered he was with the young folks. He wasn't very talkative. He politely drove me to Ivan's door, where Ivan's family seemed surprised as they greeted me.

"It was awhile later that we found out that Mom never did put the letter in the mailbox. She was sidetracked on her way out to the mailbox. It had started raining and she decided to take the wash down first. The letter was found in the clothespin bag on the next washday. Anyway, I did help at Ivan's and I did get to the wedding.

"In he morning when I heard my name called and I came downstairs, I saw at a glance that Benjamin was sitting alone in a row where another couple was already seated. I sat in the next chair, and next to me came two girls who seemed to know each other well. As they visited together, I though no more of it. As the songbooks were being passed out, the two girls were still discussing something. The man handed Benjamin a book and then tossed one to the girls, continuing on down the line. The song number was announced and the girls were still talking quietly. About that time, Benjamin looked ill at ease. The girls never noticed my plight, but Benjamin matter-of-factly moved his songbook over.

"After the wedding, one of Ivan's children had a dental appointment. Ivan was busy with silo filling, and his wife didn't drive the horse, so I took her to the dentist."

"I didn't know you drove," Clara said surprised and much involved in the story.

"I did when I was with the young folks, but I don't drive the horse Benjamin drives, so I got away from driving alone. Anyhow, it was a cold blustery day for October," Hettie continued. "As I was sitting in the waiting room, waiting till my cousin got called in, the door opened and Benjamin came in. After he hung up his wraps, he looked over the waiting room. I quickly looked in another direction, but not before seeing his forehead take on more color. My cousin was soon called in, and I went with her. When we came out, only town people were in the waiting room. We went back to Ivan's and, when Sunday came, I went home with my parents.

"We had mild weather again the next week and it stayed mild. It seemed we wouldn't be getting chilly, fall weather except for those few days. Then, the last week of November, a cold, raw wind blew up. I had gone to the neighbors on an errand for Mom. I was on the way home, coming along the field lane. Stopping to close the gate, I took a shortcut through the pasture. Rather than putting on my gloves, I put my hands in my coat pockets to warm them. Feeling something in my pocket, I pulled out a small card—like an appointment card. I read it. It was a dental appointment card for Benjamin Brubaker for October 4 at 1:00 p.m.

"I was confused as to why this card would be in my coat pocket. I took a closer look and noticed there were some words written on the back.

"The penned words read, 'If you feel it's the Lord's hand that is leading us together, when can I come to see you?' Benjamin's address followed.

"Finally I grasped that he must have put that card in my pocket that day about two months ago. Why was it on his appointment card? And why didn't I find it until now? Many thoughts went through my mind until I was able to grasp that I hadn't worn this coat since then because of the mild weather. Likely, Benjamin didn't have any other paper with him at the time. But finding it now—. Was he still expecting an answer? Maybe he gave up and asked another girl by now.

"Like I said, seeing you so preoccupied this morning and yesterday reminded me of the turmoil I experienced in the following days."

Clara suddenly gasped and interrupted, asking, "Is that where the saying originated that I have been hearing when someone is hunting for something? 'Did you look in your coat pocket?'"

"Yes," Hettie chuckled. "All our children use that expression and think it's an old family saying."

It was usually Uncle Benjamin who so dryly and seriously asked, "Well, have you looked in your coat pocket?" when one of the children couldn't find something. Even if it was the lawn mower.

After Hettie had waited on a few customers, she came back to the table and started pulling out more bags of things needing to be weighed.

Clara asked, "How did you come out of your turmoil?"

"Well, it would have been easier if I had been able to let Clarence vanish from my dreams. I fought with that a few days until a strong voice within reminded me that God could have led Clarence into my life a lot easier than Benjamin if God wanted us to meet. But knowing that Benjamin was still waiting for an answer loomed over me. All I would have needed to do would be to write my thoughts and send it to the address that was so clearly printed on the back of the card. But, it was almost two months later. Was he still interested? Maybe he had another girl. What could I do?

"I had a circle letter that I needed to take over to the neighbors. In the evening I walked over to their house, the neighbor man was out in the field doing some late silo filling, and his wife was working in the orchard. Evidently her parents were visiting, since I recognized the older man, who was in the cornfield picking up the cobs that had been missed, as Minister James Horst. He was working near the road and greeted me. As we talked, I unburdened some of my turmoil on him, trying not to go into too much detail. He had a way of questioning me asking why I thought Benjamin wouldn't desire an answer anymore. (A boy asking a girl on an appointment card that was lost for two months in a coat pocket took some explaining.)

"Coincidentally, I had a scratch pad in my apron pocket and Brother Horst had a pen so I wrote a note to Benjamin, explaining that the card had only been found that week and he could contact me at my address if the Lord was still leading him that way. In record time there was a letter in my mailbox with James's return address on it. When I opened it, I thought there was nothing inside. But, looking more closely, I found a small card in the corner. It was an outdated dental appointment care for James. What could it mean? I looked on the back of the card and squinted to read the fine print.

"It read: 'All is set. Benjamin is planning to see you at your house on Sunday evening.'

Hettie chuckled as she said, "We had things to talk about the first few evenings. It wasn't until weeks later that he admitted the struggle he endured the first three weeks waiting for an answer. After four weeks, he reasoned to himself that maybe the card wasn't found. Then he reasoned that a girl who kept a boy waiting that long was not worth getting to know. In the next weeks, he resigned himself from hoping to ever hear from me. And James had his fun putting questions to him. Benjamin was slow in believing him." A silence followed.

When Clara grasped that Hettie had come to the end of the story, she asked, "What became of Clarence?"

"Oh, Clarence," Hettie said, coming out of her deep thoughts. "As far as I know, he never chose a girl. I hadn't heard anything about him for a long time. Some years ago, I heard he was dating a widow who was older then he was, which really got the people talking. The widow broke off the relationship, and people really pitied him. I think he moved to another settlement where his brother lives."

Hettie exclaimed, "Oh, the schoolchildren are home already. Benjamin must be wondering why I haven't been back in the house at all."

That evening, as Clara lay in bed, she was listening to the voice which said, "But Sammie didn't ask you." And she thought about Merle and his coming to visit her. On and on she continued to dream. She thought that likely he wouldn't care or consider her disobedient if she helped along her naturally waved hair. Many thoughts filled her mind. Sammie's image was fading in the background. Clara couldn't sleep. She tossed and turned and prayed, but there was no rest. Finally, at midnight she promised herself she would not accept Merle's company. She was thinking about confiding in Elsie now that she understood, but then she remembered that Shannon had said, "No one needs to know."

Clara awoke the next morning feeling better, but there was still a dull pain in her stomach as she thought about giving her answer to Shannon.

On Saturday afternoon, while Clara was weighing spices, she saw Shannon roaming in the store. Anna Lois was taking care of a customer. Keeping her eyes on him, Clara waited to get his attention.

When Shannon saw Clara looking at him, he raised his eyebrows. She pointed to the back door and went outside. It wasn't long till Shannon came striding around the building.

Searching her face, he asked, "Have you got anything to tell me?"

Clara's spirit fell when she heard his mounting hopes.

"I can't, Shannon. I hope he is not disappointed, but . . ."

"I don't understand, Clara," Shannon said in confusion.

"I don't either. I thought I would accept him, but it didn't work out," she admitted.

"I'm supposed to tell him no?" he asked, making sure he understood.

Clara nodded and said, "Thanks for stopping in. I was wondering when I could tell you."

Clara dreaded Sunday dinner and the afternoon. She hoped Merle wouldn't be there. A song kept going through her mind, "In seasons of distress and grief, my soul has often found relief."

Clara's already dampened spirit fell more when she saw Merle file in with the boys on Sunday morning in church. She did manage to survive the forenoon. When she thought of going to the dinner, she now understood why Elsie had hoped Levi wouldn't be at the singing.

There were some things to be grateful for. One was that she now had a way to go to the gatherings, since Benjamin's oldest son, Charles, was going with the young folks, and he usually came home for the weekend.

When they arrived at Shannon's house for dinner, some teams were already there and more were coming. As Clara entered the bedroom to place her wraps, she heard a few people gasp in shocked surprise. Others merrily said, "You don't say?" or "What next?" Some cautioned, "Shh-shh, she'll soon be coming and hear you." Clara felt like dropping through the floor. She had no idea how the people had already found out that she had turned Merle down.

Others coming in the door said, "I don't believe this." Clara turned around and saw that Alice was one of them. Alice smiled at her and asked, "Have you heard?"

"Heard what?" Clara asked.

"Haven't you seen? Sammie picked up Caroline at church and just drove in. Peter said some of the boys said they had a date on Sunday evening, but not many people knew until today."

"Caroline?" Clara repeated.

"Yes, wonders never cease," Alice replied. The room grew quiet as Caroline and Anna came in. Later in the afternoon, those interested in going along to sing for the widows and shut-ins began leaving in groups to sing at various places. Clara and Elsie were visiting in the living room. Clara was only half listening to all that was being said.

When Shannon first talked about going around singing, she had looked forward to it, but her thoughts were dampened, knowing Merle would go along. She had seen him drive out with another boy. Now her mind was churning even more. Her heart held a nameless ache. She had turned Merle down and lost Sammie. Of course, she never had Sammie, so how could she lose him? Somehow, everything seemed to suddenly be knocked out from under her.

Somewhere a sentence was coming back to her that she heard some time ago. It had probably been about Caroline. "There should be more girls like her," Sammie had said. But no one had ever expected that Sammie would be able to win Caroline. *I wonder how Sammie acknowledged it? Whatever made me think that I would be worthy of Sammie?*

Always when a voice came to tempt Clara saying, "Would you have accepted Merle if you had known about Sammie and Caroline?" she fought it off. She must not let doubt take a hold, for she was going to accept Merle, but then she remembered she could not rest until she promised herself that she wouldn't accept him. Was it because when she had given in to the tempting thought that Merle wouldn't care if she'd adorn herself more, that she had no peace.

Chapter Thirteen

Clara hung up the last of the towels and washcloths, looking for a moment with satisfaction at the line of white wash that was swaying in the gentle summer breeze.

As she was coming back to the wash house, she heard Katherine exclaim, "Look, Clara, what we made!"

Clara looked up and saw that she and Ben James were still in the sandbox. Katherine had pressed out many sand cakes with a tin dish from her tea set, and Ben James was digging around in the sand, telling Clara a whole row of his baby language. Oh, to be happy and innocent as little children.

Dwelling on that thought, Clara went back into the wash house. Opening the lid of the washing machine, she used a stick to stir the wash and feed it through the wringer. She stirred again, but the washing machine appeared to be empty. Looking around, she saw the pile of light-colored dresses and shirts still on the floor. She thought she had put them in the washing machine, but failed to put them in after she took the towels out. Oh no, now she had wasted time, she thought as she picked up the pile and shoved it in. She had hoped to get the washing done earlier, so she could sort the tomatoes if she wasn't needed in the store.

Hettie's brother Elvin's children were helping in the store to give Clara time to take care of the house and garden while Hettie spent more time at Benjamin's bedside. He was experiencing more pain and battling with fever.

While Clara stood by the window, waiting till the load of wash was finished, she thought of the weekend that had just passed. She found herself enjoying more and more being with cousin Laura, who was only a year younger than herself. Clara had never had many doings with her. Laura was more quiet and reserved and had some good buddies of her own. But since Elsie was now dating Elva Mae's brother Harvey, Clara found herself a little misfit. It seemed it was turning out much like Alice after she was dating Peter. Clara had gradually found herself confiding in Laura. Clara was finding out that Laura was an interesting person, but her bashfulness kept her from mingling heartily with the whole group.

Clara stepped out of the wash house and started pulling the weeds that were growing there in the corner of the walk and wash house where the mower couldn't get it.

Her thoughts went to all the younger boys and girls that were joining the young folks. They seemed to be getting younger. She hardly realized that she herself was getting older, leaving her nineteenth birthday months behind.

For a moment Clara stopped pulling weeds as she pictured her sister Norma. She had seen her over the weekend at the gathering. Clara could hardly grasp that her sister was now with the young folks. She seemed to blend easily. To Clara it seemed like an extra link to be more connected with the family. Clara wondered if Norma ever had to re-comb her hair. Mother maybe wasn't in full control. Clara noticed that Norma hadn't pushed her top hair forward much, but she had somehow pushed the lower half of the hair further front and patted it neatly to the side of her face. It changed her appearance so towards how she had looked when she was a school girl. Clara had to admit that Norma had by nature a more striking appearance that she herself had.

As she hung up the load that was now washed, her thoughts strayed to the young folks.

It was more than a month since Merle had last been at a gathering. She had just about started to be more relaxed in his presence again and had secretly hoped at times that maybe Merle would be led back into her life. Since Sammie had faded out, Merle seemed more precious, but she had hurt him. Life was so difficult. For a moment she thought of Caroline and Sammie. It seemed Caroline had raised Sammie's character above everyone's comprehension.

It seemed so strange as more and more people started referring to him as Samuel. It had hardly been Caroline as Clara herself had heard her call him Sammie, so she didn't know what had brought the change about. He was becoming such a gentleman that it seemed only fitting to call him Samuel rather than such a boyish name as Sammie.

Aunt Martha's family invited the young folks for supper. Clara didn't need to be persuaded to attend. She was eager to go as that was cousin Laura's home.

The last few gatherings Clara had missed, as she felt duty-bound to stay and help Aunt Hettie with the children and the meals while Uncle Benjamin was mostly in bed and Hettie had to spend time caring for him.

Aunt Hettie had said that Clara didn't have to miss being with the young folks since other people offered to help out.

So this Sunday she did not need much encouragement. Cousin Laura had asked her to help serve the supper, and Clara was enjoying it. Clara appreciated Laura so much as Alice and Elsie soon left after supper when the couples left.

The other table waiters had left the kitchen. The dishes were washed and Laura was straightening up the countertop that held the array of unsorted dishes all stacked in an unorganized way. Clara was helping her put things away and Laura was asking about Uncle Benjamin. "So you could have off once again," she asked.

"I could have had off other weekends, too. There were people who were willing to help out, but I felt duty-bound to the smaller children. There's enough stress for them without having other people coming in so often to keep house. But this Sunday it was too good to resist."

"I was so much hoping you could come. The younger table waiters are in such a hurry to get the dishes washed and then be off," Laura replied as she was sorting the teaspoons from the tablespoons, and getting the knives and forks together that had been thrown every which way in the cake pan.

Laura asked further, "How are you making out at the bulk food store? Do you have it open?"

"Oh, sure it is open, Hettie's brother Elvin's family, you know, who live nearby were helping out a lot," Clara replied as she sorted the plates, butter saucers, and jelly dishes and put them in the cupboard.

She further explained, "Benjamins were going to bring Charles home, but Elvins said they would help."

"Let's see. Elvins. They don't have much girls' help to send, do they?" Laura thought out loud.

"Florence has helped some, even though I'm sure her mother could have used her help too, but the boys seem good at it. They seem to take more of an interest in it than Benjamin's boys do. Well, Nevin helps more than Charles ever did," Clara answered.

Laura took the smaller glass dishes and stacked them in the cupboard. Then as if suddenly hearing what Clara had said, she stopped and looked at Clara and questioned, "Elvin's boys?" She laughed a little and said, "I suppose that gives some fun."

Clara gave a knowing nod and replied, "You know, Laura, I remember my thoughts when they started helping, that Rufus would really liven things up and almost drive me up a wall after awhile. And the first few times he kept making humorous remarks and had us all laughing, but it soon got sorta old to hear regularly. Oh, well, I don't know. It seemed so put on. Like he was trying too hard to be funny. I guess we didn't give him enough attention to feed him on like his buddies did. Harold hasn't helped much. I guess he has a pretty regular job, but we have been learning to know the older twin."

Laura looked at her and asked, "Raymond?"

Clara smiled at her wondering question and explained, "You know sometimes when you really get to know someone, they aren't how you know them in a group setting." Laura looked at her for a better explanation.

The dishes now were mostly all in the cupboard and the girls sat down on the bench that was standing against the wall.

Laura's mother and dad were at the living room end of the kitchen where a bunch of girls were having a lively conversation, or maybe they were teaching others some new tricks, the way it sounded.

90

"Well, you know," Clara began. "With the young folks, when people refer to the Kulp twins, it's mostly 'Rufus so and so' and Raymond seems more like his shadow, just passing with him. So I was rather slow to catch on to Raymond's good character and witty nature. And, well, I don't know, maybe you could say he was planted a little deeper. I wonder if Raymond feels inferior at times by Rufus being so popular, I guess you might say. Raymond can be very interesting and seems respectful of others' feelings as if maybe he has had the experience of not being so easily accepted."

Laura smiled and said, "I don't know what to think. You seem to be quite respectful of Raymond. Are you trying to tell me something?"

"No, Laura, you don't understand. I'm just trying to say that I don't think many people really have a chance to know Raymond. It seems he has unused character. I mean it," Clara added. "Get that smirk off your face. I can see that you don't believe me."

"I have to tell you some things that I remember about Raymond. One day when I came in the store to work, Raymond had just finished waiting on a customer and said matter-of-factly, 'You know, our business is picking up.' I looked at him with doubt and surprise, as I hadn't thought we were having many customers—at least not more than usual. He didn't offer any explanation and went on his way stocking shelves. I was unpacking an order and set some boxes of tea on the shelf when some tumbled down. As I gathered them up, he looked for a moment and said, 'It's our business *picking up*. Yesterday we picked up twist ties; this forenoon it was brown bags.' He didn't crack a smile, but his eyes held such a twinkle that I caught on to his fun. He was right. The day before a box of twist ties had fallen on the floor when Anna Lois and I were weighing products, and he helped pick them up. Then, in the forenoon when he was trying to put more brown bags in the holder at the counter, they slipped and many scattered on the floor, and we picked them up. So, at an unexpected moment, he told me our business was picking up."

Laura chuckled. "You mean Raymond came up with that? Sounds like Rufus, but Raymond?" she questioned.

91

"If you don't believe that, listen to this one. One day I listed on paper everything that needed to be weighed. I had to do some garden work and look after Ben James, which took me longer than I had expected. When I came back in, I was quite surprised that Raymond was weighing dates. I remembered then that I had sold the last one-pound bag of dates the evening before, but I had failed to inform anyone. I asked Raymond how he knew this since I failed to put it on the list. He looked at me as if I had asked a senseless question, but I saw a very mischievous glint in his usually pale blue, sober eyes.

"'Tying the bags,' he calmly said. 'I wasn't the best scholar in school, but I learned my ABCs pretty well and still know them.'

"Not sure what he was getting at, I saw Raymond pointing to the paper with the list I had written: apricot Jello, butterscotch bits, and cocoa. He had made the first letter of each word darker, showing the A, B, and C plainly, saying he figured that these dates would probably be the next on the list.

"I guess I have to believe it," Laura said in wonderment. "But it sure isn't the Raymond we know with the young folks. Even Rufus isn't that witty."

"That's what I have been trying to tell you."

"What about when Rufus helps?" Laura questioned. "What is he like?"

"Oh, well," Clara began, "it's something like a teacher with a trying pupil. Like when he hid the scoop I was using. I hunted for it desperately until I noticed Anna Lois accusingly looking at Rufus. Or the time that I kept glancing at the clock and couldn't believe that it didn't take me longer to weigh various items. Then I caught on. He had turned the clock back."

"That sounds like Rufus; his fun gets irritating at times."

"It does," Clara admitted and added, "It's usually at our own expense!"

A few moments passed as each pondered her thoughts. Finally, Laura asked, "Do you think Raymond is a character like that among the young folks, too; but people are so taken up with Rufus's jokes that Raymond's wit goes unnoticed?"

"Maybe. I was trying to figure that out. Or Raymond is just more bashful with a group," Clara concluded.

"But you know what?" Laura asked with excitement mounting in her voice. "I was just wondering if you got the real message about Raymond. Maybe he was trying to ask you something by saying he figured the dates would be next."

"Oh, Laura, I give up with you," Clara said, playfully slapping Laura. "Let's go out and see what the others are doing. You know Ilene is his special girl," she added as they went out the door.

"You mean Ilene is eyeing him, but no one knows if Raymond has any special interest in her." Laura spoke softly as they were coming upon the girls by the swing in the yard where they were watching the boys play croquet.

"And who could resist Ilene?" Clara asked honestly.

Laura raised her eyebrows and shrugged her shoulders in a couldn't-care-less manner.

Chapter Fourteen

The hour had come. Uncle Benjamin's soul departed from his sick body. He had been lingering at death's door for a few days. Charles had been home all week, and the family had gathered around his bed a few times, but then he rallied again.

The time had come suddenly early Friday morning after he had been talking with Hettie. He suddenly gave a deep sigh and turned his eyes heavenward, as if he was seeing something.

Hettie said she heard a faint voice as Benjamin softly sang, "Soon with angels I'll be marching, with bright glory on my brow," as if he was singing along with something he was hearing. Then his soul departed. There was no time to rouse the children.

As Clara dwelled on it, she thought of the words that followed: "Who will share my blissful portion, Who will love my Saviour now?" Fresh tears washed over Clara's face at the meaning of the words, "Who would love my Saviour now?" Could the family continue in the spiritual growth that Benjamin had begun? He read Bible stories to the children; he taught the children obedience at a young age. It just seemed unfair. Clara's heart bled for the children, some too young to really understand. Little Ben James would never really remember his father. And her heart ached for Charles, who at almost eighteen, had to face life without a father. And the other boys were close behind. How could God need to take Benjamin from this earth when he was such a needed father?

When an older woman had spoken sympathizing words to Hettie on the day of the viewing, Clara heard Hettie submissively say that she was grateful that God extended the years so long, and that He didn't take Benjamin when he had his accident with the team.

Clara longed to have such a strong, undoubting faith. Hettie seemed to always see the good in things. Clara couldn't remember ever hearing Hettie murmur. She believed that there would always be a way.

The parting was hard as the children watched in innocence as their father was lowered into the grave. Many tears were shed. And now the solemn hour had come when all the friends and loved ones from near and far filed into the church, filling up every bench. Many folding chairs were set up, using every available spot, leaving narrow aisles in case someone needed to go out. When all were seated, all eyes turned to the ministers' bench, waiting on assuring words of comfort and strength in this deep sorrow that drew them together. Clara's heart thumped and a few tears slipped down her cheeks as she saw Caleb rise slowly and step up to the table.

Why did Caleb have such a heavy responsibility to offer comfort to all these people? What could he say?

Looking over the sea of faces Caleb lowered his eyes and in a trembling voice said, "We have gathered together from near and far in the echo of death. There are aged ones in our circle of loved and known ones who have long been waiting for their release. They are still waiting, for our God is in control. He fills His mansions in His order. If He only called the elderly, there would be many souls that would grow careless, thinking that they would have a long time yet. Consequently, they might fall in the way of temptation that would lead them away from ever seeking the kingdom. Thus, He calls a brother like Benjamin to touch the people and soften their hearts—to pull more souls. Far too many of His mansions are not being filled, thus He, in mysterious ways, calls to His people with a pleading call before they stray farther away—that they may come back to the fold ere the wolf destroys them.

"I have wondered why God would call a father when he is still so much needed. A few days before Brother Benjamin departed from this life, I visited by his bedside, wondering what I could say to comfort him; but he seemed to have a strong faith and was anxiously awaiting his heavenly call. I mentioned that we don't always understand God's will, but we want to submit and trust His all-wise ways.

Although the brother was weak physically, he said that at times he could not say, 'Thy will be done.' He thought he had too much unfinished work, but then he was reminded of the words from the twenty-second chapter of Matthew when the wedding feast was prepared and the bridegroom called. Those who were bidden said they would not come. Making light of it, they went on their way— one to his farm, another to his merchandise. Others were called to fill up the tables. It doesn't say that those who refused ever had another chance. Brother Benjamin said it was hard to win the victory, but he did.

"I don't remember his exact words, but he came to realize that the things of this life were not worth losing the kingdom. He didn't want anything to stand in his way. Submitting himself to God, he was waiting on His call." Caleb paused as many people wiped their eyes.

"Now, to the ones left behind. I would encourage Sister Hettie to hold on to the faith Benjamin has left behind. All things are timely. 'Seek ye first the kingdom of God and His righteousness, and all these things shall be added unto thee.' Jesus also prayed, 'Father, if thou be willing, remove this cup from me; nevertheless, not my will, but Thine, be done. But He had to suffer. Not for His sake, but so that others could be saved. And I hope that you, Sister, can trust in the same way, and that it will help others to eternal life and they will remember this when dark days come. Look to this light, like the words we all sang as children, hardly realizing the meaning—maybe not fully even now: 'Oh the mighty gulf that God did span at Calvary.'

"There was a mighty gulf there, and God sent his son Jesus to suffer and give up His life to fill that mighty gulf from sin to repentance. It could not be spanned any other way. It is like a high cliff where many people would perish if the way wasn't spanned. I grasped that the brother and sister looked at it this way. There was a mighty gulf that had to be spanned, and God saw fit to take Brother Benjamin from among us. It was not their choice, and I'm sure they pleaded for this cup to pass over, but then submitted to, 'Not my will, but Thine be done.'

"And, Sister, I would encourage you that when days become filled with dark clouds of doubt and discouragement, dwell on these thoughts. We don't need to understand; we need only to trust and let Him lead. 'For we know our afflictions work for us a far more exceeding and eternal weight of glory.' Let us not despair from that eternal weight of glory. For when the world shall be judged and the chaff shall be thoroughly fanned from the wheat, then we shall see the glory of it and praise God that He has pressed us on to gain that exceeding and eternal weight of glory. Then we shall see what the afflictions worked for us, and we shall truly say they were light and but for a moment when we see the gulf they spanned.

"Now the weight seems heavy and crushing while we look on corruptible things, but we must look on the incorruptible. To the children: you may wonder what you can do to help your mother. There's much you can do. Obey her. It helps so much. Believe, obey, and then the work is done.

"I feel unworthy to stand here when there are others that you are waiting to hear. Maybe they can share more encouragement."

Next, a young minister arose. He looked even younger than Caleb. His dirty blond hair was neatly and evenly smoothed down. His face looked solemn but kind as he looked over the congregation. Clara wondered if he was one of Hettie's relatives. Why would such a young minister travel the distance? Clara imagined that older ministers, who had years of experience in death and afflictions, would have been asked to speak. She was surprised when the young minister began speaking fluently as if he was well acquainted with speaking in front of large crowds.

Clara, imagining this young man as a busy farmer who took time off to be here, listened as he continued speaking. She saw him now as a young man leaning over the Bible and songbooks, studying the words and then coming to share the inspiration. He quoted verse after verse of comfort and admonishment from the Scriptures, occasionally linking a German song when it fit with the message.

He explained that he hardly knew this brother who was called into eternity, but out of love, he felt the pull to come and be with the church and his family and children who were left behind.

The brother, in his opening remarks, touched on the subject of how afflictions can work an exceeding and eternal weight of glory, a glory that is a blessing to us, though the affliction of now will not seem light and for a moment.

"I have been given references to German songs from the family, songs that the brother had dwelled upon during the last few weeks of his life. I have been trying to sort these in order by glancing over the words. I see they bring out a message of how the brother must have struggled to accept his lot of losing in this life and resigning to leave all behind and stretching out to the glory beyond that was beckoning him. When looking up the words, I saw a message from doubt to submission and then victory if I can bring it forth in that order. I should have had more time to study it, but maybe I could start with the song on page 287:

> *Auf christen- mench auf, auf streit*
> *Auf, auf zum ümbervinden!*
> *In deiser velt, in deiser zeit*
> *Ist Keine ruh zu finden*
> *Ver nicht will streiten*
> *Trägt die kron*
> *Des ev'gen lebens nich davon.*

"An interpretation of the song might say:

> *Up, up, and off to battle.*
> *Up, up, to overcome the world*
> *In this time is no rest to find*
> *Who will not fight the battle*
> *Will not carry the crown of eternal life.*

"You can hear the brother found comfort in these words because he found it a battle to accept his sickness, to leave the beloved family that was entrusted to him. But he acknowledged the crown of life above this and wanted to be willing to submit even though it wasn't easy. He also dwelled on a verse on page 211:

Auch Gott! vie mancher kummer macht
Dasz ich mich herzlich kränke.
Vann ich bey mancher trüben nacht
Un tausend dunge denke so tröste mein gemuthe
So gehn die seufzer zu dir auf.
Auch lieber Gott! ach merke drauf,
Und tröste mein gemuthe.

"You can see he struggled.

Oh God, how poor are my doings,
When in the night I think of a thousand things
So my sighs go to Thee,
Oh beloved God, and comfort my weakness.

"The third verse he pondered on reads:

Mein hertz sorgt zu fruhe spöt
Vie dies und das vird kimmen,
Und venns nun alle sorgen hat.
Recht angstlich durchgenommem.
So hat es doch nicht ausgericht
Drumm vill ich meine zurfersicht
Auf dicht, und sonst nichts stellen.
Gieb mir geduld, damit ich stets
Die sorgen übervinde. Und sich der anker des gebäts.
Auf deine sorgen gründe.
Der geist ist villig aber doch
Das fleisch fühlt seine schvachheit noch.
Drum sey du meine störke.

Many people wiped their eyes because they understood the message, and the young minister blew his nose and calmly continued, "It almost seems as if the brother would have written this. I'm sure he marked it because he felt heartily with the songwriter:

99

My heart is troubled early and late,
About how this and that will come,
And the cares are earnestly thought over
But have not been solved,
Then will I rely on Thee and none else.
Give me patience to overcome the cares
And have You as the anchor for my prayers,
To ground my cares.
The spirit is willing, but the flesh feels its weakness.
So be my strength.

"The brother had many a battle to turn his cares over to God, trusting Him to make a way. He pleaded that he may anchor them in prayer, that it would hold him. The spirit was willing, but the flesh felt weakness. We all know how that is. We know that God is in control and He will help us, and that He has unfailing strength; but the flesh feels its weakness. We still tend to fail to trust God. Our flesh is weak to grasp the full faith; we feel we still need to worry.

"But the brother also referred to page 185, the third verse:

Alles vas ich bin und halbe
Kommt fon deiner faterhand
Es ist dein geschenk und gabe
Seele leib, gut her und stand
Haube dank für deine treu
Melche alle morgen neu
Habe dank fur deinen segen
Un dem alles ist gelegan.

"We grasp that the brother was finding that real strength—all he is and has—comes from the Father's hand. It is a gift, a talent.

"Blessings are new each morning. What a blessing to realize that God's strength and grace are renewed each day. When we get so weary by evening and we feel we can't continue another day, we need to remember that there will be renewed strength with the next day.

100

"What were the brother's cares and things he struggled to let go? Was it the daily work or the desire to earn more money? No, I don't think so, not from the words he dwelled on in the song on page 295:

Zu mir, zu mir ruft Jesus noch
Die kindlein lasset kommen
Hab ich aus leib zu ihnen doch
Die kindheit angenommen
Ja vie ein arm elendes kind
Gebuszet und beveint die sind
Die kinder die mich horen.

"We can see that in his heart he was concerned about his children, not about earthly riches that he couldn't give up. His desire was that his children hear Jesus and follow Him to repentance. He himself felt as small as a child.

"The third verse says:

Zu mir, zu mir nicht zu der velt
Und ihren eitekeiten
Die auch kindern sehr nachstellt
Und lockt auf allen seiten
Drum sich dich for mein kinde
Und thu for ihr dein aug and herze zu
Sie sturt dich ins ferderben

"He had much concern that his children come to the Lord and not weaken when the world beckons them from every side, as the next verse says:

All that the world offers—lust and praise and what all,
If we would have it all,
It would be just like a rope or net that Satan uses to
    catch us,
Catch our souls and lead us to hell.

101

"The brother must have fought hard to give up his family and trust them to God and other loved ones. I think the brother won the victory, because he referred to page 287, verse nine:

> Ver ubenvindet, der sol dort
> In veiszen kleidern gehen
> Sein guter name soll sofort
> Im buch des lebens siehen
> Ja Christus vird denselben gar
> Bekennen for der engel-schaar.

"Now we see his thoughts were not on this world, but what is beyond, where he will be clothed in a white robe and his name be found in the book. Then he'll be known to the heavenly hosts.

"And his final thoughts went to page 292. In English it would say:

> My life is running out,
> My pilgrimage will soon end.
> Oh God, will You send me a burden bearer
> That holds me on the right voyage,
> And stay my helm till I hold out the last storm
> That my ship with fearing goes
> Right through death to the Father's land,
> And my soul stands as a lantern
> To my Jesus Christ that even in death is my life.

"Using these songs together he has left a strong testimony.

"I sympathize much for the family, the growing boys, as I was barely out of school when my father was snatched away in death in about a twinkling of an eye. He had been sick two days and no one thought it was a serious illness; but God called and he answered.

"I admit I doubted God's motive. I felt God made a mistake; it couldn't work out for good. Many people offered us comfort and sympathy, but I rebelled. People didn't understand how much we still needed Father. Two of my brothers were married; I had five sisters still at home, and Mother was never very healthy while I knew her. I rebelled to go on living. I just gave up.

"Then I had a mishap in the barn while I was grinding feed, and I couldn't work for awhile. I took time to read more, since I had to do something to pass the time. It was at this time that a late sympathy card arrived with a parable and article enclosed. I read and reread it. It slowly opened my eyes to a view that removed my depression and replaced it with such a new thought. The article was in story form, which I will now try to repeat.

"The story was about a person who passed a certain place every day, a place that he often viewed and admired. It was a beautiful meadow with thick, green grass growing like a thick carpet. There were beautiful flowers growing, and cows contently grazed in the meadow. Birds sang from the treetops. It was a beautiful place to view.

"Then one day as this person came along, he suddenly noticed a great plow had gone right through the meadow, tearing an ugly furrow through the green, thick grass, turning up bare brown ground. The plow stood idle in the furrow.

"Crying out, this person said, 'How could anyone spoil such a beautiful sight?' Instead of cows lying and chewing their cud, and birds singing, chickens were scratching around in the upturned soil for worms."

The church house had become breathlessly still. Everyone seemed to be drinking in the words and waiting to hear what comfort would come from this story. The minister paused and started in fresh vigor.

"The writer at this point referred to the meadow as our home and said, 'We had such a nice Christian family, such concerned parents who brought up their children in the admonition of the Lord, and it was a happy family.' He compared it to the meadow with flowers blooming, birds singing, and cows grazing. God, the great plowman, came one day and plowed right through the happy family—the beautiful meadow—tearing out the father, making a deep furrow and leaving the family disturbed and singing no more. Flowers—wilted smiles—dissolved, and the wife was scratching to hold onto her faith.

It went on to ask, 'How could God spoil such a happy, God-fearing family? The mound in the church graveyard standing, as the plow, still in the furrow.'"

It seemed every ear was listening, every heart anxiously waited. It was so quiet as if everyone was holding his breath while the young minister paused and wiped his brow.

Blowing his nose and trembling, the minister continued, "The article went on to say that this person's eyes were opened by an unseen hand. Like a vision, he saw a field of corn, ready for the harvest. He could almost hear the music of the wind as it swept across the golden tassels of corn. Suddenly the plowed earth took on a new beauty that he had not noticed the day before. In your mind, you can picture a nice green pasture that was there for years. Then it was suddenly plowed, destroying the sunny green meadow. But when you think of the rich, dark soil so fertile from the grass and natural fertilizer where the plowman now planted corn while we were doubting and troubling ourselves too much to notice. Then we start to understand why the plowman plowed it. Not to destroy it, but to plant there a bounteous crop. But it first had to be plowed.

"The article went on to say, 'Oh that we might always catch the vision of an abundant harvest when God, the great plowman, comes as He often does and furrows through our very souls, uprooting and turning under what we cherish, leaving for our gaze the upturned bare brown soil. Why should we stare at the plowman, the Lord? We know He is no idle husbandman. He plows and plants a crop where he purposes. We must look beyond the turned-up soil. We must look beyond death and afflictions to what it brings, and not to what it takes.'

"The article was a stepping stone for me. We had plowed under an old hayfield that lay for some years. Then we planted corn and I had noticed that it had produced a wonderful crop, bringing much more fruit forth than the hay would have yielded. I was touched; there was inner strength growing in me, a trust that wiped out the doubt. Therefore, for the children today, it's my hope that they may know God never plows a deep furrow except that He plans to raise a greater crop, yielding a far more exceeding and eternal weight of glory. I will leave off and give time to the bishop."

Clara hoped he wouldn't sit down yet. He had so much to say. She remembered that when he first got up, she had wondered why such a young inexperienced man traveled many miles to the funeral of a man so much older than him, whom he hardly even knew. But she learned it was not only the older people who have difficult experiences. She lifted her eyes to where Charles sat erect, still watching the minister who had taken his seat. It seemed Charles was still drinking in all he had said.

Chapter Fifteen

Clara looked up for a moment from her notebook where she was concentrating, marking things that needed to be ordered. There were about three orders she had to get off before the next day. Her shoulders almost ached with the load of responsibilities. She had slowly gotten used to doing the ordering while Uncle Benjamin was ill and Hettie couldn't be in the store as much. Clara had quite a time learning about all the different companies from which they ordered various items. She hoped that Hettie would take more responsibilities again, since she wasn't constantly needed in the house, but it seemed Hettie was only a shadow of the Aunt Hettie she used to know. Clara then remembered that Benjamin had done the ordering; Hettie had only helped occasionally.

Nevin and Anna Lois were trying to get things weighed, but customers continued streaming in and out of the door. Clara paused for a moment, taking in the scene. Nevin had been weighing nuts and had to quit since a lady was waiting for larger bags of roasted sunflower seeds. As he weighed the sunflower seeds, Anna Lois told him a lady was waiting for a ten-pound bag of brown sugar. Clara longed to help them, but she had to get the orders out. Clara thought Hettie would be out by now.

It was no wonder that Hettie was only a shadow of the woman Clara had always known, since half of who she was had been taken away from her. For a moment Clara pictured the scene in her mind that the young minister had talked about at the funeral. It was a real picture of how death left Benjamin's family: the flowers gone, the singing birds gone, and Hettie scratching to hold onto her faith. Yes, it was like a deep furrow plowed right through their pleasant home and family. Clara shut off her thoughts and forced her mind back to getting the orders done.

Two hours later as Clara stepped out of the store and walked toward the house for lunch, she remembered that Hettie would probably ask, "Did you get the mail?" So, she turned back and hurried to the mailbox. How she hoped to find a few letters or cards for Hettie. She recalled that three months ago during the first few weeks after the funeral, there were always three or four cards a day, sometimes seven, one time nine, and Hettie always took time to really enjoy the letters. The mail seemed to carry her, but the letters had become fewer. It seemed they were worth even more when there was only one. Some days there had been none. Then the next day, there would be one again, but the past few days, there were hardly any.

Clara understood why there was less mail. There had been another funeral in the area since Uncle Benjamin's, and there were also funerals in other settlements of the church. People were now writing to those families, but Clara still prayed that there would be a letter today. As she opened the mailbox, her heart sank. There were only a few store flyers and some bills for the store.

As Clara came into the kitchen, Hettie looked at he hopefully, asking, "No mail?" Clara showed her the mail, but Hettie didn't reach for it. Clara thought she heard a sigh. Ben James was crying. Clara picked him up and asked him what was wrong. She felt by his damp clothing that he needed a change so she changed him and started showing a book to him, telling him stories about the pictures. Soon he pointed to some pictures, offering words of his own, like "Pussy," his favorite word. Clara talked to Ben James about what the pussy was doing. Soon his eyelids began to droop and his head nodded. He opened his eyes again, but he looked so tired. Clara thought he was probably hungry since her own stomach was growling.

Clara asked, "Is dinner ready? I'd like to give Ben James his dinner before he sleeps." When Clara looked up, she saw Hettie take the soup off the stove as she wiped away tears—but more tears came. Clara got up, carrying Ben James with her while she fixed a plate for him.

By the time Nevin came in, Hettie had disappeared into the bedroom. Minutes later, Clara got Ben James. He had been nodding his head when she picked got him from his high chair, and he nestled in her arms and closed his eyes.

Nevin was saying, "Let's eat. I have to get out to the store again."

Hettie came out of the bedroom and Clara deposited Ben James in his crib.

Katherine left her dolls on the sofa and came to her place at the table. Pushing her plate and her step stool around the corner, she said, "I will sit here, then you can help me better." It warmed Clara's heart. The end of the table was so empty—always a reminder that Uncle Benjamin was missing.

Now, as Katherine innocently sat down so Mother could help her better, Clara looked at Hettie to see how she would react.

Hettie looked at her daughter fondly as she brushed the hair out of Katherine's eyes. Fresh tears came in spite of her welcome smile. A big lump formed in Clara's throat, choking out the hunger that had been there. As they were eating, Nevin talked about something a customer had said and Clara relaxed enough so she could eat.

When Clara cleared off the table before going to the store, she noticed Hettie's plate was clean. Clara hoped things would start going better, but it seemed since the letters and visits slowed down, the real sorrow was overwhelming Hettie.

Clara was wondering if she should stay in the house and visit with Hettie or go out to the store and encourage Hettie to come along. Ben James was sleeping now, and likely he would sleep awhile. On the spur of the moment, Clara hurried to the sink, got the dishwater ready, and quickly washed the dishes. Hettie looked at wonderingly.

Clara explained, "I thought that if I did the dishes, you could come out and help us at the store. We can't keep up with the work and I've been doing the ordering."

"Thanks for doing the dishes. I think I will try and nap while Ben James is sleeping. I didn't sleep well last night. I'll try to come out later."

Clara had been catching up on paperwork, but at 2:30 she shoved the books aside to help wait on customers, since there were people waiting.

Later Hettie came in the store. Clara watched as Hettie waited on customers. A few times when she was watching, she saw customers lingering and talking with Hettie. It was good for her to be out, meeting people, and listening to other people's lives and problems.

Later, as Clara and Nevin were weighing products, the schoolchildren came home and helped as much as they could. Clara listened to hear what the children were talking about so much. As she looked around, she saw two of Elvin's girls had come. Seeing Clara, they came over to her and gave her a note saying they could stay twenty-five minutes.

Clara unfolded the paper, expecting to see a list of items they needed, but it said, "There's a corn husking at Cleon's house tonight. We'll stop by for you around five o'clock, or soon after unless you have other plans. Harvey said he doesn't have room for more."

Clara knew that Cleon had pinched his hand pretty badly and couldn't use it much. Must be that it wasn't getting better. Starting to work in earnest, Clara found that the little note had cheered her. A corn-husking party sounded like an interesting event. She did feel a bit guilty for leaving Hettie and the children, but she had a way to go and she was going.

Clara was imagining that Raymond would pick her up and thought of how they would reminisce about the times and things they had talked about when he was helping at the store.

When the buggy arrived, it was Harold and Rufus who picked Clara up. Rufus kept the conversation lively, finding many amusing things to talk about along the way. At one time, Clara heard the brothers discussing Raymond. Rufus wondered what time Raymond would come home.

"Do you think he'll come yet?"

"I hope he comes since I'll be leaving before you're ready to leave," Harold replied.

"Oh, so you are going down the sawmill road tonight?" Rufus asked.

"Why not?" Harold answered him.

So, Harold was planning to take his girl home from the husking.

Some of the corn was in shocks, but there was some still in rows to be husked. Clara was husking in the rows with Laura and was eagerly listening to Laura's teaching challenges. Laura had taken up teaching this fall, and it sounded like she was really enjoying its many challenges. And she was feeling more at home at her boarding place with an older couple whose children were all married. Laura met the other schoolteacher and they were shouting together over the rows. Finally Laura went over and helped with the other teacher's row while they discussed the things they had in common.

Clara husked on, and she soon came to where her row was finished, so she went down through the rows in the direction where she heard some talking. As she weaved through the corn, stepping in one of the rows, she saw it wasn't husked. She still wasn't at the place where she heard the others talking. Suddenly she saw a boy looking anxiously over from the next row.

"Oh," Raymond exclaimed, "it's you, Clara. I thought maybe there was an Indian or a deer coming through. I thought no one was working farther over."

"There aren't anymore," Clara replied. Looking around, Clara saw both rows were husked on either side of his rows. "Are you husking alone?"

"I'm not husking alone if you help," Raymond invited, explaining. "These two rows were missed. I want to get caught up to where the others are. Sounds like it's only a little ahead here in the hollow."

Clara helped to husk the one row and they moved right along.

"Did you find anything out about Cleon's hand?" Raymond asked. "It looks as though he really bandaged it up."

"I talked with Norma. She said it got infected, and he was in the hospital for four days, but that he's doing better now. He needs to wear a sling to keep it elevated. He smashed or pinched his hand with a tool or a jack, or whatever it was," she finished.

110

"Won't be husking corn for awhile anyhow," Raymond concluded.

There was a rustling of cornstalks; then Rufus came weaving through the corn.

"My, did you lose peace with the others that you're husking alone?" Rufus asked when he met Raymond. "I was just ready to give up finding you." Then he explained, "I'm going home with Jesse. He has his half-green colt hitched and had a few narrow escapes coming here, so he would rather not go home alone. They are about to start serving the treat, and we'll be leaving as soon as we're refreshed."

"Go break your neck if you wish," Raymond answered. "I would break that colt in the hayfield, not on the road after dark," Raymond replied to his twin brother.

Rufus ruffled his hand through his hair and turned to go. Then, noticing Clara farther up in the row, he stood watching her for a moment and then, looking back and forth from Raymond to Clara, he shrugged his shoulders. Clara was glad he didn't say what he appeared to be thinking. Raymond saw Rufus staring at him and Clara.

"She's the only one who offered to help me catch up with these rows that were missed."

Rufus rolled his eyes and said, "Oh, sure," rather mockingly, and walked off. The sound of cobs being husked and merry conversations were heard ahead.

A rustling of stalks was heard as two boys came running through the corn yelling, "Everyone is invited to come to the house for refreshments. It's time to quit."

Many yoo-hoos and hoorays were heard as the young folks rejoiced.

Raymond continued husking and said, "I'd like to get these rows caught up to where the rest is husked, or no one will ever notice that they aren't done." Clara took it as an invitation and helped husk until they came to where it was done. The chatter from the crowd sounded like everyone was at the buildings already.

Clara again remembered the conversation on the way to Cleon's and said, "The way your brothers talked, you were on a job until late this afternoon."

"Yes, I was helping my neighbor tear down a barn in the next township. I thought I was tired when I came home, but the news of a corn husking drowned that out. I was told to hitch up, since Rufus didn't and he expected me to bring him home. Now he goes off with Jesse. Oh, well, my horse needed work anyhow."

"I also came with Harold and Rufus, since Charles isn't home during the week. And Harold had his evening planned," Clara admitted.

"Oh, that's right. Well, good. Then I don't need to go home alone," Raymond said as they started up the yard toward the refreshment wagon and the rest of the crowd.

"I'll let you know when I'm leaving," Raymond said as he disappeared into a group of boys at the edge of the yard who were having a jolly conversation.

The people were gradually leaving. Clara was picking up paper cups and banana peels that were tossed around in the yard and was putting the things on the wagon when Raymond came by depositing his things on the wagon.

"I'll be leaving shortly," he said. "I'll be coming around the driving shed."

Moments later as the team swung around and the sorrel horse stopped for a few seconds, Clara hopped on. The frisky horse hurried out the lane snorting anxiously as if yearning to catch up with the other teams that had left earlier.

"Okay, Lady, take it easy. Remember we have a long way to go yet," Raymond spoke to the horse as he held the lines firm. Lady snorted back and beckoned to hurry on.

Raymond's thoughts were still where he had left off after helping at the store when Benjamin was sick, and also of the funeral and afterward. "How are things going for Hettie?" he asked.

Clara found herself pouring out the contents of her heart, how she hoped to see Hettie recover from the loss and pick up the pieces and continue. But as letters of comfort and company ceased to come, it seemed she was becoming slightly depressed, showing a lack of will to go on. If only the letters would come now like they had come the first weeks when six or eight came a day and she almost had to hurry through them to get them all read.

"Maybe we should take a lesson from her experience and wait three months to send cards and letters," Raymond offered.

"It seems Hettie only sees the deep furrow plowed through her meadow of life and has no faith to envision the crop that is planted."

"The what?" Raymond asked.

"Oh, you know, what the young minister preached at the funeral. It was like a parable. He said a nice meadow is like someone's beautiful life; a plowman comes along and plows right through it, turning up a deep brown furrow, destroying the flowers and the birds that were singing . . ."

When Clara paused to catch her breath, Raymond admitted, "I can't remember now."

"You know, he compared it to what death brought, destroying their happy home. Their home was like a meadow with thick green grass and birds singing and cows contentedly grazing, but suddenly only hens are scratching for worms where the beautiful things were before. The family is looking at a deep furrow, scratching to keep faith, and asking how God can spoil something so fair. Then in the parable he said in vision-like faith we look to a corn crop that was planted in a plowed field. We can almost hear the music of the winds blowing through the heavy-laden corn stalks of a fertile field which brought forth a bounteous crop, but it had to be plowed first, then planted in faith. We have to look to the crop that is coming."

"Are you saying that we need faith to hold on till the new crop comes forth, that we don't faint in the afflictions of the furrow that was turned up?" Raymond asked, seemingly catching the idea of the parable. Then he admitted that he didn't remember that anymore. "I wasn't in a good frame of mind on the day of the funeral. I hadn't slept well the night before, so I guess I wasn't alert all the time."

Driving in silence, each thinking his and her own thoughts, Clara wondered if Raymond would confide in her as to why he wasn't in a good frame of mind. Raymond finally spoke. "I remember how one of the ministers, or maybe it was the bishop I guess, who said how it seemed Benjamin had been seeing something we did not see a short time before his soul departed from his body. He referred to the song:

> *My latest sun is sinking fast,*
> *My race is nearly run.*
> *My strongest trials now are past,*
> *My triumph is begun.*
> *I brush the dew of Jordan's bank,*
> *The crossing must be near . . .*

"At that very moment it seemed so real. I thought I felt the mist of Jordan as we look on Canaan's fair and happy land. Then the bishop went on to say:

> *I've almost gained my heavenly home,*
> *My spirit loudly sings.*
> *The holy ones, behold, they come,*
> *I hear the voice of wings.*

"The bishop had such a way of reciting it that it made the chills go up and down my back, as if I felt the air of wings flapping among the mists. When he said, 'My spirit loudly sings,' I thought I heard a faint strain of music somewhere afar off. That song has taken on a whole new meaning for me."

"I guess there is a difference as to what one remembers. I couldn't have recalled that, but we heard more that day than one could hold," Clara replied.

"If we all held something, maybe it was all gathered up," Raymond summed up, then added, "The other thing I remember was when the bishop told of a deacon who visited a widow, and he asked her how she was able to lead all her boys on the narrow way, for this bishop himself had failed in one of his sons. The widow told him to come to the bedroom door where she pointed out to him the well-worn rug in front of her bed. He saw the dents in the rug where she had prayed to God many times a day for strength and guidance for her and her family."

Clara looked at Raymond. "That was said at the funeral? I remember hearing it somewhere, but I couldn't have recalled where. Maybe you should come and visit Hettie and refresh her," she said with feeling.

"How would I help?" he asked doubtfully.

"I guess that's how everyone feels, which is why we hardly get company anymore," Clara grasped the fact. "Maybe it hasn't occurred to Hettie that it's about time for her to pick up the pieces and go visit others who have been bereaved. There was a funeral for a baby since Benjamin's funeral, and there were funerals in other districts. Maybe she should write sympathy notes to others. Comforting others as she was comforted could help her," Raymond counseled.

"See, I told you. You should go visit Hettie. Don't tell me the things," Clara advised.

"Yes, sure. I can just see her listening to her young, inexperienced nephew come with advice that I never had to use."

By now they were approaching Aunt Hettie's home. Raymond drove to the hitching rail and continued talking. He explained that after the funeral Hettie still expected them to help with the store as they had been doing while Benjamin was ill. "We did help out a few weeks, but Dad said we can't continue doing it. We need to give Hettie a chance to get a hold and become involved again to keep her mind occupied. Meeting people in the store would be like having company.

"Dad says he knows it's a heavy load, having all those boys to raise alone. The boys don't seem interested in the store, but surely they could do it. It's something Hettie can manage better than if it were a farm. It seemed Charles never took much interest in the store, and people do need hired boys. From what I gathered, Hettie would be ready to sell the place and hire the boys out, but Dad feels it's too soon to make a decision. She has to do something for an income. Only a few of the boys would be old enough to be hired out."

When Raymond paused, Clara took a deep breath and said, "I just never expected Hettie to get depressed. She always looked on the bright side of things and accepted things as they were."

"I know," Raymond said slowly. "We weren't prepared either. She took it so patiently while Benjamin was sick. Even now she doesn't murmur, but she just has no will to go on. I guess it took a while to grasp the real fact of parting. They were such a close-knit family; then half of her was pulled away and some of the roots were torn loose that were to hold the other half."

This was a new thought to Clara. In her mind she saw a tree— half of it torn away and the roots so entwined that some roots were torn up from the half that still stood. When she realized that no one was speaking, Clara pulled back the buggy robe and said, "I guess we have to do our duty to help cover the roots so that the half of the tree doesn't wilt more, with all those young, green leaves."

"And if wisdom fails us, we can always pray," Raymond added.

Clara stepped down from the buggy and thanked him for the ride and the encouragement. Raymond said, "I need it just as well," backing his buggy away and slowly starting to drive away.

When Clara got to her room, she took off her wraps and sat on a chair, her mind wandering to what Raymond had shared. It had been so long since she had last spoken with Raymond that thoughts of him had nearly faded from her memory, but now she felt she was only beginning to know him. Her mind kept recalling their conversation, thinking of more things she would have liked to share. Raymond seemed so understanding and he seemed to have some deep spiritual insights. She would have liked to share thoughts like she often longed to share with Sammie.

For a moment Clara pictured Merle; she had never really learned to know him. *I had a chance to get acquainted, but I refused it when I had the opportunity*, Clara thought.

Soon Clara's thoughts started running into each other. Maybe she was dreaming all this.

Chapter Sixteen

Clara awoke early as usual; it was only three o' clock. She could rest a few hours until it was time to get up. Already the same thoughts came rushing into her mind that usually came to her as soon as she awakened. Now some new pressing thoughts joined them.

The corn husking had been more than a week ago, but her thoughts still churned. She had been too quiet the day following the corn husking. Even Aunt Hettie had noticed and asked her if she had a date for Sunday evening, but Clara had passed it off lightly.

Clara approached Hettie a few times about things that were said at Uncle Benjamin's funeral, and they had talked more than they had for a long time. She found out that Hettie also hadn't remembered all that was brought forth at the funeral, so they discussed different parts of the sermon.

Yesterday had been mild for December and Hettie was invited to a quilting. Instead of having Nevin take her, she walked the one and one-half miles.

Clara recalled that last evening before suppertime, as she was waiting on a customer, she saw a team drive in. As it stopped at the drive, Hettie got out. Just as the buggy turned around, the driver leaned forward to pull up the robe. Clara's heart stood still when she realized it was Raymond. *What next?* she thought. *Maybe he fetched his mom, too, but no, no one else is in the buggy.*

While eating supper Clara found out that Hettie had been walking home when Raymond came along and picked her up.

Clara wondered so much if Raymond had told Hettie the things he thought she should come to realize. She sensed they must have had some deep talks, since Aunt Hettie at times stared silently for a long time, and didn't seem to hear what the children were saying.

Clara longed to hear Raymond tell her how his talk went with Hettie. She thought of Elsie and Alice. *I wonder if that's how they look forward to talking with Peter and Harvey every Sunday.* She was beginning to realize that there would be many things to share.

Clara wondered if Raymond had enjoyed Saturday evening as deeply as she had. She thought back to the time when Merle had asked her for a date, and she was in such a turmoil. Then Hettie noticed and told her how she and Benjamin had met. Clara had to think how God had led them together.

For a fleeting moment, Clara thought of how she herself had gone with the Kulp brothers since Charles wasn't home—and how things so mysteriously unfolded when she rode home alone with Raymond. Was this a leading? She tried to steer her thoughts elsewhere. She must not dwell so much on it.

The clock struck five. Time to get up. Clara felt a bit depressed and wished to stay in dreamland. She tried to pray, but her thoughts were jumbled. Her mind strayed while she tried to pray, so she finally prayed, "Lord, you know what I have need of before I pray. I pray that You lead my life as You will, not what I desire if it would lead to my downfall. I pray that You lead Raymond and guide him to the path You have planned for him. Have Thine own way." She failed to remember to pray for Hettie.

As the days wore on, thoughts kept arising, although the store kept her quite busy. The voices within battled against each other. Once, as she paused at the window, she saw the mailman pull away from the mailbox and took a quick notion to fetch it. Why was she so eager? *There's hardly ever any mail for me anyhow. Now if it was a* Young Companion *story, or there would be a letter there for me with a masculine scrawl, either from Raymond or maybe Merle, or some other boy I never thought of . . . But this is real life where such things don't happen*, she thought as she opened the lid. A circle letter for Hettie and a bunch of regular mail. Nothing special, she knew, but she was still a little disappointed.

Soon after Clara was back in the store after delivering the mail to Hettie, a team drove in. It as Dad and Mom! Clara enjoyed visiting with Mom while she was picking up things from the store. Then they went in to visit with Aunt Hettie. Later Mom came out and visited with Clara while Clara weighed 10-X sugar in various amounts.

"I wish you could be at home more," Mom said.

Clara looked up, wondering. She had thought her parents were glad she was here to help Hettie. Mom went on, "Maybe you could be an example for Norma. She just isn't very obedient in her dress and combing her hair. You went through such a stage, too, but then lay it down again." Clara remembered her struggle years ago and how Dad had talked to her, but she knew if she was honest with herself, Sammie had a lot to do with it. She had such respect for him and sensed that he wasn't fond of frills and adorning.

Mom continued, saying "Norma wants to get the parlor ready with her things. Our neighbors, Loren Weavers, are moving away and they have a hutch that they can't use at their new place, which Norma greatly desired to have. Before I was aware of it, she had talked Dad into buying it. And, she never did like the sofa we have, which I agree isn't the best. Dad gave in and got a good sofa, but I don't know what we are going to do with all our furniture!

"Dad thought maybe you could talk to Hettie. Maybe she would be interested in letting you make a parlor here. They have that sitting room that's about like a living room, isn't it?"

"Yes, that room where the parlor would be is where Katherine used to sleep. She now sleeps in a youth bed pretty regularly in my room. The room where she used to sleep is a catch-all room or what-ever.

"You mean if Hettie is agreed," Clara continued, "I could move the hutch and the sofa here?"

"Well, we have to do something with all our furniture."

Throughout the rest of the day, Clara was kept busy in the store and didn't have much time to dwell on furniture until evening. When she was putting the supper dishes away, she brought up the subject with Hettie, explaining that Norma wanted some furniture for her own parlor and her parents wondered if maybe there was room here to make a parlor to use up some of the extra furniture.

There was something in the expression on Hettie's face that made Clara continue expressing her thoughts. "I thought since Katherine seldom sleeps in that room anymore and Ben James sleeps in your bedroom, maybe we could set up that room."

Hettie smiled and said, "It sounds as if you have been dreaming." Then she admitted, "I've often desired to make up that room, but the sofa that was in there was moved to the living room about three years ago. I've often desired to have a singing or other gathering for the young folks, but there was no place for it. The living room is like another kitchen; the bureau with the Sunday dishes has a hinge broken.

"I often wanted to get better furniture, but we are not sale people. Benjamin would say, 'Wait till the boys take better care of things and Katherine wants nicer things.' I thought lately that Charles is bothered that there isn't a better room here when his buddies come here. Let's start tomorrow as we get time and clean out that room and have it ready. Let your parents know we have room."

Hettie sounded more like the Hettie Clara had always known than she had for the last five months or more.

Tomorrow came, and they started cleaning out the room. Hettie decided that it took too much effort to wash the walls, so they went to town for paint. Two of Elvin's children came and painted the once-white-dulling-to-yellow walls a light clear, clean blue. It looked so refreshing! Hettie herself had more energy and even varnished the woodwork. It looked like a new room.

Clara had sent a message to her parents that she and Hettie were looking forward to having the extra furniture, since they were preparing the room. The next weekend, Dad, Norma, and a neighbor boy came with the man who hauled the furniture.

As Clara stood admiring the room, she smiled to herself, thinking that this was almost as exciting as when she had gotten the basement parlor ready when she was turning seventeen. Was she really almost twenty?

Hettie said that if the weather was mild in February, they would make a singing for the young folks. Charles had been with the young folks for more than a year. It was well worth getting the room ready. Redoing it had somehow cheered Hettie, Clara thought. Or maybe it was that Raymond had talked with her. She was beginning to be the Hettie Clara had always known. Even Clara's own shoulders didn't seem to sag as much under the stress load as they had before.

A thought wanted to enter her mind. Clara kept pushing it away, but it was useless. She kept daydreaming of Raymond coming into the new room and they would discuss things like they had on the way home from the corn husking. *But what about Eileen? She seemed to be giving up on him because he showed no special interest in her. He was only eighteen years old, about Norma's age.*

Many thoughts ran through Clara's mind as she ironed shirts and dresses and pressed dress pants. Suddenly Clara awoke out of her dreams when Hettie asked, "What were those words you were singing?"

"Singing? I can't remember," Clara answered innocently.

"Yes, it was something like the bud of the flower may taste bad, but the flower—and something about fresh courage and dreading things."

Then Clara remembered and sang:

> *"Ye fearful saints, fresh courage take,*
> *The clouds ye so much dread*
> *Are big with mercy and shall break*
> *In blessings on your head.*
> *His purposes will ripen fast,*
> *Unfolding every hour.*
> *The bud may have a bitter taste,*
> *But sweet will be the flower."*

"The words have a lot more meaning now than they had when we sang them with the young folks and didn't concentrate on the words," Hettie said thoughtfully.

*   *   *

It warmed Clara's heart to see all the people arriving on this mild February evening. They had worked hard all week to clean the house for the youth to gather and sing. Throughout the week, a fleeting thought went through Clara's mind. "Suppose no one shows up?" But the buggies were still arriving and everyone seemed glad to come.

Hettie seemed to be enjoying herself as many girls surrounded her. Two months ago Hettie would not have been ready for this. Clara still marveled at how redoing the room to make a parlor had seemed to lift Hettie out of her overwhelming sorrow and gloom. *Guess a change of some sort was needed*, Clara thought.

As the girls filed into the kitchen to begin singing, Clara looked for a moment at the third girl from the door, wondering if visitors came for the singing, until she realized that it was Amelia Oberholtzer from the Lone Oak district. She had forgotten about her. Clara had seen her in church last Sunday and was informed that Amelia was helping at Russel Newswangers. On Sunday Amelia had three of Russel's children along, and it seemed the children were quite fond of her, and Amelia seemed to enjoy the children as well.

Now, seeing her, Clara noticed Amelia was quite common looking. At church she had looked so kind and motherly that Clara hadn't noticed how common she was. At church she had looked as if maybe she was an older girl, having all the children with her, but now she looked like a young girl.

When the singing was over, Clara noticed that Amelia had Ben James on her lap and was talking to him. Katherine was standing in front of her, eagerly listening. Apparently Katherine asked Amelia something and she answered Katherine, continuing to talk. It looked like they were having an interesting conversation. Katherine was patting Amelia on her arm, sharing in the conversation too. Katherine usually wasn't one to make up with strangers or even to talk much with people outside the family. *Amelia must have some magic tact that pulls children*, Clara thought.

Later Laura slid in a chair beside Clara and asked, "Who's the girl who is holding Ben James? Is she Hettie's relative?"

122

"No. She is helping at Russel Newswanger's home. Russel's wife needs to take it easy for awhile. Eunice had been there, but it was too heavy a load for her to manage—with all the little ones—so Amelia came from Lone Oak."

"Is she an older girl?" Laura asked.

"I took it for granted that she was," Clara admitted and continued, "but I found out she is about my age. Then, of course, I'm not as young as I used to be."

Clara, still speaking to Laura, asked, "By the way, where were you last Sunday evening when we were at Emory's house for supper?"

"Oh, I was catching up on some sleep," Laura said rather gratefully and explained, "I had such a full week at school. I went to a wedding at Beaver Creek. Getting everything ready for a substitute teacher always requires so much work, I needed another day to recover. I had put in late hours and I took the opportunity to get some sleep. I don't suppose I missed anything," she added.

Clara tried to make it sound as though she had missed a lot. On the spur of the moment, Clara asked, "Don't you sometimes feel—well, get a craving on Sunday evening when so many girls our age and younger are dating?"

"Didn't I tell you that just last Sunday evening I desired to sleep?" Laura chuckled matter-of-factly, stating, "My mind doesn't have a lot of time to roam when I'm teaching school."

"There are teachers dating though, as far as that goes," Clara said, not ready to believe Laura was as innocent as she appeared to be.

"But I bet they take it out on their pupils on Monday, like some of my teachers did when I was going to school," Laura said rather forcefully.

Clara almost ached to be as satisfied and content as Laura appeared to be. Most of the girls were in the living room part of the kitchen and appeared to be playing some new tricks on the others. In fact, the boys seemed interested, too.

Laura had gone to talk with Elizabeth, also a teacher, and now the people were hunting their wraps and songbooks and hurrying out the door, some of them thanking Hettie for arranging the singing.

Clara was gathering the drinking cups and putting the cookies from the refreshment table back in the container. She turned around when someone said, "I didn't even ask if you have a way to go home tonight."

Who would be saying that? She turned and faced Raymond as he tipped his cup. For a moment she thought he was thinking she was going home to her parents, but then she saw a mischievous glint in his otherwise sober eyes. She smiled.

Raymond chuckled and looked on silently for a moment. Clara thought he was about to say something, but then he picked up his songbooks and went to get his wraps.

Clara's heart was deeply touched. Tears of yearnings misted her eyes when she reached her room. She longed to talk to Raymond about things that had happened since the corn husking. Did he also desire that? Was that why he asked if she needed a way to go home? Would he have asked if the supper or singing would have been elsewhere, or was he only kidding? Clara had no way of knowing, but she felt the longing to share her thoughts with someone who understands and cares.

Earlier that evening Clara had been told that her sister Norma was about to start dating a brother to the woman who lived where Frankies used to live—Ezra Horning. He came to the area sometimes from Dry Ridge.

My, she didn't know her sister was that popular, but Mom had said Norma dolled up the parlor so that Clara would hardly recognize it. Norma also adorned her hair in the latest fashion.

Clara thought of the parlor they had organized at Hettie's. Having her own things there was precious, but then it also made her long more to be able to use the room as her friends were using theirs.

Over the next few weeks, Clara spent many a moment pondering the few words Raymond had said that evening. He had wondered if she needed a way to go home? Was he only teasing because she needed no transportation that evening?

Chapter Seventeen

Clara had only a moment to talk with Alice, as Elsie and Caroline had things to discuss with Alice, too. Some of the couples were making plans for other than going to Eli Gehman's home for dinner and to Earl Sensenig's for supper. Clara felt rather rejected. *Elsie and Alice have so many things going that they don't share with me. Their lives are centered on Harvey and Peter. Well, I still have Laura.*

Clara made her way out of the church and almost walked into Amelia who was outside the door. She had Russel's children and was buttoning their coats; one needed to have his shoe tied. Amelia cheerfully smiled at Clara, taking Clara by surprise. She remembered to return the smile only after Amelia had already looked over to the little girl who was asking her something.

"Sorry, what were you saying?" Soon Amelia was leading her little ones to Russel's carriage. Clara thought, *Amelia seems so interested in the Oberholtzer children, and the little ones look up to her so trustingly.* Amelia was waving good-bye to the children as Russel got in the carriage.

Amelia likely was also going to the dinner place. She was friendly enough but usually stayed in the background. *She surely isn't here to allure a boy*, Clara mused to herself when she again noticed Amelia's unattractive appearance. Her bonnet covered her head well, hiding her hair which was obediently combed back.

Clara rejoiced when she met up with Laura. She thought she had missed her. Just as she began speaking to Laura another woman came up to Laura and began talking. This woman was the mother of Leonard, one of Laura's school pupils who had been sick during the past week. When Clara thought their conversation was coming to an end, another teacher, Elizabeth, came and asked about the upcoming teachers' meeting, going in the forenoon to visit school.

Charles came driving down to pick up Clara. *He may as well. I don't belong to anyone anyhow.* Clara had a notion to go home with Hettie and the children, but then she remembered they were invited away. Charles had an amused grin on his face as he stopped to pick her up. He was chuckling about something that Rufus had said to Harvey as a joke, and Harvey at first thought he was serious.

Soon Charles was humming a merry tune. Leaning out of the buggy and having some good-natured fun, he saw Harold and Reba, his steady girlfriend, following closely behind them. When Harold pretended to pass as Charles was holding his horse in, Charles spirited up his horse. Soon Charles pulled the horse almost to a halt, and Harold pretended to be upset at him. Charles guided his horse further over on the road so Harold couldn't pass. Just then another sound was heard from behind them as a buggy came up beside them. Clipping on past, Raymond and Rufus leaned forward and waved at Charles and Clara.

Speaking to his horse, Charles said, "Okay, Duke, let's go."

Wanting to make sure Harold had enough time to visit with Reba, Charles chuckled and said, "Harold was crying the blues, saying the week was so long, because Reba had gone away over last weekend. He acted like he was going straight to Reba's house instead of going to the dinner place. I wonder why he is in such a hurry now."

After Duke was warmed up, he wanted to keep going. They passed the buggy ahead carrying Elsie and Harvey. "Save some dinner for us until we get there," Harvey waved to them.

Clara, smiling, turned to Charles and said, "If I wouldn't know you, I would think this is the first weekend you are with the young folks."

Charles smiled a lopsided smile and said, "We need to have fun at times."

It just didn't seem quite like Charles. Clara finally asked, "Why so eager?"

126

"The weeks seem long. It's so good to be with the young folks on Sundays before going to Willis's for the week."

"Don't you like it there?" Clara asked.

Nodding yes, Charles said, "I like it well enough, but I have no young folks to meet with during the week."

There were more teams coming up behind them. Duke wasn't quite as spirited anymore. Looking in his rear-view mirror a few times, Charles saw Caleb's family coming up right behind them. When they pulled out around them and waved, Charles now seemed to be in a deep thought. Clara waved at the little faces peeping out the carriage window. Paul Henry and Hannah Mae were taking turns to look out. *They mustn't be going home for dinner*, Clara thought.

Soon Charles guided Duke on the dirt road which led them to Eli Gehman's lane. As Clara stepped down from the buggy, she saw Paul's buggy was close behind. Paul usually drove alone, but Amelia was with him now, since Paul lived only three miles from Russels. The farms in that direction were a bit scattered.

Clara couldn't believe that the afternoon was already spent. She hadn't eaten until the second seating. Some of the girls decided they should sing for the grandmother who lived in the little house attached to the main house. Clara and a few other girls had stayed after they finished singing, since the grandmother wanted to know who they were and the names of their parents and grandparents. She was quite talkative and more stories began to unfold; however, it was all rather interesting.

Clara wondered, *Will I have so many stories to tell when I get to be her age? Stories about how I got the hutch, had a basement parlor, moved in with Uncle Benjamin and Aunt Hettie, Benjamin's death, and how I worked in the bulk food store for the rest of my life? And how my friends all got married and I didn't fit in anywhere and my sister caught a tall, dark, handsome fellow from another area? Maybe I will work for her some day.*

"Clara! Clara!" an urgent voice was calling, bringing her back to life. Jumping up, she asked, "What's wrong?"

The young girls at the door said, "Charles is ready to leave." Looking toward the window, Clara saw a few teams hitching up,

127

and, yes, Charles was waiting. She ran to the other house to search for her wraps.

Clara wished she was going home and could tell Hettie the things the grandmother had shared with them, rather than going all the way to Earl Sensenig's house for supper. Well, she would try not to think about it. *Raymond had not seemed to notice that she was around. Why go and have more disappointments when it hurt so much to see him, longing to share her heart with him and listen to him relate as well?*

"I was almost ready to think you had left with someone else. No one seemed to know where you were. Raymond said he had seen some of the girls go to the smaller house earlier," Charles said as he greeted her.

Clara just looked at him. He had no idea what an effect his few words had on her. She wished that a thought or word of Raymond wouldn't affect her so much. Did Raymond see who the girls were? Why did he notice?

Suddenly Charles looked over and said, "I thought I was supposed to pick you up. Didn't I bring you?"

Clara looked at him and said, "I'm here."

"I see. I hadn't heard from you."

"You weren't very talkative either, were you?" Clara asked Charles.

"No. I don't have the habit of talking to myself, but now that you are conscious, I may as well talk. I have to tell you that you'll be charged to ride with me tonight."

"Oh, yeah, surely not because I talked too much?" Clara asked.

"No, but I want you to talk to Amelia tonight and ask her if I can see her next Sunday at Russels."

Clara gasped, then echoed the words, "Amelia Oberholtzer! Please, Charles, I don't know how to ask people."

"You may as well learn," Charles answered reassuringly, not showing that he heard her alarming tone of voice.

"Amelia is a few years older than you are," Clara reminded Charles.

"Does it matter?" he inquired.

"But, Charles, I hardly know her. I can't do it. Maybe she even has a friend back home. I wouldn't know."

Charles, smiling, said, "I gathered from Paul that she isn't dating."

"Why don't you ask Paul to ask Amelia for you? I would rather not since I don't know her better." Clara brightened at the new thought.

Charles chuckled at her and admitted, "No, I can't ask Paul for fear of getting him upset at me. Maybe Paul himself is thinking about asking her. Here I thought you would rejoice if I'd ask a girl. Now you almost discourage me."

Clara was getting nervous. "I'm not discouraging you from asking Amelia but, how would I say it? I mean, suppose I don't ask right. She is almost a stranger to me," Clara finished.

"How do you think I feel? It wouldn't be any easier for me to make it through the first evening if she accepts me, but I fear I won't be accepted. Paul need not know that I asked."

"You say it would be hard to visit with her the first evening, but it's your choice. I didn't talk you into anything. Have you ever talked with her?"

"Not really, but I know she is the most beautiful girl I ever saw, and I want to know how she feels about me before she goes home. Tell her if she has no answer tonight, to let you know sometime next week before Sunday." *Charles isn't taking no for an answer,* Clara sighed to herself.

Stumbling down from the buggy in a dazed state of mind, Clara wanted to go somewhere deep in the forest and walk and walk to think things over. How would she tell Amelia? She was clenching her fist so hard she realized it was hurting. If Charles had been her brother, she might have exploded in front of him.

It was such a surprise that Charles was attracted to a strange girl who was such common clay. What had attracted him to Amelia? Then Clara remembered how Russel's children looked up to her, smiling, as Amelia listened to each of their interests and concerns.

Clara remembered when they arrived at the dinner place that forenoon, that Charles had grown quiet during the last stretch of the way. She remembered that Caleb had passed them and when they arrived at Eli Gehman's house and Clara stepped down from the buggy, she saw Paul's horse was directly behind them. *They must have been following us, since Caleb had passed.* Clara hadn't noticed who had been following them after Caleb's buggy has passed, but likely Charles knew since he had been watching his rear-view mirror several times. Charles likely knew before Caleb had passed. Now she understood why Charles had suddenly stopped talking and seemed to be in deep thought.

Clara had been at the first seating and was helping with the dishes, wiping the last of the dishes while the table for the second seating was being filled. She noticed that Amelia was at the table, the third from the end. Just then the boys came in, filling up the remainder of the table. She saw Rufus, Shannon, and Peter filing in. In the next group Raymond was leading, followed by some younger ones with Charles and cousin Levi. As they were being seated, Clara suddenly noticed that Charles was right across the table from Amelia! The room had grown quiet as the young people paused for silent prayer.

After the bread had been passed, as Clara wiped the last kettle and some stray silverware, she took a quick glance at Charles who was waiting for the meat platter to be passed to him. She also noticed the beads of perspiration on his brow. No one was talking at his end of the table. Further up, Rufus and Dennis were having a jolly conversation. Clara wished that for Charles's sake, someone would talk at his end of the table. She decided she would leave the room. She couldn't watch this.

Clara lifted her eyes further to see if Amelia was aware of Charles, and just then Earl Sensenig's grandchild came tottering behind the table, crying for her mother. Amelia reached for her, picked her up, and got a cracker from the plate of cheese and crackers. She gave a cracker to the little girl, talking soothingly to her. The little girl looked trustingly at Amelia and said, "Kacker?"

Amelia softly said, "Yes, you may eat it." The tears were drying on the child's face as Amelia talked to her.

Sliding over on the bench where she was sitting, Amelia placed the little girl between herself and Elizabeth. Just then, a bowl of mashed potatoes was handed to Amelia. Taking a serving, she passed it on. The little girl struggled up on Amelia's lap and reached for the glass of water. The boys on the other side of the table started chuckling as Amelia helped the child with the water.

Clara glanced at Charles. He wasn't perspiring anymore. He was looking at the little girl for a moment as she played with the fork and waited her turn for the potatoes, watching Amelia expectantly. As Charles watched Amelia, she was smiling so kindly to the little one. Cousin Levi was trying to pass the bowl of noodles to Charles, nudging him back to life.

Clara escaped to another room. She wasn't going to watch this; at least the child had broken some of the strain. Clara wished Charles would know she hadn't talked with Amelia yet so he could relax and not be so nervous.

It was such a nice evening. Different groups of girls took a walk out the field lane which went out to a single railroad track, separating the neighbors' fields. The track was seldom used, perhaps only once a week to get lumber to the lumber yard in a nearby town.

It was while they were coming up the railroad track near the field lane that Clara hurried to catch up with Amelia, who had turned onto the field lane. The other girls in the group continued walking further down the railroad track. Some of the girls had stopped and were lingering.

Clara asked Amelia, "Do you have any younger brothers and sisters?"

Looking surprised, Amelia said, "Oh, I didn't know anyone was coming with me. No. Well, yes, I have younger brothers and sisters—a whole row of them."

"Little ones?" Clara asked.

"Well, not anymore. They are growing up. Kenneth is four already. The three little boys, as we call them, are now four, six, and eight. We had to let them grow up; they just didn't stay babies. My

131

twin sister always says she thinks I will have a children's home some day," Amelia chuckled.

"Your twin sister? Are you a twin?" Clara asked, wondering if she heard correctly.

"Yes, Sylvia is my twin sister. She is about to marry her Freddie, and she gets upset with the little boys, who have a way of getting into her parlor and misplacing her things. Sometimes they dig up the flower bed that's near the parlor door."

"It seems like you like children," Clara summed it up. Then she added, "It's a wonder you aren't a schoolteacher."

"Oh, I really wanted to teach school, but we were always so busy with produce. Dad didn't want me to help out at Russel's for such a long time, but it was so necessary. But my weeks of helping at Russel's are limited," Amelia explained.

"Oh, so you won't be here very long?" Clara asked.

"That depends on how things go at Russel's. Probably no more than a month."

"Would you be interested in having my cousin Charles Brubaker come and get acquainted with you next Sunday?"

"What?" Amelia asked as she whirled around. "I don't know who you are talking about. Are you talking about a big boy?"

Clara smiled. "Yes, he's my cousin and lives where I'm working. You know, they had a singing there a few weeks ago. His mother, Mrs. Benjamin Brubaker, is a widow since Charles's father died last August. Charles is the oldest of the children."

"And he wants to visit with me?" Amelia asked in disbelief.

"Yes, he told me to ask if you are interested."

Amelia walked on, pulling a weed to chew on while she thought. "Was that where a six-year-old girl and a little boy were with us at the singing?"

"Yes, Katherine and Ben James, who is three."

"I remember the children, but I'm not sure who Charles is. I probably know him, but I didn't learn all the names yet—who belongs to whom," she confessed.

"Do you remember the boy who sat across the table from you this evening during supper?"

Thinking for a moment, Clara said, "There was one wearing a yellow shirt and one wearing a pale green shirt, who was too bashful to look up—"

Amelia was beginning to remember when Clara cut her off, saying, "That was Charles."

Taking a deep breath, Amelia thought out loud, "He's the one who drives that frisky black horse and who seems mature in spite of his boyish looks. I . . . never learned to . . . entertain big boys," she stammered. "I only know how to entertain little people. Maybe he could bring Ben James along, or whatever you said his name is," Amelia finished.

Clara nodded and informed her, "You don't have to answer tonight if you want to think it over."

"I'm afraid that would make it worse. I'd surely get cold feet. It—it's all right, if he wants to come. Maybe he will do the entertaining. Pray for me. I've never done such a thing before, but it would be interesting to get to know him. If he noticed me, he must be— well, I will wonder all week and will have bitten off all my fingernails by Sunday!"

That evening, as Clara was riding home with Charles, eager for him to ask her about Amelia's answer, she asked, "How did it feel to sit across the table from Amelia?"

"Don't talk about it. When I first realized it, I was afraid you had talked to her already and I got so warm. I was about to get up and go outside, but I was trying to believe you hadn't talked to her yet. Then that little girl came to the rescue, easing the tension. Have you talked with Amelia?" he asked anxiously.

"Yes. After she figured out who you were, she said you could come; but she wants you to bring Ben James along. She likes to entertain small boys."

Charles chuckled, surprised. "Does she think I'm a spy? The way you said, 'bring Ben James along,' sounds like your brother Benjamin—like Joseph told his brothers: they can't come unless they bring Benjamin along."

"I think she feels like the spy. It seemed she was startled that anyone would notice her. She said she has a twin sister who is about to marry."

"Twin sister?" Charles repeated, surprised.

"After I started talking to Amelia, it was easy. She wasn't sure who you were until I said you were the one who sat across the table from her. She wondered if you were the one wearing the yellow shirt or the one wearing the pale green one, who was too bashful to look up."

"Please don't talk about that meal. I was glad the child came and cooled the atmosphere."

After Clara was in bed, still very wide awake, she thought of Charles. He had admitted it wasn't going to be easy to visit with Amelia, yet he wanted to so much. *Even if I didn't want to ask her, apparently Amelia impressed him, and now he has a chance to find out if she is agreed. It doesn't matter how deeply I long to share with Raymond or how much my heart is stirred, it's a longing that cannot be stilled. We girls can only pray and wait on God. Charles doesn't know how it is to feel this way and never be able to find out. I have to endure it.*

Chapter Eighteen

The wind of the past few days had blown away all the drab, dark November rains. The sky above the church building was full with white clouds moving into each other and rolling on, with more clouds rising into wind clouds. They were so arranged that the sun shone through bravely. Not only had the wind chased the rain away, it had also brought a chill in the air. The chilling temperatures caused the congregation to pull on wraps and beckoned them to seek warm shelter to do their visiting, rather than staying outside.

Since the new church house had been built the past summer, Clara was glad there was now room to put on her wraps in the anteroom and to visit with friends. Previously she had to get her wraps, throw them over her, and wiggle herself outside to stretch out her arms to pull them on, in order to allow room for others to get their wraps.

Now the church was only two and one-half miles from Hettie's place, instead of seven miles. But there were also disadvantages, too. Now she didn't meet her parents, sisters, and Cleons in church very often. However, Caleb and Virginia were usually there unless the ministers switched. Calebs had three miles to church instead of the nine they previously had had.

Clara thought of the many changes coming with time, things she had never imagined. She was still trying to get used to the fact that Uncle Walter was ordained as a minister since the new church was built. He was Cousin Levi's dad. Clara had been relieved when the ordination slip was found at the head of the class, rather than going to the end where Sammie sat. He had been married only a few months.

135

Being a minister was hard for Uncle Walter. Clara was hoping he'd develop more confidence in himself and be more at ease.

Russel, the young deacon, seemed easygoing and submissive, willing to work with what was given him. It had been hard, but he seemed submissive. The younger ordained leader also had little children to sit with him on the bench unless other people took them. Russel's tiny baby, whom Amelia had helped to care for, seemed healthy after its tiny start.

Little Hannah Mae, at Clara's side, pulled her skirt and said, "Let's go to Grandma's."

Clara, looking up, said, "Yes, let's go see if Mother is ready."

As Clara made her way over to the women, Aunt Hettie came and deposited Lena Jane in her arms. Lena Jane was crying. Hettie asked, "Are you going with Calebs?"

Clara nodded as Hettie gave her the diaper bag and said, "I just changed her, but her bottle is empty. I guess she is still hungry." Clara tried to get Lena Jane satisfied; but it was Hannah Mae who succeeded in cheering her tears. She romped around, pulling at Lena Jane's foot, talking baby talk to her.

Finally Virginia came with sleeping John Wayne on her arms, offering to exchange him for Lena Jane. Virginia calmly listened to Clara's explanation as to why Lena Jane's eyes were tear-stained. Virginia decided to fill up the bottle at the water cooler, which Lena Jane took happily, playfully kicking at Hannah Mae who was pretending to take her bottle.

Clara marveled at Virginia's relaxed way with the many little ones who were entrusted to them, while still fulfilling the church work. Musing, Clara thought, *I would make a poor mother. I wouldn't have thought of putting water in the bottle to help the child until we get to Grandma's.*

As Clara came to the carriage, Caleb and Paul Henry were waiting. Paul Henry chose to sit with his dad. Virginia was coming, too. Lena Jane rejoiced at the sight of Caleb, reaching out to Daddy's welcoming arms, telling him of all her troubles in her own baby talk.

Clara enjoyed conversing with Paul Henry and Hannah Mae as they drove to Dad and Mom's house for Thanksgiving dinner. The

136

whole family would be there. Occasionally Clara spoke with Virginia, but the children were keeping her attention. They had so much to tell.

The few times Clara overheard Caleb and Virginia's conversation, they were discussing when the ordination would take place in another settlement, trying to decide if they could go because of a wedding invitation. Later she heard them discussing someone they had met at the funeral yesterday. An aged man from the church had died, but Clara hadn't been to the funeral.

Clara was wondering when Caleb and Virginia got time to do their work, take care of their children, and take care of their church responsibilities. Virginia didn't go everywhere with Caleb. Clara heard them discussing whether their neighbor, Anna, could keep the children if they decided to go to the ordination, or if Eunice could come for the day.

Later, as Clara was helping with dinner preparations, she looked at her sister Loretta, wondering whose baby she was holding. Finally, she asked, "Is this really Howard?"

"Of course, it is," Loretta said, carrying him on her hip.

Clara couldn't believe how much Cleon's baby had grown already. He was only a baby the last time she had seen him. "I guess I didn't notice him the last few times we were at the same church. He surely favors his mother."

When Clara made a trip to the basement for a jar of pickles, she decided to look in the parlor. She had seen it since Norma had reorganized it, but that was a long time ago. She couldn't remember the details. "Oh!" she gasped, sighing as she opened the door. She stood for a moment, surveying the array of things on the coffee table in front of the sofa—a dainty candy dish, seashells, a pencil holder, and a little cedar chest with a picture of a deer prancing through the woods. Clara opened the little chest and gave out a cry of shock. A picture of Ezra was inside! (The church actually forbids photos and pleads with the young folks to avoid the pride and idolatry to which it leads.) Quickly closing the chest, she noticed the shiny, elaborate newspaper/magazine rack. Rubbing her fingers over the smooth varnished oak, she noticed the various compartments. There was also a corner shelf hanging on the wall, each shelf holding trinkets. The stand next to the sofa was covered with a plush bureau scarf like the one on the hutch, the fake fur resembling fluffy white carpet. A few candles in pretty holders were on the stand. The fireplace shelf held many knickknacks, scalloped, laced edges bordering the material on the shelf.

Clara studied the arrangement of flowers on the corners of the mirror. The sun catcher attached to the window glistened in the light. The afghan on the sofa blended well with the sofa and the rest of the room. Finally, Clara's eyes caught sight of the attractive wind chime hanging by the other window. Two of the longer chains held a glittering glass heart. Reaching for them, she saw Ezra's name on the one and Norma's name on the other.

Feeling like an intruding child, Clara remembered to take the pickles to the kitchen. At the top of the stairs she met Norma, who was wearing her sparkling royal blue dress with glittering flowers of the same shade of blue pressed in. Her white apron had a row of royal blue flowers stitched across the top with clear blue ribbons tied at each end, an identical border at the top edge of the pocket.

Norma's face looked flushed. Her hair was neatly patted with the bottom half flowing out further than the top, forming a scalloped edge. "Oh, I was just ready to go down for the pickles. Now you came after all. I thought Mom said you went for them. We're ready to eat."

Caleb and Dad sat at the end of the table. Loretta sat next to Paul Henry and Hannah Mae so she could help remove the dishes.

Clara looked at her sisters, Mildred and Sylvia. She could hardly believe how Mildred was growing up; she was tall but more slender than Norma and herself. Mildred didn't need to doll up her face; she had a neat appearance by nature. Her dark hair was so thick, it hung front in a natural way, evenly framing her broad face. There was a dimple in her left cheek.

What was Cleon teasing Loretta about? Looking up, Clara was surprised to see Cleon sitting at the corner next to Dad. She realized Ezra Horning was talking to Loretta. *Of course, he would*

138

be here; he is considered family. No wonder Norma looks flushed. Ezra's dark eyes sparkled. He had a full head of hair swirled up over the back. His hair was neatly trimmed with round corners around his neck and ears.

In a deep, rich voice, Ezra was reminding Loretta about something. "You know you haven't found that quarter yet."

Loretta shrugged her shoulders as if she didn't care. Norma looked at Ezra, their eyes speaking volumes.

Looking at Loretta, Ezra said, "I told you you wouldn't find it." Apparently Ezra had dared the girls to find the quarter he hid in the parlor.

Most of the others around the table had their attention on the little ones seated at the table. Howard cheered with glee when he saw Cleon. Lena Jane sucked her one thumb, her other hand pointing to the pudding with marshmallows, and exclaimed, "Candy, candy," as her dark brown eyes looked at her daddy.

The dishes had been washed, and Clara went to the door to let Hannah Mae out. Wearing her wraps, she stood begging by the door. As Clara closed the door, she stood for a moment looking down the road. Seeing a few people walking, she looked again. It was Norma and Ezra. *I wonder where they are going. They must have a lot to talk about after driving here from church. He'll be taking her home this evening, and likely they are going to the supper and singing at Elvins tonight.*

For a fleeting moment Clara thought of her longing to share things with Raymond. She would be satisfied if she could only ride with him to the singing and share things without going for a walk. She pictured Norma's glamorous parlor and thought, *I guess it's no wonder no one ever came to see me, if that's the kind of parlor it takes to interest someone.* She remembered the ruffled sheer curtain in hues of white, light blue and clear blue that hung over the glass in the door. It reminded her of gentle, flowing water. Even its design was like soft waves, or perhaps like clouds. Maybe it was a picture of "cloud nine," which she had never risen high enough to see.

Later in the afternoon, Virginia asked her sisters where the children were. "Loretta is with them," answered Mildred.

A little later Paul Henry came leading a crying Lena Jane. He said she was in the basement and couldn't get out. As Virginia picked her up and soothed her, she asked, "What do you have here?" Opening her little hand, a broken candle fell to the floor. At the same time, Mildred had picked up Hannah Mae, who had come to the top of the stairs. In one hand she held postcards and in the other she held seashells. They all knew the girls must have been in Norma's parlor.

Virginia looked hopelessly at her younger sisters and said, "We'd better straighten things up before Norma comes back." Mildred took the seashells and postcards and headed downstairs as Virginia admonished her daughters.

Mom said, "They don't know these things aren't toys. Dad calls it a jewelry store, and I'm sure they didn't leave it in the mess it was in a few weeks ago when some of the younger ones from Ezra's district came on a Sunday evening. Ezra and Norma had walked to Ezra's sister's house and the parlor was a sight by the time they came back. The boys left the parlor door open and hid under the basement steps. Norma was humiliated, since she had no idea anyone was still around."

Cousin Levi offered to pick up Clara and take her along to Elvin's place where the young folks were invited for supper. On the way she found herself telling him about Norma's parlor. "I suppose she didn't do it all at one time—probably bit by bit so that her parents weren't aware of it," Levi assumed.

"I'm sure, since I keep seeing changes every time I go there. I was wondering why my parents allow her to do it, but maybe you have a point. She probably did it gradually. It's no wonder no one ever came to see me, if that's what it takes to draw someone," Clara admitted.

Levi looked at her and asked, "Would you want Ezra to come see you?"

"No," Clara answered decidedly.

Levi asked further, "Didn't someone want to see you at one time?"

Clara looked at him questioningly, trying to remember. Did Levi do the asking? No, it was Shannon who asked her for Merle. She turned to Levi and asked, "How would you know?"

Levi shrugged his shoulders and admitted, "Merle confided in me one day back then."

"I had other things on my mind at the time, and when I was at a wedding, I saw he found another friend."

Levi drove in silence awhile, as if he were thinking about something. As if thinking out loud, he said, "I guess Elsie had other things on her mind, too."

"Do you think she had Harvey on her mind at that time already?" Clara asked, surprised at the new thought.

"I know she did. I just hadn't been aware of it. Sammie informed me of it."

"There are more girls around. What are you waiting for?" Clara asked softly.

"A lot of boys asked me the same question," he said, then concluded, "I wonder, too, but it takes more bravery than I have to ask after being turned down one time. It took all I had to ask in the first place."

They drove in silence until Levi started talking about how his life had changed. Clara had always thought Levi was affected somewhat when his dad was ordained to the ministry. Sharing her thoughts, Clara said, "I guess it was an adjustment in your family when you dad was ordained, but it was such a relief to me that Sammie and Caroline were spared, having been married so recently."

Levi blew his nose and said, "They would have been young for such a load, but probably Sammie would have learned faster and adjusted better at his age, his mind so young." It was true. Recalling Bible verses and Bible stories didn't come easy for Levi's dad. Maybe if it would be one's own dad, one would find it hard to accept.

At length, Clara said, "It seems there are more and more changes to accept in life."

"Are you talking about Charles getting a job in the Lone Oak district and moving there, and Nevin taking the job Charles had, and you not having Charles to depend on for a way to get around?" Levi asked.

"Well, I would have had to get used to that anyhow, even if he was dating around here. I would often have had to look for another way, but, yes, it takes some adjusting. Charles had me spoiled. Elvin's boys offer transportation at times.

"One of the adjustments that I wasn't ready for is Alice and Peter being married. I may as well prepare for Elsie to leave us, too."

"Yes," Levi replied, "I know what you mean. I changed friends a few times already. And maybe if we could see the changes that are coming in the next years, we would despair. I believe it's good we can see only part of a day at a time."

Clara was thinking deeply of the truth, "part of a day." Yes, this evening could even bring changes.

It was hard to see Charles moving out, but it was wise he could make such a move, rather than always going back and forth on weekends like he did the first half of the year. Since Willis didn't like to see Charles quit working for him, it was decided to let Nevin, since he was sixteen and interested in farming. He was missed in the store, but they could make out. Hettie helped so much and Anna Lois was a good worker. At times, others helped when Hettie or Clara had a day off.

*   *   *

Clara looked a moment at the moon that was silently making a clear little light. It was almost full. Clara was heading over the fields on her way home from Elvins. It had been such a full day and seemed like longer ago than just this morning that she was in church and went with Caleb and Virginia to Dad's for dinner. She had enjoyed the talk with cousin Levi, who seemed like a big brother. And Laura was so talkative tonight. So often her thoughts were so school-related and about other teachers, but tonight was interesting.

Clara didn't like to admit it, but the evening had been a disappointment, leaving her with an empty feeling. Seeing Raymond a few times had stirred her longings. But Raymond hadn't given her any sign of recognition.

142

Chapter Nineteen

It was a dreary January Sunday afternoon. Hettie had been writing a letter and then took a nap with Ben James. Clara was helping the other boys play Probe. Clara popped a few batches of popcorn and stirred up lemonade as she and Laura visited and the boys continued to play Probe. When Laura asked Clara if she had been sewing for spring, they went upstairs where Clara showed her the piece of material she was thinking of using.

Laura admitted she still had fabric to make for the winter, but "I had no mood. School was rather sluggish."

Clara smiled, "You have been teaching more than a year. You know those days come with January and they pass again."

"I know, but it's getting to me. How can I help the pupils?"

"You don't sound like your usual self. You usually have such a positive outlook, and school keeps you going," Clara said in disbelief.

"I know it used to keep me going, but I failed my pupils last week. Poor Michael was in tears when I belittled him for not knowing the two-times tables. He was used to my taking time to help him and challenge him to catch on. And fifth grade—I had them enthused that we would be having a geography quiz, like baseball spelling. They had been so listless in their lesson, and they started getting eager about it and looking forward to it last week. Then I disappointed them by not having it prepared.

"On Friday, when I passed out papers for the second grade, everyone raised their hand as if they didn't know how to do it. I got a little irritated and went to Erla's desk to read the first sentence and discovered I had given them the seventh grade's work sheets. I quickly gathered them up and said I would give them their sheets.

"In the last session, when I had put the poems on the board for the upper grades and passed out the books for them to copy them into, the room got quiet. I looked up and wasn't sure what their facial expressions meant, as if copying a poem was the oddest thing I ever asked them to do.

"Louie Dave, in the back row, glanced at me and then looked at his classmates. He shoved his hands through his hair, letting it flop in each direction. Then he raised his hand. I wasn't sure I should ask him what he wanted, since I thought I saw a smirk rising in his eyes and playing on his lips. The other pupils watched him expectantly. I bit my tongue and tried to ask calmly, 'Yes, Louie?'

"In a gruff voice, as dryly as only he can talk, he asked, 'Shall we copy our poems in our penmanship books?' He looked at me so soberly, but I could see he was laughing inside for being so wise to point out my blunder. I heard some snickering as he asked and felt my face getting warm. To cool off, I said, 'It might give you good practice, but if you don't want to, Louie Dave, you can pass out the poem books.' Louie rolled his eyes in a circle as he got up and passed out the poem books, as if he were a hero."

Clara was laughing until she wiped tears as she had heard many Louie Dave stories. He wasn't really mischievous, but school would be bound to get boring without him in the classroom.

"And I dread Monday morning," Laura said. "I wonder what the pupils told their parents."

"Maybe things will go better again," Clara predicted.

"How so?" Laura asked anxiously.

"Well, you haven't told me yet what was robbing your mind that you weren't thinking what you are doing," Clara said.

Laura stared at the floor. She blew her nose, her eyes glistening with unshed tears. This wasn't like Laura; she would usually laugh things off. She cleared her throat and said, "Everything was all right till Tuesday evening when I came home and found the letter. He wondered if I would accept his company. He asked if it would be all right for this Sunday. If I need more time to think it over, let him know when, and if I don't see it as the Lord's will, he would accept it.

"I don't know how many times I started writing an answer. On Thursday evening I finally got a sensible letter together, but I couldn't mail it. The message didn't sound right. I thought on Friday I could do better, but writing went worse. I just wish he was someone I had a reason to refuse. I thought everyone knew I planned to be an old maid schoolteacher all my life."

"I still have no clue," Clara said leaning forward with interest. "It must be Dallas from York County or the young widower, as much as it presses on your mind."

"Clara," Laura cried in alarm, "it's only a few months since Evan's wife died. I would have much reason to refuse them both. I thought I could refuse Raymond Kulp, too, but . . . but . . . but . . ."

Clara drew a deep breath to extend to Laura her congratulations, but all that came out was a moan. No wonder! Clara wouldn't have been anymore startled if Laura had struck her across the face. Clara finally managed to say, "Well, why would you want to refuse Raymond?" Her voice sounded rather strained, but Laura didn't seem to notice. Clara took a sudden chill, goose pimples running up and down her arms.

"I told you I want to continue teaching school. I can't have other things on my mind. I never considered Raymond. I thought he belonged to Ilene. What happened to that?"

"I guess Mark is giving her some attention," Clara answered, remembering the latest gossip she had heard. "And what did you tell him?"

"I wrote him many letters telling him I'm not interested and I don't feel it's the Lord's leading, but none of them sounded right. I mean, when I thought of him receiving the letter, I rewrote it. If only I had a reason to turn him down. I always considered him as one of the younger boys, but I guess he is only a little over a year younger than I am. If it would be Rufus, I wouldn't have any trouble writing the reasons. Rufus would just read it and say, 'Oh, she isn't interested, so I better look elsewhere.' But Raymond—I mean, if you noticed, he has matured; I don't think he asked lightly. And the longer it goes till I answer, the more likely he will think I am considering and I feel there were things in his letter other than what the words revealed. I don't know how to answer."

"You mean you are afraid he is like cousin Levi, still sensitive from when Elsie turned him down? He hasn't gained confidence in himself since," Clara offered.

"Yes, that well explains the feelings I was trying to put into words," Laura said with feeling.

A silence followed as both girls sat thinking. Then Laura asked, "What would *you* do?"

Clara chuckled in spite of herself and said, "He didn't ask me, but if you can't write to let him know, maybe you could tell him to come on Sunday evening and you could explain."

Laura thought deeply for a moment, then looked up at Clara and rose from the bed where she was sitting. "Thanks for listening. Maybe I could do that because my conscience doesn't let me send the letters."

By bedtime the shock wore off and Clara could cry out her disappointment into her pillow. Tears flowed freely, relieving the tension. Life was so perplexing. How she longed for a deep conversation with Raymond, and Laura had no desire for him. More tears fell. Why had she let herself be drawn to him? He was so understanding and seemed to think deeply, as Laura put it. "If you have noticed, he has matured to manhood," she had said. Clara should have known she wasn't worthy of him. Clara vowed she would never again build up her hopes when she had no cause. She would pray to God to guide her to the path He had paved for her.

*   *   *

The rain gently fell, dreary gray clouds all around. Typical April weather, brought more showers, but it didn't dampen the spirits of the ones in the house seated around the kitchen table playing Probe.

Clara had played awhile with Roy, Landis, and Earl. After getting tired of it, she gave Hettie a chance to play a few rounds.

Landis, taking another handful of popcorn, asked Earl if he had a "U," claiming they had guessed all the other vowels. Earl shook his head no and the other players rejoiced when the card said that an opponent on Roy's left had to expose a card. Earl turned up an "N" with the next letter an "M." Only an "H" at the beginning of the word, with only one letter turned down. It didn't take Hettie long to guess the letter "Y" when it was her turn, which made the complete word "hymn." They continued to play.

Clara got up and saw the rain was still coming down steadily. She had thought of going to Elvins to see if she could go with Lawrence to Adin's house, where the young folks were invited for supper; however, when she saw it was still raining, she decided to stay where it was dry unless Lawrence offered her a ride. Going into the parlor, Clara thought of stretching out on the sofa and maybe taking a nap, but first decided to open the curtain to let in some light. Instead of lying down, she sat on the rocking chair, idly watching the rain fall.

Katherine came to the door and asked if she could come in. Carrying her doll, she sat on the sofa, her doll beside her. Clara knew what Katherine would do. Jumping off the sofa, she got the old *Ideals* books from the shelf and climbed back onto the sofa. As she showed the pictures to her dolls, Katherine started telling imaginary stories to the doll. This was what she usually did when she was in the parlor; sometimes she used magazines for songbooks. Clara wondered if she, too, had that much imagination when she was her age.

Clara reminisced, remembering how eager she had been to go with the young folks. It had seemed that the enjoyment would never fade, but where was that urge now? She remembered her cherished plans and dreams, and now they had faded. Her friends had had strong dating relationships and later left the young folks to step into marriage. Even Elsie had married in February.

Clara then thought of Laura. Wasn't that back in January that Raymond had asked Laura? Laura wasn't interested in dating, but she couldn't bring herself to disappoint Raymond. At Clara's suggestion, Laura had given Raymond permission to visit and talk things over. Here it was April and they were still seeing each other.

When Clara had asked Laura about it, she said, "We are still discussing it." Clara had expected Laura would eventually come to the place where Elsie and Alice came after they had dated awhile. They got that look in their eyes that seemed to say they weren't telling you everything anymore. But Laura—Clara couldn't really pinpoint Laura's character. She didn't freely talk about dating or about Raymond.

When Raymond was in the group of young folks, Laura seemed to silently gaze at him occasionally, as if he were a glittering star that hung on a thin thread. Even though Raymond at times sent a cheery smile her way if they passed each other, she seemed embarrassed. Whenever Raymond was at a gathering and offered to take Laura home, he always came and addressed her politely saying, "Laura, are you ready to leave?"

Laura barely nodded and didn't raise her eyes enough to see his kind, friendly expression as he turned to get her wraps. Raymond seemed to be so thoughtful of her. Clara couldn't grasp how Laura kept from responding. It still almost hurt to see how merciful and understanding Raymond was, or tried to be; and Laura seemed to refuse his attention.

Clara reached for the notebook in which she had started copying poems that she had found. The poems seemed to describe her struggles, as if someone was speaking guidelines for her. She had copied the first one when Benjamin and Hettie had received the book, *Streams in the Desert*, while Benjamin was ill. It had described the dreams she had, the longings of Sammie and Raymond that were quenched, and the struggles she had to be submissive when her friends' dreams were fulfilled, taking away what she had with them. Maybe the entry touched her even more because it was dated March 17, her birthday:

> *I'll stay where you've put me, I will, Dear Lord,*
> *I was eager to march with the ranks and file,*
> *Yes, I wanted to lead them, you know.*
> *I planned to keep step to the music loud*
> *To cheer when the banner unfurled,*

To stand in the midst of the fight straight and proud,
But I'll stay where you've put me.

I'll stay where you put me, I will, Dear Lord,
Though the field be narrow and small
And the ground be fallow and the stones lie thick
And there seems to be no life at all.
The field is thine own, only give me the seed;
I'll sow it with never a fear.
I'll till the dry soil while I'll wait for the rain
And rejoice when the green blades appear.
I'll work where you've put me.

I'll stay where you put me, I will, Dear Lord.
I'll bear the day's burden and heat,
Always trusting Thee fully when even has come,
I'll lay heavy sheaves at Thy feet.
And then when my earth work is ended and done
In the light of eternity's glow,
Life's record closed, I surely shall find
It was better to stay than to go.
I'll stay where you put me.

Many people praised Clara for staying and helping Aunt Hettie with the store and the family, but there were times she yearned for what her friends had. Living in their own houses with their husbands, using their hope chest treasures, living out their hopes and dreams.

Turning the page, Clara saw she had copied from the scrapbook that Hettie received after Benjamin's death. It was so well written. Clara thought of the disappointments that came over the years, remembering, too, the sermon that was preached when she and others were baptized. They were told that Satan will tempt them and try them to test their faith, just as he did Jesus.

These poems were becoming a greater treasure than the quilts, rugs, and things in her chest. She read the lines again. She had already read them so often, she knew them by memory. She found it easier to learn them when she discovered the poems could be sung to a familiar tune.

Disappointment, His appointments—
Change one letter, then I see
That the thwarting of my purpose
Is God's better choice for me.
    His appointment must be blessing
    Though it may come in disguise
    For the end from the beginning
    Open to His vision lies.

Disappointments, His appointments—
Whose? The Lord Who loves me best
Understands and knows me fully
Who my faith and love would test.
    For like earthly loving parents
    He rejoices when He sees
    That His children accept unquestioned
    All that from His wisdom flows.

Disappointments, His appointments—
No good things He will withhold.
From denials oft we gather
Treasures of His love untold.
    Well He knows each broken purpose
    Leads to fuller, deeper trust.
    And the end of all His dealings
    Proves our Lord is wise and just.

Disappointments, His appointments—
Lord, I think it then as such
Like the clay in hands of potter
Yielding wholly to Thy touch.
    All my life now is Thy moulding,
    Not one single choice is mine

Let me answer unrepining,
"Father, not my will but Thine."

Clara turned the page and saw the verse she had copied from the birthday card Anna Lois had given her with a gift. It was such a surprise to her that Anna Lois thought to give her something. In the card she had written:

Guide me to those who need my help,
Teach me to see their need
That I may speak the word of cheer
And do the kindly deed.
  And if the work Thou dost appoint
  Is one the world counts small,
  Make me content with my lot
  And faithful in it all.

As Clara read the words, "make me content with my lot," she wondered if at times Anna Lois also longed for a caring husband and yearned to be a mother, but had to accept a lot that didn't seem as worthy. *But Anna Lois always seems so cheerful, and it sounds like she and her maiden friends have interesting times together.* Clara wondered if maybe Anna Lois sensed at times that Clara was feeling disappointed. As she reread the two verses, she suddenly became aware that she could sing them to the tune of "God Moves in a Mysterious Way."

Clara must have fallen asleep because suddenly she heard Paul and Landis at the door calling, "Supper is ready."

Several weeks later Clara was reading her Bible as she took her hair down, a practice she had started some time ago so she would have a routine to guarantee that she wouldn't neglect reading the Word. Suddenly, reading Ephesians 4, she realized what she was reading and read it again. It seemed to say what the poems said—to be satisfied in our calling. "I therefore, the prisoner of the Lord, beseech you that ye walk worthy of the vocation wherewith ye are called."

Clara took a moment to copy the verse in her notebook of poems. As she opened her notebook, she saw the verse she had copied earlier from Hettie's *Streams in the Desert*:

> *In the center of the circle*
> *Of the will of God I stand.*
> *There can be no second causes;*
> *All must come from His dear hand.*
> *All is well, for 'tis my Father*
> *Who my life has planned.*

Throughout the weeks, Clara had continued reading the entries in *Streams in the Desert* for each day. There were so many uplifting messages and poems. Sometimes she had almost marked something she really liked, then remembered it wasn't her book.

Hettie, noticing Clara's interest in the book and seeing her copying some of the pages in her notebook, surprised Clara by giving her a copy of her own, which she cherished deeply.

*   *   *

The mild September day was stretched over with a clear blue sky as far in the heavens as one could see. The young folks were arriving at Caleb's house for dinner.

Clara was standing at the kitchen counter pouring pudding in the dessert dishes, garnishing it with whipped cream and graham cracker crumbs. As she gazed out the window and saw a group of girls enjoying the soft breeze, Clara noticed Laura standing on the porch with her back resting against the post. Clara was eager to talk to her and hear how school was going. Since there were more students each year, they had to make two rooms this year, with Laura teaching first, sixth, and seventh, and eighth grades.

As more buggies came in the lane, Clara saw Raymond Kulp stepping out of a buggy and unhitch his horse. Her mouth dropped. Was she seeing right? Why was Laura already here? Then she remembered that Laura might have come with her brother.

Since the new church was built, the youth were somewhat separated. Clara tried to remember—had Laura been at Echo Valley this forenoon? Since she had come to Caleb's home last evening to help Virginia, she hadn't arrived until the girls were filing in. They had set up the table in the morning and left immediately after church was over.

* * *

The last of the dishes were washed. Some of the girls helped since Virginia had to feed John Wayne and put the food away. Clara saw that some of the boys had gone out to their buggies for their songbooks. Apparently they were going to sing. Likely Caleb had asked them to sing.

When Clara walked by the window as she was putting the tea towels in the wash house, she saw some of the younger boys hitching up their teams. Some girls, including Laura, stood on the walk, wearing their bonnets, waiting until the boys drove up.

"What's going on?" Clara asked in disbelief.

Eunice, who was standing nearby said, "Oh, some of the younger ones want to go over to the ridge and climb Cedar Hill since it's such a nice day. I guess some of the girls are going, too, and some have to take their sisters home before they go.

Just then, Laura's brother Sidney drove up and Laura climbed in, as other buggies drove up to pick up the girls.

Clara glanced over at the other end of the kitchen where the boys, with their songbooks, were seated in a circle. Cousin Levi, Raymond—Clara gasped. She had finally resigned herself that Laura had changed her mind and accepted Raymond, although she didn't act quite like her other dating friends.

As the weeks continued, Clara thought it strange, but satisfying, to have Laura remain with the group after the dating couples left the gatherings. When Clara asked Laura about her and Raymond taking a break, Laura had replied, "I didn't say anything about taking a break. I always said I want to teach school for many years."

"And Raymond doesn't want you to teach school?" Clara had asked.

Laura's face had colored as she said, "He doesn't care if I teach, but a relationship interferes with my teaching. I guess he didn't believe I always wanted to remain a teacher."

As Clara weighed bags of tapioca and clear gel, her thoughts wandered. Laura didn't talk much about breaking up with Raymond, but she seemed rather withdrawn. At times she didn't even bother coming to the gatherings. Raymond seemed more like himself—cheerful and manly, not paying any attention to girls.

Clara wondered how Raymond could appear as usual, since it was Laura's decision to break up their relationship. Yet she seemed to be more affected than Raymond.

Disgusted with herself, Clara realized that the old struggle was returning. She hadn't realized how good it had felt to not have tempting thoughts of Raymond. She thought she had won the victory, but now these tempting thoughts were coming back again. She was disappointed with herself that she left them bother her.

Chapter Twenty

Weddings were becoming quite a usual event to Clara. So many of her cousins had married during the past year, and now this fall, even more were getting married.

This wedding was in the Spring Hill District where her Uncle Eli David lived, her mom's brother. Clara had never been to this home before as it was their son Andrew who was marrying Peter Horst's daughter, Edna Mae. Usually when the Reiff cousins married, the wedding was in the Dry Ridge area where Norma's Ezra lived; however, Eli David lived in the Spring Hill area.

This was the fourth of Eli David's sons to marry, and the ceremony was always in a different house. Emma Mae and Lucinda were the only girls of the Reiff cousins near Clara's age who weren't married.

From the upstairs window Clara saw the hostlers taking the teams that were still arriving. She recognized some of her younger cousins, but she didn't know quite a few. Likely, they were Edna Mae's relatives or neighbors.

As Clara watched, she noticed the one hostler seemed very energetic. He was everywhere. He was average size, not really tall. It was amusing to watch him. When he talked to the people as he took their team, he had a friendly grin on his face, losing no time in putting the horse away. So soon he was back again. Sometimes he just tied the horse quickly and took the next horse. When he had time, he put the horses away.

There were other hostlers around, but the one Clara was observing had a handsome smile and seemed to be friendly with everyone. When he raised his eyebrows, he had an innocent look. It seemed to Clara that she had seen him before. But where? Who? There was something about his expression that stood out. He was not what the world called homely, for that meant simple and plain. He was rather striking. He seemed to make everyone relax. Even if he was taking a horse and another team arrived, this boy still greeted the people, even though another hostler took the horse. Regardless of the situation, he brought smiles to the visitors' faces.

Clara asked Lucinda who the hostler was. "Oh, that's Frankie Snyder's Bennie. They used to live in your area. He is so ambitious and, well—ah—he is the cream of the crop," she added.

Clara was stunned beyond words. Bennie! She couldn't believe this was Bennie. Where had the years gone? He was no Sammie, just growing up the way he was raised, nor was he Johnnie, pretending to be something more. She hardly noticed how Bennie was dressed. Clara hadn't remembered that this was the area where Frankies now lived.

As Clara's name was called to go downstairs to be seated, and she was making her way through the hall to the stairs, her sixth sense alerted her that she was being watched. She met the glance of a boy with deep, clear blue eyes that seemed to ask, "Who are you?"

Moving on downstairs as more names were being called, some as couples and some as singles, Clara saw this boy walking alone and looking timid, as if he did not want people to notice him. Those clear blue eyes held an expression that Clara couldn't identify.

He wore his hair rather short, more like a man would than a young boy. He was combed modestly and didn't need long hair to toss over his head. What stood out the most to her was his pure white shirt which made him look well dressed. The current trend was to wear a shirt with figures and designs on a white background.

Throughout the day as Clara looked up, she met those very blue eyes searching her. He quickly looked away when they made eye contact. This happened when she walked to the dinner table. She saw him watching her from the table as she walked past. After dinner, when the young people returned from a walk and were crossing the porch, she looked up without thinking.

There he stood on the porch with a few other boys. A faint smile appeared and Clara assumed that perhaps she had smiled too. She was taken completely off guard. Shifting his posture, he looked away, as if he had been caught intruding.

Clara tried to find out who the young man was. He couldn't be one of the Snyder boys. Sammie was married and she knew Johnnie. Clara continued to study his expression when he couldn't be seen. She noticed he made up with other people and seemed friendly. Later, when some of the young folks were having fun during supper, as they usually did at weddings, he didn't take part in it. He continued visiting. After supper, he was visiting with Peter Horst, the man of the house, and with the married children who were helping with supper.

Clara asked Norma who the young man was. She looked at him and shrugged her shoulders saying, "I don't know," and went her way.

Clara had been visiting with Susan, who was waiting on the table, when Mrs. Peter Horst came toward the pantry with her hands full. Clara opened the door, and asked, "Who is the boy wearing the white shirt?"

"Oh, that is—ah—ah, let me see." Trying to remember his name, she finally said, "It's Virgil Stauffer, Mahlon's son." Clara repeated the name to herself; she had never heard the name before.

When it was time to go home and Clara was stirring through the pile of clothes on the bed, looking for her wraps, she couldn't locate her sweater. *It has to be here somewhere*, she thought as she looked under the bed. Well, she would have to go through the pile again.

Two girls came into the room. As they went to the dresser, looking for their bonnets, they were talking in low tones. Clara didn't pay much attention until she heard them say something about "Virgil." She paused a moment as she tried to catch the conversation.

One of the girls said, "I thought maybe he'd go back to Minerva."

157

"He had his chance," the other one replied. They were talking so softly that Clara could hardly catch the words.

Hearing the name "Minerva" again, the other girl said, "But her mother said . . ." Clara couldn't hear the rest.

"Oh, do you think?" the other one asked doubtfully.

Clara finally found her sweater and was on her way. As she passed the girls she heard one say, "Maybe it's better this way."

"But I pity Minerva. She surely tried."

Clara didn't stay to hear more. As she hurried downstairs and outside, she thought the van was likely waiting on her.

Coming to the kitchen entrance, Clara met a few boys. One said, "Here comes one of them."

Looking up to see who had spoken, Clara and saw it was one who had come in her van load. Apparently they were waiting for a few people. She also noticed further over stood—what was his name? As he was talking with someone, his blue eyes met hers, his smile widening. It had been so unexpected that Clara froze and just stared, quickly vanishing out the door.

*   *   *

Over the days and weeks that followed, Clara found that leaving the settlement and all the miles in between had not been enough to dissolve the force that was pulling within her. Many mornings she awoke early, tempting thoughts plaguing her mind. *Was it a coincidence that their glances met? Was he really watching her? Why?* Those clear blue eyes—she could still see them. She tried to determine the expression they held. Had he smiled a few times? He looked so decent—his blue eyes, his so-white shirt, and neatly combed hair. He looked pure. She thought of the words, *"Demuth ist die schanta tugend, denn sei zierte unser jungend"* (that is what it was, the humbleness, a beautiful virtue, it adorns our youth and the old people even more).

Clara spent many a moment recalling the conversation she had overheard at the wedding. She wondered what the girls had been talking about. Who was Minerva? Virgil was alone at the wedding.

Maybe he broke up with Minerva. She thought deeply over many unanswered questions till her mind wearied.

Over the weekend, she saw Raymond again in the group and found more struggles stirring. She wished she could get a hold of the submissive feeling she had had while Laura and Raymond were dating—when temptations didn't beckon her so. At times her longings could hardly be stilled.

Clara told herself if she were living a *Young Companion* story, a letter would arrive in the mail with a masculine scrawl and it would be from Virgil. They would get acquainted and she would listen as he told of his ideals of life. She imagined many different reasons of what his expression held. Clara felt sure she wouldn't have to lower her standards. He seemed to have high standards. Didn't this Minerva respect them?

As the days continued, Clara was letting herself be discouraged. There was no letter.

At times the Kulps sent a message that she could go along to a gathering. A few times Raymond came alone to pick her up, but he mentioned nothing about Laura. Neither did they get into any serious subjects, until one evening, on the way home from the supper. They had been silently driving along when Raymond, stirred out his thoughts, said, "So Amelia's dad is buying a farm for Charles."

"A farm for Charles?" Clara gasped in echo.

"Hettie hasn't told you?" he asked.

"No, I haven't heard a thing along that line. Charles was home the other day and was working on the meadow fence. I noticed while I was working in the store that Hettie was outside with him, and it seemed they had lots of things to discuss. I assumed wedding plans were brewing."

Then Clara asked, "So you think Charles would move to that district?"

"Her father," Raymond started explaining, "is a great one in produce farming, and this farm is what he needs for that. No big barns or silos, the buildings weren't too well kept, but it's good farming land. It's sixty acres, a little bigger than a young couple needs for produce farming. I guess at one time it was two separate farms, like one forty acres and the other twenty acres. There are buildings at each end of the farm. The one barn is in better shape, but the other house is more suitable. Maybe they'll sell the one house; they'll figure out something."

Then Raymond also mentioned, "We never know what changes life brings," and added, "Dad says there is some talk about ordaining a bishop for this area. There are now two churches and Bishop Allen also has West View to look after besides Lone Oak, his home district.

"Surely not Uncle Walter. He was only ordained," Clara said in concern.

Raymond drew a deep breath and said, "I believe it's about two years, and he is older. I have been thinking so much about Caleb." There was a sense of pain in his words.

"Oh, Clara groaned, "I wasn't thinking about Caleb. There is Lloyd yet. Surely the people wouldn't subject Caleb to such a weighty lot."

"It's easy to think so," Raymond said as he turned in the drive. "But we have to remember it's not what man thinks, for God is in control."

Clara thanked Raymond as she got out. She was sorry the conversation had to end; Raymond seemed to have such deep spiritual reasoning.

Clara tried not to let her time with Raymond affect her, but it had touched her heart. Raymond shared things with her that Hettie didn't confide in her. He was so mature. She found that the encounter eased the struggles somewhat that had been luring her since the wedding.

*   *   *

Clara winced as the pain throbbed in her head. It was about a week since the ride home with Raymond, and last night she hadn't gone to sleep till late. Now she awoke so early with the feeling that something was piercing her brain behind her eye. She thought eating breakfast would help, but as soon as she got up from the table her head throbbed again. It hurt so much she even got an upset stomach.

Hettie had gone to the barn to help the boys. Clara held a cold washcloth over the pain for awhile. Swallowing a few aspirin, she got the keys and headed out the door to open the store.

Clara felt depressed at the sight of the store. She felt like running out the lane to the neighbors' big meadow and on down to the woodland. She longed to go out to where the steers were grazing leisurely beneath the tall trees, wishing to let her mind unwind until it was done.

Clara wanted to go anywhere but to the store. She ached to talk to someone who understood her longings. Her notebook with the collection of poems didn't appeal much to her. The battle was raging.

Anna Lois, waiting for Clara to open the store, greeted her cheerfully. Anna Lois began getting the assortment of bags that she would need when she weighed the products, picking up where she left off last evening. Clara heard Anna Lois softly singing as she went about her work.

"This world is not my home, I'm just a passing through. My treasures are laid up somewhere beyond the blue. . . ."

Later, as Clara was filling the dairy case with cheese, she again was aware of Anna Lois softly singing:

> Let but my fainting heart be blessed
> With that sweet spirit for its guest.
> My God, to Thee I leave the rest,
> Thy will be done.
>
> Renew my will from day to day,
> Blend it with Thine and take away
> All now that makes it hard to say,
> Thy will be done.

Clara hurried out the side door and went into the utility shed where they kept supplies. There she left the tears come till she felt a release of the tension that had been mounting. She prayed to God to forgive her anxious heart and pleaded for submission to be able to say, "Thy will be done."

After washing her face in the restroom, she came back to continue filling the dairy case, feeling grateful that her head wasn't throbbing anymore.

There weren't many customers in the forenoon, making it possible for Clara and Anna Lois to visit while weighing bags. Anna Lois invited Clara to come to her place for dinner the next Sunday.

"I'm having my friends over. You know, you often heard me talking about Frances, Lisa, Annetta, and Joann. This will be even more interesting since Ruth, Verna, and Doris are coming from Lone Oak, and if Mabel can have off, she and Katie will come from Spring Hill, too. Maybe Lena is coming; all depends on how her mother is doing."

At times Anna Lois talked about the good times they had together, and Clara knew Frances and Annetta pretty good from the times they stopped in at the store to talk with Anna Lois.

Clara decided that she would go for dinner and maybe join in the visiting awhile before coming home and finding something else to do or somewhere to go.

But the visit had turned out to be quite interesting. The girls all welcomed her, as if she belonged with them, and as if they all knew her. "Oh, you are the one who works with her in the store."

Frances was telling about how her cat disappeared for three days, and how she hunted for her, finding her penned in the buggy shed.

Joann told about how her dog rose such a fuss one night that she couldn't sleep. Verna declared she would get rid of any dog if it kept her awake. "My nieces and nephews live across the street. I can have them over if I want someone to talk to; then I send them home and get a good night's sleep."

Mabel then related something her little niece said. It was so funny and reminded Doris of what her nephew had said. Clara found herself relating something Paul Henry had said when he was younger.

Ruth said, "That sounds like my first grader," and went on telling what he had done.

162

A lot of chuckles were heard. Lena said, "Like my mom. Last Saturday morning she was so confused. She was waiting for the train, and every time my nephew came around with the lawn mower, she thought the train was coming."

The girls grew sober and asked, "How is she doing at night? Can you get your rest?"

"Well, yes and no. Early in the morning she thinks its already time to get up. At times she has the kettles on the stove for eggs and oatmeal before I'm awake. If I start losing too much sleep, my sister-in-law stays with Mom while I sleep during the day."

Sometimes a few conversations were going on at one time. Clara was beginning to feel like one of the group. When they talked of some of their married friends who they seldom got to see, she knew what they meant. She and Elsie and Alice used to be together; now the times they met were few and far between, since both of them lived in other settlements.

Someone was asking Anna Lois about her parrot and if he was still learning new words. She told them that when her brother and his wife went on a trip, they kept some of their children. The parrot got well educated during that time.

As the parrot hopped from one perch to another cocking his head, Clara asked, "What do you think he will say about today?"

Annetta said, "Let's all be quiet for a moment and see if he has anything to say."

For a moment all conversation stopped. The bird, looking from one to the other, with a clear, unmistakable voice, rang out, "Thank you!" A burst of chuckles and laughter rumbled throughout the crowd. Someone asked, "Was that the bird?"

Some of the girls laughed so much, they needed to wipe their eyes with their handkerchiefs. That led to more conversation—what they had heard other birds say at other times.

Suddenly, Joann jumped up from her chair and exclaimed, "There's a buggy coming up the road! I wonder if Erma is coming. Did you say something to her, Anna Lois?"

"Yes, I did say something to her. She thought she wouldn't come home until tonight. Maybe she came home sooner."

163

As the buggy came up over the rise, Joann and Annetta said at the same time, "Oh, it's just some young boys."

Resuming their conversation, the girls discussed the new job Erma was planning to start—staying with an older lady.

Clara was gripping the side of her chair to keep from rushing over to the window to see who the boys were who were driving past.

These girls aren't even real, Clara's thoughts exploded. When she calmed down, she heard a few girls admonishing Anna Lois about something.

Katie asked, "What's this I'm hearing?"

Anna Lois shook her head and held it as if she was all perplexed.

"Oh," Frances said, "I asked Anna Lois if it was Evan coming to see her. He probably saw there were so many people here that he drove on. I did hear he has been seen around this area a few times during the evening."

"Yes," Lena chimed in. "Some people approached me, too. The poor man can't go anywhere without people trying to track him down."

Anna Lois said to Lena, "Okay, if he comes around, I'll send him over."

Verna said, "Like my brother when he was a widower," and she told of his experience. Doris and Ruth started smiling; they knew what she was going to say.

Annetta said, "Not like the one in West View—" and the stories continued. The subjects changed from one to another faster than one could follow. Anything from trying to behead a rooster to having someone knock on your door to borrow money. Older girls were thought to have a lot of money.

When Clara came home, she had much to share with Hettie. The enjoyment of the afternoon had reminded Clara of years ago when Elsie, Alice, and she were together. But she was still shocked to know that none of the girls—not one of them—was interested to know what boys were passing by. She was still wondering if these girls weren't real, or if she perhaps hadn't yet learned to overcome the dreams of her youth. Maybe she wasn't real. As she pondered, she clung to the ray of hope that maybe the struggle eases as one gets older.

Chapter Twenty-One

Clara pinned her hair up. She had read awhile and then taken a refreshing nap. The house seemed so quiet with Hettie and the children away for dinner, but they would probably soon be home.

Clara had not planned on going to the young folks' gathering for supper at Eli Fox's home; however, when cousin Levi offered to pick her up and urged her to go, she changed her mind. *Oh, there he is already.* Clara hurriedly put in the last few hairpins, put on her covering, and got her bonnet and sweater, hoping a sweater was enough for the mild March weather.

As Clara climbed on the buggy, Levi teased her, saying, "What's the matter? You don't have that eager look you had when you were seventeen and going to a young folks' gathering."

Clara chuckled and asked, "Do you?"

Brushing his hand across his face, he said, "I'm afraid not. That's why I offered to pick you up. I don't want to be the only old one there."

"How about Laura? Of course, you never know if she will be there. And she is younger than me," Clara answered her own question.

"She'll probably be there and will leave soon after supper," Levi stated matter-of-factly.

"I've never been able to figure out Laura. She and Raymond were dating quite a while. She's the one who caused the break-up, yet it seemed to affect her more, and still does. Raymond goes on as if he never really cared, but I can see he still respects her as much as ever. Are they dating in secret, or what? Laura just isn't the same," Clara wondered.

Levi stared ahead as if in deep thought. Looking up, he said, "I used to wonder, too. Then I talked to Raymond a few times. When I got him started and he knew I was sincere and not just nosy, he was ready to talk about it. He told Laura if she just wants to teach school, she should teach school as long as she wishes. He won't stand in her way, and whenever she is ready to date, she shall let him know. He said he would wait and that's how they parted. Raymond never gave up. He just goes on living, waiting until she's ready." Levi looked at Clara to see if she caught on.

Looking at Levi blankly, Clara asked, "And why doesn't Laura happily go about teaching as she did before? She seemed more like the old Laura when they were dating."

Levi chuckled as if he knew something. Looking at Clara, he asked, "Have you ever tried to imagine how hard it would be to live with the fact that someone is waiting for you to make a decision. I think Laura thought he would soon be interested in another girl, but anyone can see he is still thinking of Laura and would wait seven years for her if he had to. Laura's resistance is getting low."

"Do you think Laura would tell him if she would desire to have him come again?" Clara asked unbelievingly.

Levi smiled, "Hardly, and Raymond began realizing that, too. He told me he met Laura in town one evening the other week after school and asked her if she has any desire to continue seeing him. She told him he could come, and they had a date last Sunday evening. No one found it out since the young folks weren't invited anywhere specific for supper on Sunday."

This was almost more news than Clara could absorb. No, Clara couldn't begin to imagine how it would be to know Raymond would take you anytime. Speaking her thoughts, Clara said, "I could never understand how Laura could do this to Raymond," adding, "How can she resist? Surely you know girls who would accept you if you asked them."

Looking at Clara helplessly, Levi shook his head and said, "I wouldn't know which one. You have no idea how hard it is to ask, fearing denial."

"But if there is a girl who impresses you or is drawn to you, you have the right to ask her how she feels. You don't have to live with anxiety and longings." Clara's words came from deep within her heart.

"It isn't as easy as you think," Levi replied.

They drove in silence for a while, Clara hoping Levi wouldn't ask any questions as to why she said what she did. Finally, Clara said, "You said I don't look as eager as I did when I was seventeen. That's a fact. Going to the gatherings leaves me feeling like a misfit. Even the ones who seemed so young when they joined the young folks are marrying already, and the ones who have just now started going with the group seem so young. I never thought I'd be with the young folks when my sister Mildred went out with them. I thought I was getting old when Norma joined the young folks." Clara sighed and rolled her eyes.

Levi laughed and said, "And now Norma is married, but she did marry rather young."

"But Charles is married too," she reminded him and added, "I admit I'm starting to feel a little more comfortable when I'm with Anna Lois and her friends. It's rather interesting. Some of them are only four years older than I am."

"Maybe I should check in with them, too," Levi mused.

"I dare you. Which one can I ask for you?"

"Didn't you tell me that not one of them was interested in seeing who the boys were who passed by on the road?"

"Did I tell you that?" Clara asked, staring at him.

"You didn't tell me, but I heard about it," Levi answered. No amount of coaxing made him admit how he heard about that. Clara didn't remember if she told Hettie or who she had told, but how would Levi have heard? Regardless of how he was informed, it must have impressed him since he remembered.

Levi, aroused from his thoughts, said, "You seem to think it's hard to grasp or accept the fact that Mildred is old enough to join the young folks. You wouldn't want to keep Bennie waiting longer, would you?"

Clara gave Levi a bewildered look.

"Haven't you heard? That's why Bennie Snyder keeps appearing in our area every so often. He has an interest in Mildred."

Clara drew a deep breath and muttered dryly, "Give me strength."

Levi laughed heartily.

"They are both remarkable," Clara said, after having time to think about it.

"You mean Mildred is remarkable for who she is, after the influence Norma had on her?"

Clara's thoughts continued. *It seems Norma's influence never bothered her. To think what Mildred would be able to do with her hair, but she never seemed tempted. And she need not be. Just the natural shape of her eyebrows and her dimple make her attractive enough.*

"But Bennie?" Clara said, questioningly. "He is somewhat older than she."

"I guess that doesn't matter," Levi replied, "if Bennie wants to wait around."

Clara was thinking of Bennie at the wedding—the energetic hustler. He'll probably find things to do to make the time pass.

*   *   *

Clara felt out of sorts. It was a nice cool May day, but the sun was gaining over the clouds. Clara wished she could fight the discouragement and rise higher in faith like the sun gained over the clouds.

Last weekend she had gone to the young folks' gatherings again, but she felt like a misfit. Laura left early with Raymond when the other couples left. Laura was starting to be more like Elsie and Alice had been. Laura's eyes held a joy she didn't share with Clara. With Bennie in the area, Clara realized that indeed he was noticing Mildred, but she couldn't blame him. Mildred was a nice girl and had a pleasant countenance, which she didn't spoil by dolling herself up.

Clara felt another pang as she thought of how they had visited in Norma's home the other week. It touched Clara's heart to

168

see the quilts on her beds—the ones she had had in her hope chest. And the bureau scarves on the dressers were the ones Norma had made herself. It tugged at Clara's heart to see Norma's dreams had been fulfilled. She noticed the salt and pepper shakers with matching toothpick holder that her aunt had given to Norma. This same aunt had also given Clara a set. Everywhere she looked, she saw the things that had been in Norma's hope chest, things she had collected over the years.

It pained Clara's heart to realize that her own hopes and dreams weren't fulfilled. Norma had often gone against her parents' counsel, but her life still was blessed and fulfilling. Clara had to wonder why the joys were denied her when she sought to obey her parents and respect the church. She knew she must not feed on self pity, but it was hard to understand. She had tried so hard to live in God's will. Why were all her cherished plans and dreams denied?

Clara received much praise for staying with Hettie and the children, but her longings went beyond what the praises filled. Charles and Amelia had been home one day last week. They seemed like such a happy couple. Charles made a wise choice, even if it wasn't outward appearance that attracted him. Even so, he had said that Amelia was the most beautiful girl he had ever seen.

For a moment Clara thought back to the day when Eli David's son Andrew married. She still remembered Virgil's humble spirit, the white shirt he wore, and how neatly and modestly his hair was combed. She still wondered why it seemed he had been watching her. For weeks and months she had secretly hoped to find a letter in the mailbox until just the sight of the mailbox depressed her.

The struggle increased when the *Young Companion* arrived, containing a story about a girl finding a letter in the mailbox with a masculine scrawl. Even if it wasn't from the boy she had hoped it would be, it was still a letter. There was no letter in Clara's mailbox.

Since the family wasn't ready yet to leave for church, Clara decided to walk and enjoy nature and the cool, pleasant spring breeze. The walk was refreshing—the birds singing so merrily. The trees and bushes were adorned in their spring outfits, and wildflowers decorated the roadway. Occasionally a sweet fragrance from a bush or a plant filled the air.

Pausing a moment along a deep ditch, where it would hardly be noticed, Clara saw a little blue wildflower blooming in simple beauty. That little flower was satisfied to bloom down in the ditch.

Clara thought of the words, "I'll stay where you put me; I will, dear Lord." But she was also trying to recollect a verse she had read at one time about a little flower blooming somewhere unseen, unnoticed.

The walk to church had refreshed Clara. She spoke with a few women she met as she entered the churchyard. Some of Anna Lois's friends had greeted her and made her feel welcome.

It wasn't until the ministers filed in that Clara realized she felt a little disappointed. She then realized that she had been hoping there would be a visiting minister who would bring some stirring message forth to challenge her and to refresh her wilting faith. Uncle Walter had the opening, touching on different subjects. Clara had hoped he would continue on in more detail. He had touched on temptations. "When you overcome temptation, it's a victory. Each victory will help you overcome another temptation. We must keep fighting." He referred to the Old Testament, going deeper into the subject. Clara wasn't able to follow or grasp it.

Without thinking, Clara found herself watching a young mother with a cute baby. The baby looked so trustingly at its mother. Next, she noticed a man who was watching his son who was sitting on the little boys' side. Clara tried to steer her thoughts back to the sermon, but so soon it strayed again. Suddenly everyone was starting to kneel for silent prayer.

Clara was sure Uncle Walter had asked the congregation for prayers so that the spirit could speak further through the brother, but she hadn't even heard him. She had noticed a woman from another district and tried to figure out who she was. She was disgusted that her mind roamed so easily.

The congregation rose again, then sat down and waited expectantly for the deacon to read the text. It was getting unusually quiet. Clara looked up and saw that Caleb still hadn't given the Bible to Russel, but was paging through it. Deacon Russel patiently waited. Clara breathed a prayer that Caleb would be given strength to bring forth the Word, wondering how long it would take him to find the text. Surely he must have one in mind. Finally Caleb handed the Bible to Russel, and Russel rose and announced the text in 1 Corinthians, chapter 10, the first fourteen verses.

As Russel began reading, Clara heard it was based on what the Israelites endured in the wilderness. Verse six says, "Now these things were our examples, to the intent we should not lust after evil things, as they also lusted." It said more about not tempting Christ as they did, nor murmuring as some of them murmured. It again said in verse 11, "Now all these things happened unto them for an example, and they are written for our admonition." Suddenly Clara sat up, becoming more interested as he read verse 13, "There hath no temptation taken you but such as is common unto man: but God **is** faithful, who will not suffer you to be tempted above that ye are able; but will with the temptation also make a way to escape, that ye may be able to bear it." Clara was drinking in the words like a wilting flower receiving water.

Russel read only one more verse, then said, "These are the words I was asked to read. I wish the Lord's blessing to what comes further."

Clara noticed that Caleb was still paging around in his Testament, as if searching for something. As he slowly rose and made his way to the table where the Bible was lying, he opened it to the text. Looking at the congregation for a moment, he then looked down at the Bible.

When he lifted his eyes again, Caleb slowly started speaking, saying (this is translated to English), "I greet you in the name of our Lord Jesus Christ. I wish His peace, which is higher than all else, to be with us this hour. For without peace no one will see God. I would have desired to listen longer to the lesson the brother was bringing out, but everything has its time."

Clara felt guilty because she had not gotten anything out of the opening sermon since she couldn't keep her mind focused. Caleb said, "I trust you have all prayed that the Spirit will speak further so something of benefit can come from it. We of ourselves cannot speak unless the Spirit speaks through us. And I feel like I am coming to class unprepared. I had been reading another text last night and this morning, This morning, when the brother made mention of temptations and working to win the victory, I felt led to some other Scriptures. I trust God will speak what He wants out of this. I, the servant, want to try and do the work He wants done.

"Chapter ten, verse one, says, 'Moreover, brethren, I would not that ye should be ignorant, how our fathers were under the cloud and all passed through the sea.' It's a reminder for us how those before us were in afflictions when they knew not how to go further. They couldn't go in their own strength, but had to rely on God, Who made a way to guide them. What does it say? A fire guided them by night and a cloud by day. When they came to the Red Sea, they murmured, 'Why couldn't we have died in Egypt? Weren't there enough graves there?' Their enemies were behind them, and the sea was before them, but they were told, 'Stand fast and see what the Lord will do unto you today.'

"Do we get discouraged and think there is no way to go on? What's the use? We have to stand fast and see what the Lord will do unto us today. He made a way. The murmuring of the Israelites proved they didn't have their full trust in God. Not like Abraham did when he went to offer up Isaac. With God all things are possible.

"He dried the waters up so there was a path for them to go through. Do we stand fast and trust God will remove the obstacles that block our way? It is mostly the obstacles in the distance that discourage or worry us. We let down our trust like the people there at the Red Sea. Once God opened the waters, but their joy was short-lived because their enemies started following, taking the path the Israelites had taken. They feared again, but God is almighty. He made the water roll back when they were almost through. Their enemies had just entered the water and they were destroyed. The Israelites were saved because God was leading them. He is faithful; why don't we trust Him?

"I was thinking about this the other day when my little son clasped my hand and took a few steps. I gradually released my hold and his walking was fine. As soon as he realized I wasn't supporting him, he sat on the floor. I couldn't lead him anymore because he

172

wouldn't walk. Is that why we get discouraged? We think God isn't guiding us anymore, so we give up. We want God to do all the guiding. We lose trust and don't even do what we have the strength to do. If my son had kept trusting and had stepped on, I could have given my guiding support when he faltered. But when he gave up trust, I couldn't lead him.

"The Scripture goes on, saying how they 'were all baptized unto Moses in the cloud and in the sea; and did all eat the same spiritual meat; and did all drink the same spiritual drink: for they drank of that spiritual Rock that followed them: and that Rock was Christ.'

"That's how we can continue on our spiritual journey; we look unto the cloud, unto God who is guiding us. We were baptized in His name. We are blessed in eating and drinking of that Rock. We have the Spirit that feeds and refreshes us. He speaks to us in a still small voice. He feeds us as we read His Word. And He speaks to us through us poor human ministers. How often do we hear His voice within speaking to us when we err and guiding us on again.

"But if we live for our own pleasures and serve men and ignore His voice, His voice will become still. Further on the Scripture says, 'But with many of them God wasn't well pleased: for they were overthrown in the wilderness.' They lacked faith. They did not trust the cloud that was leading them. They murmured because they weren't satisfied with what they were fed. They wanted other things. Had they not tempted themselves after other food, they would have been satisfied with what they had to eat. They murmured so much that Moses' faith was tried. They pressed so hard on him complaining that he once struck the rock when he was supposed to speak to it.

"We might say that was long ago. How does that help us, or why refer to it? What does the next verse say? 'Now these things were our examples, to the intent we should not lust after evil things, as they also lusted.' They lusted after other food. Was the food evil that they lusted after? No, the food was not evil; the lusting was evil. They weren't satisfied with what God had provided for them.

"To make this easier to understand, we could compare it to a girl who had a good enough life. But she lusted after other things.

173

The things she wanted were not evil, but it was evil to focus on what she wanted and did not have. If it weren't for these other things tempting her, she would be satisfied. So it was with the food. If we could resist the things that tempt us, we would be satisfied. But if we give in, we aren't satisfied anymore with what God has provided for us, even if it is sufficient.

"Another verse says," Caleb flipped through the Testament. "I think it is in James." More pages rustled as he picked up the Testament and said, "Here it is in the first chapter of James, verse 14. Maybe starting at verse 13, where it says, 'Let no man say when he is tempted, I am tempted of God: for God cannot be tempted with evil, neither tempted He any man. Verse 14 says, 'But every man is tempted, when he is drawn away of his own lust, and enticed.' Mark that word *Gelocket*—enticed, beckoned.

"We lure ourselves. It is like beckoning a dog to come, calling him to us. When we do that with lust, it becomes more than lust. The next verse says, 'Then when lust hath conceived, After we beckon it to us, it conceives and it brings forth sin.' That's when it becomes sin. The Israelites lusted after other food. They murmured, then became so enticed to it that they weren't content with what they had anymore. They didn't just give it a passing thought. *'Wish we could have so and so.'* It mastered them. Going back to our parable, it isn't sin if a girl admires a certain boy, but when she is drawn away by her own lust, if it overtakes her, and God's will can no more rule her life, then it brings forth sin.

"When we beckon the lust, when we sin to have something, what does it bring? Death. Not always a death of the earthly body but death of the spiritual kingdom within us that used to guide us and speak to us when we erred. We have overruled the Spirit within and silenced it. Like it says here, 'Then when lust hath conceived, it brings forth sin: and sin when it is finished, brings forth death.'

"I could mention many things as examples. Maybe members of the church lust after something we don't allow. They let themselves be enticed; it beckons to them. Instead of passing it off and saying, 'Well, we can't have that,' soon they feel evil against the church and against the ministers. The lust is then fulfilled; it brings forth sin. They leave the church.

"That which they cannot have means more to them than the church. They feel everyone is against them. It brings sin and then death to the kingdom within them. The next verse says, 'Do not err, my beloved brethren.' What need is there to say more? We can see what it brings. It's not a fairy tale. To err is to entice. We can't help to lust after things, but we do err if we beckon it to us.

"Back to the text, 'Neither be ye idolaters, as were some of them.' Idolatry is anything we depend upon or value higher than God." Caleb continued reading the next verses about fornicators and not tempting Christ and not murmuring as some of them did. He made some remarks, mostly a review of what he already had said, saying again, "'All these things happened unto them for examples: and they are written for our admonition.' It cannot be denied. We are people who let ourselves be tempted. The Scripture says, 'Wherefore let him that thinketh he standeth take heed lest he fall.' We might think at times we are able to withstand the temptation and think we are strong, but the next temptation could make us fall. We have no reason to look down on others and think we would have done better, that we wouldn't have allowed ourselves to be tempted like that."

"The next verse, verse 13, has so much instruction and encouragement. 'There hath no temptation taken you but such as is common to man: but God **is** faithful.'" Caleb put emphasis on that sentence and more so as he continued, "'Who will not suffer you to be tempted above that ye are able; but will with the temptation also make a way to escape, that ye may be able to bear it.'"

Caleb laid down the Bible and drew a deep breath, saying that first sentence has much encouragement, and asking if the congregation understood its meaning. "'There hath no temptation taken you but such as is common to man.' We don't have to be ashamed of the temptations that come to us. We don't have to think, *But my temptation is different. It's so strong*, because it's common to man. We all have them.

"Jesus knows. He was tempted too by Satan, but He didn't give in. He didn't beckon it. What does it say about the temptations

175

that try us? How can we endure?" Caleb asked in a kind voice, as a teacher would ask his first graders a question regarding the story they had just read to see if they knew what they read. "It says, 'God will not suffer you to be tempted above that ye are able, but will with the temptation also . . .'" Caleb stressed the words, "'make a way to escape that ye are able to bear it.' It does not say he will take the temptation away, but will make a way to escape that ye are able to bear it. If He took the temptation away, you wouldn't have to bear it anymore. So we don't get rid of the temptation; we are given a way that we are able to bear it.

"I now think back to the time I was a young boy and went traveling. We visited a place where there was an older minister living at one end of the house, and we got to talking. The minister somehow got to this verse, and I hadn't really been aware there was such a verse. I asked him how come there are people who have nervous breakdowns or sink into temptations if it says God **will not** suffer you to be tempted above that ye are able to bear it?

"The old minister rocked in his rocking chair a few moments and then bent forward saying, 'Read that verse again. It says that with the temptation, God also makes a way to escape that ye are able to bear it. He will make a way.' He continued, 'If people are rebelling and enticing the lust, they will not see the way He made to escape.'"

Shivers ran up and down Clara's spine as Caleb used such a gentle, but urgent pleading tone as if she was hearing the old minister herself.

"We won't escape from the tempter but escape enough that we are able to bear. We have to be soldiers to fight it and be able to stand. I now remember something I read in a paper. It was, I think, a Sunday School paper or something like that, and might be fitting to include in this thought, making it a little easier to understand. It was based on a story with which we are very familiar of when Adam and Eve were in the garden and the serpent tempted them, saying, 'Did God say you cannot eat of the fruits of every tree in the garden?'

"And Eve replied, 'We can eat of all the trees but one. For God said that if we ate of that tree we would die.' And the serpent said, 'God knows you surely wouldn't die, but you would become wise like God.' Then they started noticing the fruit. It looked good and tempted them more because they knew what they would gain. They didn't think about what they would lose: peace with God. They just thought of how wise they would become.

"The Sunday School paper further said that if Adam and Eve could have laughed off the words of the serpent, we could never be wise like God; we couldn't handle that, then the temptation would have left. But they beckoned it. Think what trouble it brought them as they overestimated themselves. Is that the cause of our temptations?

"If a man is tempted after riches, thinking if he could get enough money he could buy a farm, then he would be satisfied. So he takes some dishonest ways to get it. He never stops to realize that if he had so much wealth, there could be temptations he couldn't cope with. He didn't need the farm, but thought of how much more money he could make. But then there was a wet spring, and he couldn't get the crops out. When he did get a renter, it was one who didn't keep things in shape and who neglected farming. God had a reason for withholding that wealth, but the man took his own way and suffered for it.

"Or like a boy who so desires a certain girl and goes against his parents' counsel. He believes it's a leading and the parents just don't understand, so he takes his own way. He despairs. He didn't consider that God would have led him to her if it would have been good. He didn't know he couldn't live peacefully with her. We are too much like Adam and Eve. When something appeals to us, we are tempted to go after it. We beckon the lust and entice it till we meet up with sin when we could have taken the way of escape. Jesus didn't give in to temptation when Satan showed Him all he would give Him if He served him.

"The last verse, verse 19, says, 'Wherefore, my dearly beloved, flee from idolatry.' Why is that verse right next to the one of being tempted? Because if we serve anything more than God, if something stands in our way, that we cannot give up, it's idolatry. We are serving it rather than God.

"It seems fitting to turn to the first chapter of 1 Peter, verses 6 and 7 to close this text. Verse 6 says 'Wherein ye greatly rejoice, though now for a season, if need be, ye are in heaviness through manifold temptations.' It's only for a season that we are tempted. Verse 7 says that the trial of your faith, being much more precious than of gold that perisheth, though it be tried with fire, might be found unto praise and honor and glory at the appearing of Jesus Christ.'

"Gold is tried by fire, but the Scripture says gold perishes, and the trial of your faith **is much more precious** than gold. So, these temptations are the trials of our faith, as temptation makes our faith purer and stronger. Although we have to give up the farm we so much wanted, or the girl we so desired to have, or the things the church denies us, if we can fight on as a soldier, we have something much more precious than gold. And the trial of our faith may be found in praise, honor, and glory. When? Not here, but at the appearing of Jesus Christ. I will leave off and let it for others to testify."

Clara wasn't the only one who wiped tears as many changed positions.

Lloyd said he could testify to the message as God's Word, and he didn't want to take away the thoughts of what was brought forth, but he said, "My mind goes to Hebrews, chapter 12, verse 4, where it says, 'Ye have not yet resisted unto blood striving against sin.' Our temptations may be hard to bear, but we have not yet resisted unto blood against sin. This is a thought to remember when we think the way is hard. I leave off for further testifying."

Russel said, "I also wish the blessing to what was brought forth. It can be testified as God's Word. My thoughts went to 2 Corinthians, chapter 4 when the brother talked about the trial of our faith and what it earns for us at the appearing of Jesus Christ. Verse 16 says, 'For which cause we faint not; but though our outward man perish, yet the inward man is renewed day by day.' And verse 17 says, 'For our light affliction, which is but for a moment, worketh for us a far more exceeding and eternal weight of glory.'

The Scripture says our afflictions are light and for a moment, yet they seem to drag us down and seem to be endless. But like we heard at a funeral some years ago, when at the judgment day the chaff from the wheat shall be thoroughly fanned, we see that it was our afflictions that worked for us the exceeding and eternal weight of glory, we shall surely say they were light and for a moment. Yes, they work for us. Now we feel they work against us, but they make us gain that weight of glory. For His cause we faint not. I wish the Lord's blessing to all and leave off."

Caleb stood again and said, "I am glad for all the thoughts that were brought forth, so let us come and pray before we part."

Clara wasn't the only who was impressed with the service. The song leaders had chosen to sing the song on page 303:

Alle christen hören gerne
Fon dem reich der herrlikeit
Den sie meynen schon fon ferne
Dasz es ihnen sey bereit
Aber vann sie hören sagen
Das man Christi kreutz musz tragen
Vann mon vill sein yünger sein
O so stimmen venig ein.

Lieblich ist es anzuhoren, Ihrbeladne
Kumm zu mir
Aber das sind harte lehren
Gehet ein zur enga thür
Hort man hosanna sigen Lauts gut
Laszts aber sagen kreutz' ge! ists ein andre tone
Und ein jeder lauft davon.

Clara just blinked at the words, and as they sang the last verse, tears came unbidden.

Lasz mich uber alles achten
Vas die seele an dir findt
Sollt leib and seel fershmachtend
Veisz ich doch dasz sie gevinnt

179

Dann du bist in allen leide
Jesu! lauter trost and freude
Und vas ich allhier ferlier
Findt sich besser doch in dir.

Translated:

All Christians gladly hear
About the kingdom of glory
For already from a distance
They think it is prepared for them.
But when they hear it said
That one must bear Christ's cross
If one wishes to be his disciple
Ah then only a few join in

It is pleasing to hear, "You burdened ones,
Come to me."
But these are hard teachings, "Enter in
At the narrow gate"
When one hears Hosanna sung,
It sounds good
But let "Crucify!" ring out,
Then it's a different tone
And everyone turns away.

Let me consider what my soul finds
In Thee higher than all other things.
If soul and body should languish
Yet I know that it (soul) wins
For thou Jesus art pure comfort
And joy in all suffering
And whatever I lose here I will find
Better in Thee.

*　　*　　*

After church Annetta asked Clara to go along to her place for dinner, but she had no desire to go. Someone offered her a ride along to where the young folks were going for dinner. She didn't take that offer either. She knew if she'd go away all afternoon, by evening she wouldn't remember much of what she had heard. She wanted to go home and digest it. Maybe she would make a few notes of some of what she had heard so the Spirit could speak through the ministers to her.

Clara knew the hours Caleb spent in the bedroom reading. That was how he knew where to find the verses that were given to him. How could they come to his mind if he wasn't acquainted with them? *What would their efforts help if we all went away and enjoyed ourselves and forgot what was brought forth and didn't get the value out of it?*

Clara spent the afternoon weighing again what she could recall and tried to make a writing of it to put in her collection of poems, etc. She wanted to remember what Caleb said about the story of Adam and Eve. It was such a new thought.

How many times she could have prevented her heartaches if she had not coaxed the temptations, but had passed them on thinking, *I could never be a wife for Raymond*, or if she would have accepted that she would never get acquainted with Virgil. She felt grateful that God had made a way of escape that she didn't pluck off the forbidden fruit. She wanted to try and not murmur so much and wait to see what the Lord had in store. She wanted to trust that God would open the Red Sea when there was no other way, and trust that God knew when to open it. God had made a way to escape. He led Laura back to Raymond.

Clara felt humbled at her small faith. God showed His strength today. He spoke through the ministers. *We needed no visiting ministers to stir and build our faith and guide us.* As she paged through her notebook, she noticed a poem she had copied into it, but didn't remember from where. As she read the lines, they took on new meaning, something she hadn't captured before. She studied it till she could quote it by heart:

181

My Father's way may twist and turn
My heart may throb and ache,
But in my soul I'm glad to know
He maketh no mistakes.

My cherished plans may go astray,
My hopes may fade away,
But still I trust my Lord to lead
For Father knoweth the way.

The night be dark and it may seem
That day will never break.
I'll pin my faith, my all, on Him
Who maketh no mistakes.

There's so much now I cannot see,
My eye is still too dim,
But come what may I still can trust
And leave it all to Him.

For by and by, the mist will lift
And darkness turn to day,
Then looking back we'll praise His name
Who led us all the way.

She discovered it could be sung to a tune. There was so much she could not see, but Clara wanted to trust God to lead her. He who always knows the way, for by and by, the mist will lift. The question kept going through her mind, *What lays beyond the mist?*

182

Chapter Twenty-Two

This had once been home, Clara thought as she was spending the day with her parents and sisters. She realized she was now more like a guest. She had helped Sylvia husk a few baskets of corn; now she was enjoying the time helping Mother quilt. Loretta was mowing the yard, and Sylvia was cleaning the bedrooms.

A few times Mom had started to get up, saying she had to something, and Sylvia had breezed into the kitchen, saying either, "Don't bother, I'll get it," or "No, Mildred wants to do it when she gets home." It seemed Mother was only the manager at home; the girls were doing most of the work.

Rachel, Cleon's wife, had come over on an errand, bringing her two little boys along. They had stayed awhile, and Rachel helped to quilt while they visited together.

As Clara and Mother were stitching and talking, Clara asked what had been pressing on her mind during the last few months. "Doesn't it seem strange or hard to understand why the bishop lot fell on Caleb? He is so young, and they have little children. Lloyd and Walter would have had children to go along with the work and children old enough to stay alone when their parents needed to travel."

"Well, it doesn't matter what man thinks. God is in control. We prayed and trusted He would do what He knows is best," Mom answered, then added, "I had hoped Caleb wouldn't need to carry it, but when the qualifications of a bishop were read, I thought it described Caleb's nature. It will be hard for them with their little children, but God will provide, and the children will grow up. We have to think of the things that make it easier for them. He is sober. He is not quick to speak. When he needs to talk with an erring member, he won't speak too hastily. He is patient and long-suffering and not quick to anger. I'm sure the people will help with their chores and keep the children. It seemed there was always a way when he was a minister, and I trust it will continue to work out."

Mildred came breezing in the door, coming home from her job at the butcher shop. "Oh, so we have company," she rejoiced as she saw Clara. "That's nice that you don't need to sit alone at the quilt." Looking at Mother, then at Clara, Mildred asked, "Are you staying overnight?"

"No, but I'll stay for supper," Clara answered as she continued to stitch.

"What are we having for supper?" Mildred asked, pulling a package out of her bag.

"Oh, we are having what is likely to be the last fresh corn of the season," Mother answered.

"Here is a pack of sausage. It will taste good with the corn and potatoes. I think there's still time to make it," Mildred said, placing the package on the counter.

"Oh sure," Sylvia said, starting to make supper.

"What's wrong with it? Is it another package that has been laying around two days?"

"No. This time it's fresh. A man who came to pick up his meat didn't have enough containers along, so some of it didn't fit in. He told Erma and me to take the rest along home," Mildred explained.

"Well, Sylvia, you were going to heat up the leftover beef and gravy," Mom said. "Put that back for another time. Maybe it wouldn't have been quite enough anyway."

Mildred sat on one of the chairs and asked, "Clara, where were you on Saturday evening? We had a good singing. The gang from Lone Oak was over and the singing was beautiful," she exclaimed with enthusiasm.

"I was in bed. I slept so well," Clara said pleasantly.

"I know I slept good after I came home. The cool autumn air is good for sleeping."

"Where's Dad?" Clara asked.

"I guess he's went to Cleon's to tinker in the shop. It's Friday, the day Cleon shoes horses. I suppose he is talking to the people who bring the horses," Mom said as she pulled her chair over further to start quilting a new row.

"That's right. This is Friday already. I should get to work if I want to go to the quilting at Ella's house tomorrow afternoon," Mildred said, jumping up from her chair.

"Do you have to work Saturday forenoon?" Mother asked, looking at Mildred. Mildred nodded her head as she walked through the kitchen.

As Sylvia prepared supper, she occasionally asked Mom's advice. As Clara and Mother continued quilting and visiting, Clara saw Dad walking up the road. It was about suppertime.

"Here comes Mrs. Harnish for her milk," Sylvia exclaimed. "Loretta, you'll have to get it. I still need to mash the potatoes and shake the flour for gravy. The pickle jar is empty so I will need to fetch something sour yet for Dad."

Jumping up, Clara said, "I'll fetch something for you."

"Get red beets. We haven't had them for awhile," Sylvia ordered.

Clara easily found a can of red beets on the well-laden shelves in the basement. As she was leaving the cellar, she decided to peek into the parlor to see how Mildred had arranged it by now. The parlor door was partially open. As Clara pushed it open farther, she saw that Mildred was in there dusting.

"Oh, it's you," both sisters said at the same time. Clara noticed the blue and white cloud-covered curtain wasn't on the door anymore. Instead there was the regular green curtain to pull down. Commenting about that, Mildred said, "Why would I want that curtain? It's just another thing to keep clean. Whenever anyone opened or closed the door, they had to touch it," she answered matter-of-factly.

"What do you have here?" Clara asked as she walked over to the corner. "A table in the parlor? Is that in style?" she questioned.

"In style," Mildred mocked. "I guess it's Bennie's style. He loves putting puzzles together and some are too big to fit on the card table. For awhile I put a piece of plywood on chairs while we worked on puzzles, but it was a mess, so I put this table in here," Mildred explained.

"A puzzle? It looks like a game of Probe to me, only set up for one player," Clara responded.

"We finished the puzzle the other Sunday, and Bennie urged Dad to play a game of Probe. Dad wasn't interested, saying it took him too long to think of a word, so Loretta helped play a few rounds," Mildred explained.

"You mean Father comes into the parlor and plays Probe with you?" Clara asked unbelievingly.

"The other time Dad helped, we played in the kitchen. That was before I had this table. I have a feeling Dad got a word ready for Sunday."

"What's this?" Clara asked, walking over to the windowsill. There was an iron structure of a man standing on a platform.

"That's the fisherman. Try throwing him in the water if you can." As Clara pushed the man over, he always bounced back up. She tried several times, but he always managed to keep from falling overboard.

Clara, now laughing, asked, "What is it anyway?"

"Oh, Bennie found it somewhere when he was traveling, and bought it. It has caused many a chuckle. The poor guy has a hard time hanging on when a bunch of boys drop in on Sunday evenings."

Clara picked up the Rubic cube lying on the sofa, looking at it questioningly.

Mildred smiled, saying, "Bennie can get one solid color on every side. Now he's trying me how to do it, but it doesn't make sense to me yet."

"Since when do you have a View Master?" Clara asked as she noticed one with a pack of reels on the stand.

"Bennie brought his View Master along last week. He got some reels when he was in Canada. We didn't take the time to look at all of them yet," Mildred exclaimed.

"Clara! Clara!" Sylvia ran down the stairs saying, "I thought you came down to fetch red beets. Were you hunting for them in the garden? We're ready to eat and couldn't find either of you." The others were already sitting at the table waiting to eat as Clara and Mildred came up from the basement.

After silent prayer, they began to eat. "Have you seen that the jewelry store is out of business?" Dad asked Clara. "It's now an activity room."

Clara nodded and smiled as she replied, "Yes, I noticed."

As the conversation continued during the meal, Dad said, "Caleb stopped at the shop today to pick up horseshoes. He said if it suits, they will drop little boys and Lena Jane off here on Sunday morning. Since they're going to West View and going out this way, they'd rather drop them off here than leave them with the neighbors as they usually do. I don't know if they're taking the two older ones along."

"Isn't West View Allen's district?" Mother questioned.

"Yes, it would be, but Allens are in Canada. The graveside services for Peter and Alice's stillborn daughter will be held on Sunday afternoon and Calebs decided to go in the forenoon."

"Peter and Alice had a stillborn daughter?" Alice asked, shocked.

"That's what he said." Dad continued, "I guess that means Walter would have to conduct the church services alone unless a visiting minister comes."

Mom nodded, "I guess we all know why they plan to ordain another minister. Caleb needs to be free to go when he is needed elsewhere."

By the time Clara arrived home, there was a message that Peter and Alice had a stillborn daughter whom they named Alta, and that Clara could ride along with Calebs if she desired.

*　　*　　*

A small group had gathered at the church where the viewing was held. Clara's whole being was smitten when she saw the little angel. The baby looked as if she was sleeping and that Clara should pick her up and cuddle her. She couldn't imagine how Peter and

Alice's hearts must ache, giving up this child they had been anticipating. Her heart bled for them.

Caleb said, "The Lord has given and the Lord has taken. Blessed be the name of the Lord. Jesus said, 'Suffer not to let the children come unto me.' I thought we could use the passage in John, chapter 9, where it says, 'And his disciples asked him saying, Master, who did sin, this man, or his parents, that he was born blind?' Jesus answered, 'Neither had this man sinned nor his parents: but that the works of God should be made manifest in him.'

"So we feel today, it's not for anyone's sin that this baby was born and called home instantly, but that the works of God should be made manifest in him. I have to think back when I was a schoolboy, and my parents laid a baby away. I asked Dad why God didn't let us keep the baby and he said, 'God is above us and can see the pathway ahead of us, and it must be that this baby would have had a very hard road ahead. God was kind and took the baby to Him, so it didn't have to walk the rocky road.'

"It made me feel good that God was so merciful, and I feel God must have seen this little one deserves rest, too. May it be a balm for the parents today. He knows what we cannot see. She is now safe with Him. We do not mourn because she can have rest, but because we must stay here and cannot follow her. You can rejoice that you now have family in Heaven. He has taken a little lamb to get the big sheep to follow, I trust Heaven is nearer than it was before.

"I will recite a poem while the grave is being covered. Mother gave it to me when I was grown and started going out with the young folks. She said it was sent to them when my brother died. I have read it many times when the tempter was luring me. It was a challenge to live for what is right, to not bring shame to my name.

I'm just a little baby
And I didn't linger here.
I went straight to be with Jesus
And I'm waiting for you there.

Many dwelling here where I live
Waited years to enter in,
Struggled through a world of sorrow,
And their lives were marred with sin.

So, dear parents, don't you sorrow;
I'm not held in death's cold tomb.
I have gone to be with Jesus;
Wipe those tears and chase the gloom.
    Thank you for the life you gave me;
    I'd have liked to have brought it fame.
    Had I lingered in earth's shadows
    Might instead have brought it shame.

Though you miss me, please remember
I'm of all God's lambs most blessed.
I'd have loved to stay there with you
But our Shepherd knows what's best."

There wasn't a dry eye in the little group. Everyone's heart was touched.

Chapter Twenty-Three

There had been a steady stream of customers during the forenoon, keeping Clara occupied. She was kept busy waiting on customers while Anna Lois and Hettie did the weighing and the stocking of shelves. After the steady stream ceased, Clara joined the others, twist-tying and putting labels on the bags.

Anna Lois said that Lena told her that the young minister who had been at Benjamin's funeral had stopped in to visit her mother.

"You mean he was in the area and there was no special church services?" Clara asked, surprised and disappointed.

Anna Lois nodded, saying, "Lena said they had been to another area and just passed through here on their way home."

"I wonder why they didn't schedule a special church service," Clara murmured. "I would so desire to hear him again."

"According to Lena, they begged him to stay, hoping to have a church service the next day, but he could not be persuaded. He said they needed to go home," Anna Lois exclaimed.

"What difference would another half day have made?" Clara asked.

"It would have been a day and night longer," Hettie reminded her.

"But so what. They were traveling anyhow," Clara reasoned.

"Maybe they had something that needed their attention at home," Hettie reminded her, adding, "I would also have desired to hear him speak again."

Clara waited on two more customers. Later Hettie laid a letter on the counter for her. Glancing at the letter, Clara saw that it was from her sister Norma. Quickly bagging the customer's items, Clara eagerly tore open the envelope, not even waiting to read it until the next customer was checked out.

Seeing it wasn't much more than a note, she read, "Sending a few quick lines your way to let you know our baby has arrived. It's a little girl. She weighed seven pounds, fourteen ounces, so she is not real small. She doesn't have much hair. Ezra's mom says she looks like her babies looked, with a chubby, broad face. She is always hungry, sleeps, and is hungry again. It doesn't matter if I'm done eating or not. She is the boss now. We named her Carrie." Norma had drawn a smiley face which made Clara chuckle. Her heart warmed at the memories. When Norma was small and tried to say Clara, it came out as Carrie. The name had stuck for awhile. Clara almost envied Sylvia who would be helping Norma for a few weeks.

As Clara prepared to dress for church, she saw the new maroon dress hanging in her closet. The day was finally drawing near when she would be wearing it. There were only four more days until Raymond and Laura's wedding. She was asked to be a gift receiver, along with Raymond's single aunt, who was a little older than she was, and a couple other friends.

Clara was looking forward to the wedding so much that she almost forgot the solemnness of today. This was the day that names would be taken to ordain the minister to relieve Caleb since he was now a bishop.

As Clara was removing her wraps at church, she smiled warmly when she saw Laura. Laura's eyes seemed to smile, but her expression was more solemn. Clara greeted her, asking if the cookie baking went better. The ones they had baked before hadn't turned out good enough for the wedding.

It seemed that Laura didn't want to talk about cookies. She quickly responded that the baking went better the next day, but there was still a lot of work to do.

Clara was happy to inform Laura that Hettie had said she may come a day to help if she was needed. Laura didn't seem interested in talking about it just then, so Clara didn't pursue it any farther. Maybe later she could ask which day she should come.

During the service, Clara noticed that Laura, who sat in the bench in front of her, seemed to be deeply affected by the sermon. It was a touching sermon. Some visiting ministers were present, and the church was reminded that God already knows who will be given the work of preaching the Word, saying this man has been spared from his mother's womb to preach the gospel, and in the following days, His will would be revealed.

Clara didn't understand why Laura would be so deeply touched. She thought her upcoming wedding would be foremost in her mind and that it would somewhat exceed the occasion of today. *Surely Laura isn't having doubts now so near to her wedding day. She seems so happy since she and Raymond are dating again.*

It seemed like a long span of time that the church sat in silent suspense. The ministers and the bishop had gone to the entry room. Every now and then someone went into the room to give a name they felt the Lord led them to give, or just to give their blessing. Finally, as no one moved and the anxiety seemed to mount, the ordained men filed back to their places.

Clara looked at Caleb again. He was a sober, quiet person, usually calm and steady, but now he looked distressed. Clara thought there was almost a look of pain. Clara watched the other home ministers and noticed that Walter took a quick look at the boys' side, then hung his head. The whole church waited and it seemed hard for Caleb to begin speaking. Clara was beginning to wonder if any names were brought in that were not in good standing in the church, since there seemed to be an unusual strain in Caleb's voice. Usually Caleb spoke steady and with assurance. Now he tried to steady his voice as he began to read the names.

Clara was holding her breath so hard, fearing she'd hear Sammie's name, that she almost didn't hear what he was saying. She heard Eli Fox's name, followed by two of her cousins, both who were Laura's brothers. Willis, the deacon, was also in the lot. There were several names of men mentioned, who Clara didn't know well, except for seeing them in church.

Clara thought he had given all the names when, in a trembling voice, Caleb said, "and Raymond Kulp." A deeper hush fell, as if no one was breathing. Clara was sure she didn't hear right, but then she saw the tears blinding Laura's face.

The rest of the week was a blur. It was the most stressful ordination that Clara had ever attended. Michael Hoover, the young minister who had been at Benjamin's funeral, had a part. He said that love drew him to the service since there were a few young ones in the lot. He shared, "I was once at your place and thought God wouldn't ask me to do this work. I was so young and there were wiser and more experienced men in the class. But, as high as Heaven is above earth, so much higher are His thoughts than ours. We don't always understand His ways. An older brother greeted me on the day I was ordained and whispered, 'God chose a weak one so that He can lead him. A man who is strong in himself cannot be led.'

"I could tell you how very weak I was, but I don't want to take the time away from all the others that I look forward to hearing. I do want to share a poem that was given me soon after I was ordained. I often had to read it over and over when doubts set in, when the load was heavier than I could carry."

Clara noticed he wasn't reading; he was reciting. He recited the poem in such an expressive tone that Clara felt shivers going over her. Tears welled up in her eyes at the truth of the words so full of the tender mercy of God.

> *One day when my burden seemed greater*
> *Than my body and spirit could bear,*
> *Weighed down by the load, I faltered*
> *Beneath my sorrow and care.*
>
> *And I cried to the heedless silence*
> *As I walked where I could not see.*
> *Where is the strength that is promised?*
> *Where is the strength for me?*
>
> *And suddenly out of the stillness*
> *A voice came clear and true,*

"My child, you are striving to carry
A burden not meant for you.

"For the thought of the years outstretching
Before you has darkened the way,
While the only strength I have promised
Is the sure strength day by day."

I took one step and found it
Quite easy indeed to take,
And the burden slid from my shoulder
And my heart that was ready to break.

Gave thanks that my eyes were opened
And my shoulders were eased of their load.
As step by step I was strengthened
To walk the roughest road.

"I had to read this poem many times to remind myself that when the load was getting too heavy, I had to recognize what made it heavy were the days and years stretching out before me. It's not the load of today, for we have strength today. It's when we also carry the load meant for tomorrow that we lack strength. God has promised strength for today, renewed strength day by day. This is promised to us.

"A minister once was getting weary of his lot and was going to resign. It was just too much for him. Then the bishop asked if he would preach just today. The minister said, 'Yes, I can do that.' The bishop said, 'That's all we ask of you, and that is all God asks of us—to endure our lot today.' If there is a tomorrow, there will be strength for that, too. It's the years stretching out before us that darken the way."

Everyone at the ordination could see that the load was pressing hard on Raymond all forenoon. Was it only because he was so young? The tension had come to a climax as Caleb started at the head of the class, taking the books one by one, leafing through them,

194

hunting for the paper, handing them back, and reaching for the next one. The suspense was getting uncomfortable and finally broke when Caleb came to the end of the line and found the paper in Raymond's book. Many tears were shed, relieving the tension. It was almost a relief to have the suspense lifted. Suspense is always harder than knowing.

Dinner was served at Earl Garman's home to all the relatives and travelers before they returned home. Clara wanted to ask for a copy of the poem that was read, but she was told that Michael left right after church. Clara couldn't believe that they wouldn't stay for dinner before going on their seven-hour journey. What difference would a few more hours have made? They had no bus to meet. They were traveling by van.

There had been no special church services announced for the new minister, since the wedding was planned for Thursday. It had earlier been decided that the newly-ordained minister would attend and speak at the wedding, but now plans had to be changed. Church services were scheduled for the next day, since ones with experience said Raymond needed to speak before Sunday. If he would think about his new responsibility of preaching during the rest of the week, doubts would overwhelm him.

Clara hadn't attended the special church services, since people were needed at Aunt Martha's to help prepare for the wedding.

The wedding was a little different than originally planned. Some people were there who otherwise wouldn't have been invited. On short notice, a few ministers were invited who had also been ordained before they were married. The service also had a different theme than it would have otherwise. Clara felt sorry for Laura and Raymond because they had this extra responsibility on their wedding day; but they seemed to hold up well under the circumstances. Many expressed their gratitude that the wedding was this week and not a few months later.

A few days later, as Clara lay in bed still trying to adjust to all that had happened, she was in awe of Almighty God. He knew the way ahead. He knew why He denied what she had craved. He knew

195

that Raymond's life would take him down a path of life she wouldn't have felt equipped to walk. The poem was taking on newmeaning:

> *My Father's way may twist and turn,*
> *My heart may throb and ache,*
> *But in my soul I'm glad to know*
> *He maketh no mistake.*
>
> *There's so much now I cannot see,*
> *My eye is still too dim;*
> *But come what may I still can trust*
> *And leave it all to Him.*
>
> *For by and by the mist will lift*
> *And darkness turn to day,*
> *And looking back we'll praise His name*
> *Who led us all the way.*

Already some of the mist was lifting, and Clara could see that God was wise to deny her longings. She wanted to trust more.

Aunt Martha told Hettie that Raymond hadn't been himself for the past two months, but they thought he was nervous about the wedding. Not understanding why that would affect him so much, they encouraged him to break up with Laura if he had doubts, rather than live in an unhappy marriage. Raymond told his parents that the struggles he was having was not about his upcoming marriage. He had told no one except Laura how the upcoming ordination was pressing on him.

A few days later, while reading a poem in a Christian magazine, Clara suddenly paid full attention when she came to the third verse. She found herself skipping over the first two verses, not grasping the meaning.

The Peace He Gives

I know not why my pathway leads
Through valleys rough and steep,
But this I know while walking there
I've found communion sweet.

With those I love and best of all
With Him who climbed for me
Beneath a heavy cross,
That led to Calvary.

I know not why so many props
Have gently been removed;
But I do know through every loss
His arms unfailing proved.
I have no reason, not at all,

To doubt His precious Word;
Though all I have be swept away
His voice would still be heard.

Above the storm, and as I lift
My tear-filled eyes to Him
The great Creator, Lord of all
He whispers peace within.

It was the following words that seemed to speak to her:

So as I look beyond today
I pray that I may share
This peace He gives with those who have
A greater cross to bear.

How those words expressed her feelings. *Laura and Raym* *ond had greater crosses to bear*, she thought. *Why had I so yearned* *after him?*

She also remembered the words written in the book, *Streams* *in the Desert*:

> *Thou doest so soon forget*
> *Forget that He has led thee*
> *And gently cleared the way*
> *On clouds He poured His sunshine*
> *And turned the night to day.*
>
> *And if He helped thee hither, too,*
> *He will not fail thee now.*
> *How it must wound His loving heart*
> *To see thy anxious brow.*
>
> *Ah, doubt no longer*
> *To Him commit thy way,*
> *Whom in the past thou trusted*
> *And is just the same today.*

Those two sentences stood out: "How it must wound His loving heart to see thy anxious brow."

Clara hoped she had learned to trust more.

Chapter Twenty-Four

Clara hummed softly to herself as she left the kitchen and walked down to the store. She had put the roast in the oven so it would be tender by suppertime when the schoolchildren came home and Hettie would be back from Lone Oak District. Hettie had taken Ben James along, but the other children were all in school.

Walking down the lane toward the store, Clara noticed that the snow was quickly disappearing. Only small patches remained here and there. There was water around the patches that remained, showing that even they would soon be melted. The February air was more moderate.

A carriage that had been at the store was now leaving, and a woman came out the door, carrying a bag and walking to the only car in the parking lot. It wasn't a very busy day in the store, which was good, since some days it would be almost impossible for Anna Lois and Clara to tend the store alone. There were days when there was a long line of people waiting to be checked out.

As Clara entered the store, Anna Lois was straightening things on the counter, putting a few bags away. Anna Lois sat on the chair, giving out a sigh.

Clara looked at Anna Lois questioningly as she stated, "It's been rather slow today so far."

"Maybe that's good," Clara responded, "since we have to watch the store by ourselves today."

"I think slow days are more tiring than days we have to keep stepping. There's too much time for us to think about ourselves and others," Anna Lois said as she walked to the office. "Do you think we should get the spice order together, or could we wait another week?"

Shrugging her shoulders, Clara asked, "Was the butcher here already to get his order? I guess Hettie got that together last evening."

"No, he wasn't here, and I wasn't able to locate his order," Anna Lois said as she looked at the many notes tacked on the desk.

Removing a note, Anna Lois handed it to Clara. It said to be sure to check the plastic bags and get an order together. Clara nodded her head and was off to the packing area, checking the bag supply. Some were quite low. She had barely begun to write out the order when she someone was ready to be waited on. Anna Lois was busy in the office.

A half hour later, after waiting on several other customers, Clara went into the office and found Anna Lois sitting in the chair, munching on an apple. She looked as if she was coming back from a deep thought.

"Have you despaired with the ordering?" Clara asked.

Yawning, Anna Lois admitted she wasn't concentrating on the orders.

"What have you been concentrating on?" Clara asked, seeing a sheepish expression on Anna Lois's face, as a child caught in mischief.

"Honestly, I'm getting rather curious," Anna Lois said as she straightened up in her chair and expressed her thoughts.

"Did you say Hettie went to Charles's house again today?"

Clara nodded her head yes. Clara waited for Anna Lois to tell her what was so unusual about that.

"I don't know, maybe I'm imagining things. Wasn't it just last week when Charles was here for most of the day, and had his little daughter along? Later in the week Hettie was over in that area. Now she went again? It seems strange to me that she went again, since she usually waits a few months before going over there again."

"Well, the others were going and she went along," Clara said, not convinced of anything suspicious. Clara knew Hettie was fond of her little granddaughter, Saloma, and Amelia seemed like a real daughter to Hettie. Clara wasn't sure either what the occasion was that Charles had been home last week. Hettie hadn't been in the store much that day. It seemed they had a lot to talk about. Since Amelia hadn't been along last week, it was too good for Hettie to resist going along when she heard there was a van going that way.

As if guessing Clara's thoughts, Anna Lois said, "I don't know, but Hettie seemed rather quiet since she came home last week. I'm wondering if she really is just going to Charles's place when she goes to Lone Oak, or if we don't know everything." She talked softly as if she was afraid to let her thoughts be known, and there was a mysterious look in her eyes.

"Well," Clara said, "Hettie's mind did seem somewhat preoccupied after Charles left here. So often when Hettie spoke, it was something about Charles or Amelia or little Saloma. I guess it stirs up memories for Hettie to see Charles and Amelia with their young family—memories of when she was young and shared her life with Benjamin. I think she minds it that Benjamin isn't here to enjoy the grandchild. Saloma is such a little sunshine, and looks so much like her daddy. And Charles seems to look more and more like his father."

"I guess time will tell if it's Charles and his family who have been on Hettie's mind," Anna Lois said, sounding as if she doubted Clara's reasoning.

"Surely you don't think Hettie is seeing someone, do you?" Clara asked, astonished.

"I just don't know. Has she been receiving any letters lately?" Anna Lois asked.

"I don't get the mail," Clara admitted.

"Well, we'll see. Eventually we'll find out," Anna Lois smiled.

Late Saturday afternoon, when it was time to close the store, Hettie locked the main door while there were still things to finish up. Usually they didn't lock the doors until after hours, and they often allowed people in who came after closing time.

Hettie came back to them and said she would pay them now for their last two weeks, as usual. Then she said, "It's about time we start discussing things. I was offered the chance to move into the other house on Charles's farm. I decided to take him up on the offer, since the boys are often over there anyway, helping with the produce. They'll be there more during the summer and none of the boys have taken any serious interest in the store so far. You two will get the first chance to take over the store and can even buy the house if you are interested. Maybe you would want to live in the house together, or you could ask another girl to live with either one of you, if you are interested. I will let you think it over for a while before others hear about it."

Anna Lois had gasped when Hettie started speaking, asking her a few questions now and then. Hettie was planning to move the last week of March or the beginning of April. Anna Lois was in deep thought, a wistful look rising in her eyes. Clara was too stunned, not knowing what to think.

As time went on and the news spread, friends and family encouraged Clara to join Anna Lois to take over the store and live together in the house, or to get another friend to live with her if Anna Lois decided she didn't want to move. Anna Lois and Clara had many discussions.

Anna Lois seemed to have an eager attitude, as if her wildest dreams were coming true—having her own home and a job right there—a job she was already familiar with. And it sounded like Annetta was considering helping with the store, too. How much she helped depended on what Clara decided to do.

For some reason, Clara had doubts. She daydreamed of how it would be to share the house and business with Anna Lois, or maybe Anna Lois would stay with her parents and Annetta would join Clara in the house. Clara felt disturbed; too many doubts were rising within her.

As the weeks passed, Anna Lois was waiting for Clara to make a decision so she would know how to continue. Clara wished she felt as eager as Anna Lois did. Clara's parents had come over to discuss the situation. Mother said, "You must know what you want to do. Do you really enjoy the store work and want to continue to carry it on with Anna Lois and Annetta?"

"I really enjoy working with Anna Lois, and I'm experienced in the work, but I can't make such a decision. I don't plan my life; things never go as I plan."

202

Clara's parents said they would help her with buying the house, if that's what she wanted to do. She would have to discuss with Annetta and Anna Lois as to who would share it with her. Anna Lois was giving Annetta first chance since Anna Lois lived so near to the store already, and Annetta would have to travel a further distance. Anna Lois wanted Clara to help with the business.

Many evenings Clara thought things over, waking early the next morning, still pondering over the decision. She had often thought about living with Anna Lois or Annetta, because she wouldn't want to live alone. But her thoughts never went further.

Mother said, "It's your nerves. You have never made such a serious decision before. Remember, you wouldn't be marrying the job; you could always give it up if you decided to do something else."

"But I don't plan my life," Clara told Mother, and Mother reminded her that she has to, to a certain extent. Everyone was encouraging her to take the chance and rejoiced that she had such a great opportunity. Still she was scared.

Anna Lois was becoming eager for a definite answer. As the end of March approached, Hettie and the children planned to move the second week of April.

One evening when Clara got the mail, she found a letter from her sister Virginia. The short note asked her to come for supper on Wednesday evening. "If you can't make it for supper, come in the evening anyway." *She likely wants to ask me to stay with the children for the weekend or sometime when they need to be away,* she thought. *At least it gives me something else to think about.* Clara didn't have much hope of discussing the situation with Caleb and Virginia, since neither of them were very talkative. *They'd tell me I have to decide.*

The store wasn't very busy on Wednesday afternoon so Clara went to Caleb and Virginia's for supper. Happy children welcomed her at the door. Hannah Mae eagerly showed her a paper she had done in school, and she also showed Clara her loose tooth. Paul Henry told Clara about his rabbit that had eight little ones, but Lena Jane just smiled.

The two little boys had been bashful until after supper when they began talking to Clara. Earl David showed on his fingers that he was two. They were so eager just to have someone there. Lydia Ann toddled around, sucking her thumb, happy with the attention she was getting. As Clara tried to catch her, she would quickly run away.

Lena Jane stood on a chair while Clara washed the dishes, rinsing them for her; but Clara could have done it faster alone. Lena Jane chattered about her many childish interests. The boys went to the barn with Caleb.

While Clara was putting the dishes away, Hannah Mae told her how Earl David cried so much at Abner's. When Clara asked Virginia about it, she was told that that happened about three weeks ago when Caleb and Virginia went to Ohio. They left Earl David, Lena Jane, and Hannah Mae at Abner's house. Earl David had cried so much it left a big impression on Hannah Mae.

Later, Paul Henry, Earl David, and John Wayne came in. The little boys showed Clara the handkerchiefs someone had given to them. Clara saw that Caleb was sitting at the other end of the kitchen; he must have come in the back door while she was talking with the children. Soon the boys were building a block tower and Clara entertained Lydia Ann while Virginia folded the wash.

Virginia asked, "So, are you planning to help Anna Lois run the store and stay in the house?"

Clara was getting so weary of that question. "Oh, I don't know. People expect me to do that. I do enjoy the work, but I don't know. I wish I didn't have so many doubts." Clara sighed.

"Well, you must know if that's what you want to do," Virginia said as she shook out the diapers and folded them, one after another.

"All the people tell me that, but I never planned my life. When Benjamin got sick and I went there to help, Mother had so many other girls to help her, I stayed there," Clara simply said.

Clara noticed Caleb glance toward them. She thought he was going to say something, but instead rested his head in the palm of his hand. When Earl Wayne came carrying his one shoe, Caleb picked him up and put on his shoe. Lydia Ann came over to Caleb and also crawled up into his lap. Hannah Mae showed Clara pictures that her friend Malinda had made for her.

Virginia put the clean diapers in the dresser near the sofa and began folding the small underwear while Clara folded the towels. Virginia asked Clara, "Is there any kind of job you would like to do? Something you have dreamed of doing, but couldn't because you were tied up with the store?"

"I really haven't dwelled so much on jobs, since we were always busy with the store," Clara answered.

"And you aren't really enthused about living in the house with Anna Lois and taking over the store, I gather." Virginia questioned.

"Not as much as other people. Well, it just doesn't seem real. It seems something is saying I shouldn't," Clara said, sharing her honest thoughts. "Mother seems to think it would be a good idea, but—oh, well, I wish I wouldn't feel so doubtful. Everyone expects me to help Anna Lois take over the business."

Caleb got up to get a drink for Earl David, lingering in front of the sink. After a while he said, "If you feel doubtful in making a decision, it might help to have another option to choose from."

Virginia looked at Caleb as if she was waiting to hear more, but he spared his words. Virginia said, "We have been talking and wondered what you would think about helping us out." Clara waited to see what Virginia had in mind.

"We have a canning kitchen in the basement," Virginia explained. "I only used it the first few years we were married, since I like to do the canning in my regular kitchen where I can be with the children and hear them when they waken. We thought we could remodel to make a nice little kitchen. That way you wouldn't have to live with all the children's noise. You could have some privacy. The other room is where Caleb had his woodworking tools. He doesn't have time to use them anymore, so that could be made into a bedroom. Caleb says it wouldn't take too much plumbing to put a full bathroom in there."

"Regarding work," Caleb spoke up, almost wistfully, "it would make our load a lot easier if we had someone here. The children could stay here when we go on trips or errands. We often come home too late in the evening to pick up the children and get them out of bed. It takes time to go after them the next morning. Getting neighbors or someone to stay here with the children is getting more difficult. The children prefer that someone comes here to stay with them."

Clara's mind reeled. "But would I always have work? I mean, the times when you aren't going anywhere?" Virginia looked at Caleb. Caleb's expression seemed to say, "You may as well suggest it."

"Well," Virginia said, sounding almost like a child who was afraid she was asking for too much, "with the summer coming, there will be a lot of work besides just looking after the children. We've been discussing that, too. Do you enjoy sewing?"

"I haven't done much except for myself. I like it after I get started. When I stayed with Benjamin and Hettie, I made aprons for the dish detergent bottles and also clothespin bags to sell at the store. That wasn't a success. It seems people just came for groceries, not for crafts. Why do you ask? What do you have in mind?"

"The dry goods store about three miles down the road is looking for someone to make slips and nightgowns. There was something else but I can't remember what. The woman who had been making them is getting too old to continue and someone from another area was sewing for them, but it hasn't been working out too well. Sometimes the customer wanted to show them what she preferred, and shipping is too expensive," Virginia explained.

"Let's go down and see the basement," Clara said, getting up, feeling quite enthused.

As Virginia showed Clara what they thought could be done, Caleb also came downstairs with Lydia Ann on one arm and Earl David on the other. John Wayne bumped down the stairs on his seat, hands, and feet.

"We could put a partition here and move this. You could put a refrigerator here. The bedroom would need to be cleaned and painted," Virginia said.

Clara was getting more enthused as Caleb showed how he could make it, but then Clara thought of something. "But your children will grow up and I wouldn't be needed anymore."

Scratching his head, Caleb said, "We are looking at the need of today. If we could already see the purpose you have in those tomorrow years, then you couldn't help us. When that time comes, there will be someone needing you. Maybe by then your parents will need help. We don't want to beg you," Caleb added, "but it would make our work a lot easier."

"Even if you have to do a lot of work to get it ready?" Clara questioned.

"Sure, that won't mean much, and since the rooms aren't being used anyway, it's more worthwhile."

Before Clara left, she told Caleb and Virginia she won't need more time to think it over. She said she is willing to help however she can. Later in the evening, she felt so—she didn't know how to express it. It was as if she had been feeling her way through a fog, not knowing where to go and now she could see more clearly. She then became aware of the song she was singing:

> *For by and by the mist will lift*
> *And darkness turn to day,*
> *And looking back we'll praise His Name*
> *Who led us all the way.*

It felt like she had been dragging along the past few weeks and now she was moving more easily. As the mist lifted, Clara could see where to go instead of stumbling along. As she lay in bed, drifting off to sleep, another poem came to her mind:

> *The thought of the years outstretching*
> *Before you has darkened the way*
> *While the only strength I have promised*
> *Is the sure strength day by day.*

Clara's heart gave thanks that her shoulders were eased of their heavy load as she recited the poem she had heard at Raymond's ordination.

Chapter Twenty-Five

Clara rejoiced when she received a letter from Mother. She had written to Mother about the details of her decision, feeling sure that Mother would be in agreement. Since Annetta was helping regularly in the store, learning all she could before Clara and Hettie quit, Clara could take the time to read her letter. Also, since Hettie was so busy packing her household things, one of Elvin's girls was helping, too.

Clara read:

Dear daughter,

Your letter surely surprised me. I thought you would be staying in Hettie's house and having one of your friends live with you. I thought you liked the work, but, of course, it never occurred to me that you could help Caleb and Virginia and even have your own quarters. It sure is nice of Caleb to do the work of making your own living quarters. It will be handy for them with less planning when they need to go away, and the children can stay at home instead of going off to different homes. God always makes a way.

No, Virginia shall not move one of her beds to the basement for you. She'll need her spare beds when she gets visitors, which happens often. We are shopping for a bedroom suite. You know we give each of the girls bedroom suites as they need them. I had been thinking we should get one for you, but it didn't seem practical since you had no room to put it. I wasn't going to get one for Mildred yet, but there was a sturdy one at the auction place. It went for a reasonable price so we got it and put it in Cleon's house. Mildred says you can have that, since there is still time to get one for her. We'll see, since she already has quite a few things stored in it.

I did get a table and some chairs at the second-hand shop in town. Cleon said they have a love seat you can have. Someone gave it to them and they put it in their built-in porch for the time being. Likely you wouldn't have room for a sofa anyway, so Hettie may as well keep the sofa.

I want to go through my spare dishes. I have some I never use that you may have. Tomorrow we are going to look at a refrigerator that we saw advertised. Ezra's sister said she had a rocker-recliner you can gladly have which someone gave to them.

We'll deliver the things after we get a bedroom suite, or after we decide if you can have the one we bought for Mildred. At least you have your hutch.

We are having parlor problems here. Sylvia would like to have a parlor with her things, and I suppose it won't help when Mildred moves, since Loretta is eagerly waiting for her seventeenth birthday.

Sylvia is not dating yet. If she has someone lined up, I don't know about it. The three sisters have so much going on that I can't keep up with it all. I suppose I'm not supposed to either.

*   *   *

Hettie's twelve-year-old son Earl helped Clara get the pony hitched, and she was off to Calebs on Saturday morning. Clara was eager to see the furniture her parents had sent over for her. Next week she would be moving into the basement quarters of Caleb and

Virginia's home. This afternoon she'd stay with their children since they were going to visit a few elderly and shut-in members.

As Clara came into the kitchen, she saw Virginia sweeping the floor, getting ready to wash it—part of the weekly cleaning. Lydia Ann was crying. Virginia said she had awakened early this morning and later was taking a nap; however, the little boys were so loud they wakened Lydia Ann and Hannah Mae wasn't succeeding in comforting her.

"Here, I'll take Lydia Ann along down to the basement," Clara said, taking her from Hannah Mae. Lydia Ann's sobs ceased as she put her thumb in her mouth.

Downstairs Clara oohed and aahed when she saw the breakfast set. The tabletop was tan with matching tan chairs. There were even two leaves included. Mother hadn't mentioned that it was a breakfast set. Clara had pictured a table with some odd, mismatched chairs. She marveled to herself when she saw the loveseat. It had wooden arms and such a neat design in the upholstery. *And what's this? Oh, a serving cart! That will be handy to put beside the sink since the sink is small. Oh, no, here is a small cupboard with two doors to set beside the sink. I can put the serving cart next to the gas stove.*

Suddenly, Clara was aware that someone other than Virginia was upstairs talking. Soon the door opened, and who but sister Norma with baby Carrie came downstairs.

"Norma!" Clara gasped.

"I stopped in at Mom's before going to Ezra's sister's house. Mom told me about the basement rooms you were getting ready and I immediately took a notion to have the driver drop me off here while he takes a few of the other women shopping for a few hours. I was hoping you'd be here. I'll be going to Ezra's sister Barbara later.

"This room sure looks different with light blue linoleum. I remember the old brown flooring that was in the canning room. But where is the bedroom suite?" Norma asked.

"I didn't see it yet," Clara said as she took baby Carrie from Norma. "Oh, my, she is heavy," Clara said.

"I know," Norma answered and added, "maybe she'll soon start crawling and won't need to be carried everywhere."

When Clara opened the door to the room which she planned to use as the bedroom, there was the bedroom suite! "Oh, look! It's not the one they had gotten for Mildred. The color isn't as nice a shade as hers," Clara said as she wiped her fingers over the gray suite, "but it has a bookcase headboard—something I've always wanted."

"And look at the deep dresser drawers and the nice mirror. See all the room you'll have in the chest of drawers," Norma said, sounding enthused.

"It might not be such a beautiful shade, but I do like the handles," Clara thought out loud.

"Let's set up the bed," Norma said, as Clara sat Carrie by Hannah Mae on the floor and Lydia Ann sat close by, adoring her and looking very pleased. Hannah Mae was eager to watch Carrie while the sisters set up the bed.

"Where do you want this?" Norma asked. "Along the wall with the dresser next to the door? Can we put the chest of drawers along this wall?"

"But where will we put my hope chest?" Clara asked.

The sisters rearranged the furniture a few times, finally deciding that the chest of drawers would have to be placed in the kitchen-living room area, so the chest could be in the bedroom.

Clara looked around and said, "I wonder if Mother sent any covers and bedding. I guess Virginia has some extra ones."

"Covers and sheets," Norma repeated. "Here is your chest. Don't you have any sheets? And you have quilts!" she said eagerly opening the chest. She dug around and exclaimed, "Here is the pink-and-white-checkered sheet set that I was always envious of. Where did you get it?"

Clara looked dazed. It had never occurred to her that she would be using the things in her hope chest. Was this the fulfilling of her dreams and hopes?"

"Who gave you this sheet set?" Norma repeated the question.

"Let me see. I got the set when I hurt my leg when I was twelve. It was in the sunshine package from Daniels. They used to live were Carls live now."

"Look, here are the bureau scarves you made when you were laid up with your foot. Let's see how they fit your dresser and chest of drawers. Do you have another set you'd rather use?" Norma asked as Clara was still trying to grasp everything that was happening.

"And here are the pot holders we made in school," Norma said, fondly looking at them. "Mine have been washed so often already and I scorched one on the burner. Oh, well, I am a sloppy cook; things don't stay nice. Which quilt do you want to use on your bed?" Norma asked, seemingly unaware that Clara was in a daze, trying to grasp the facts.

Clara began catching some of the enthusiasm and picked up a salt and pepper shaker set with a matching toothpick holder.

"Oh, yes," Norma said, "that will make it look like a kitchen with that set on the table. I like mine so much and always think of Aunt Barbara Anna."

Of course, this is my house, Clara reasoned to herself. *I may as well use the things,* she thought, as she placed a rug on the floor that Aunt Martha had given to her when she was learning to crochet. It looked so cozy in front of the sink.

"I guess I'll use this quilt. It's the first one I made and it's not so light colored," Clara said as she lifted it out and spread it on the bed.

"Look at this block," Norma said. "Remember when we both had dresses like this and we got into Grandmother's porch? She had just painted some of the chairs and I got my dress stained?" Norma reminisced.

"I had forgotten about that, but I remember this dress," Clara said, pointing to another block. "I wore it the first time I went to church with my hair up."

Norma, looking at a box containing a candy dish, asked, "Didn't you use this in your parlor? I'd put it on the sink and keep candy or snacks in it and remember Edna, your teacher."

212

As the sisters reminisced and continued to go through the hope chest, they found many things that Clara could use in her few rooms. Something kept tugging at Clara's heart. She had secretly dreamed that some golden day would come when her dreams would be fulfilled. She thought she would not be doing this until that time came, but since Norma was so enthused Clara was beginning to feel enthused, too. She had to get used to the idea. They were finding towel sets, dishcloths, and tea towels. Some had been given to her as a gift for being a table waiter at weddings when she first started going with the young folks.

"Oh, this pink set," they both said at the same time as Clara pulled out a towel set. "I always remember Barbara Anna and when I had to stay there while the rest of the family went to Wisconsin on a trip. She gave this set to me and I had wanted to use it right away. Mother said I should keep it and maybe someday I would have my own house. I must have been about five or six years old."

"I just remember hearing about it, but it sure is pretty," Norma said fondly. "Is that my driver blowing the horn?" Norma walked over to the door and looked out. Coming back inside, she said, "I didn't think they'd be back this soon," as she picked up Carrie who was becoming discontented.

Clara followed Norma upstairs and they were both surprised to see that Virginia had prepared dinner. No wonder the baby wasn't content; they had forgotten the time.

Clara was putting the dishes away as Caleb and Virginia were getting ready to leave. Virginia dressed John Wayne, preparing to take him along. "They say it seems old people are cheered at seeing a child sometimes. It works best to take just one along, because John Wayne and Earl David sometimes chase each other around."

There was a knock on the door, but before Caleb got there to open it, the door opened. "Laura, what brings you here?" Clara gasped in surprise, thinking they may be going along to visit the elderly.

"Is Raymond here, too?" Caleb asked Laura.

"No, he just dropped me off. He's going to Kinsman Hardware Store. He'll be back. Are you heading out to Andrew's already? We thought we had a few hours."

"No, we are visiting some others first. I guess we could meet there around three o'clock," Caleb informed Laura.

"That's what I understood, so I thought I'd come over awhile to see the kitchen corner I've been hearing about," Laura said smiling at Clara.

Caleb, Virginia, and John Wayne were on their way. Clara remembered that Andrew's mother, who lives with them, had asked to be anointed so Raymond and Laura were also going to join them there. Laura sat on the sofa and they began their visit. She asked about the store and about Annetta and Anna Lois's plans to share the house. There was so much to discuss.

Clara noticed that Laura looked toward the window occasionally as if she were watching for Raymond. Several times Clara started to say, "We can go down to the basement," but Laura always kept on talking, drawing Paul Henry and Hannah Mae into the conversation, too. They enjoyed interacting with grownups. Suddenly, Lena Jane said, "A horse is coming."

"Surely not Raymond already?" Clara asked. "We haven't been to the basement yet." Looking out the window she said, "I don't see any horse."

Laura asked Clara about her furniture and Clara told her about the bedroom suite. Laura didn't make any move to get up, although Clara thought they should go to the basement. Paul Henry roused up and said, "I hear people talking. Sounds like they are in the basement."

"Are you sure?" Laura asked.

Clara then heard what sounded like a door closing. "Let's go down," she said. "I want you want to see my things." As she made her way toward the door, Laura lingered behind, becoming interested in one of the plants on the windowsill and asked Clara the name of the flower.

There was a soft knock on the outside door, and Laura smiled as she turned to follow Clara. "Anna Lois!" Clara gasped. "I thought you were tending the store!"

"I was," she mused, "but Elvin's children are watching it right now. I had to come over to see your little house."

Laura, Clara, and the children followed Anna Lois out and through the outside basement door with Clara leading. As she opened the basement door she gasped and holding her hand over her heart, exclaimed, "What?!"

As Clara stood there frozen, everyone started laughing. She didn't know from where everyone had come. Annetta, Lena, Frances, Lisa, and Joann were there. Also, those who came from other communities were Ruth Verna, Dorcas, Mabel, and Katie, plus their neighbor Wayne's wife. "Come in, come in," they sang out.

"How did you all get here?" she asked, coming out of her stupor.

Continuing to laugh, one of them said, "The ones who came in the van walked in the lane and others just walked. Some have their teams behind the barn."

Hannah Mae's eyes got big and she said, "Look at all the presents over there!"

Clara groaned out loud as she saw all the packages on the table and on the sink.

"Come on, Clara," they chorused. "Open them! It's your housewarming party. We want to see what you got, too."

Laura opened one of the doors under the sink and said, "Look! It's empty! Get these packages opened!"

"I believe Hannah Mae and Paul Henry would be willing to help you open them."

The children eagerly ran to the table and Clara followed them. "Look!" Paul Henry exclaimed. "I found a dishpan full of things." As he picked up a few things, he named them. "Jello, noodles, and I don't know what this is."

"Here is a bottle of soap to wash dishes and a small kettle," Hannah Mae explained, as Clara also opened some of the gifts.

"When you marry, you don't get to open your own gifts," Laura said.

"Yes, we do have **some** advantages," Annetta replied, placing extra emphasis on the word some. That brought chuckles from across the room.

"Look, these cans don't have any paper on them!" Paul Henry said.

"That's for the times when Clara doesn't know what to make to eat. She opens one of those cans," Joanne replied.

Paul Henry thought for a moment and said, "But maybe she wants soup and it could be a can of pears."

The girls laughed and said, "Then she must just eat fruit for that meal."

"Candy!" Hannah Mae said from the other end of the table.

"And I found marshmallows and peanut butter," Paul Henry chimed in.

"You knew about this," Clara said, looking at Laura. "That's why you tried to keep me upstairs."

Laura nodded and said, "I sure did. I was trying to keep you occupied so you wouldn't see the people coming. When Lena Jane saw a team, no one believed her since it was gone by the time the others looked."

"Did Virginia know about it?" Clara asked as she opened another bag.

"No, I didn't tell them since there were enough who almost left a hint slip. Here comes Raymond," Laura said as she went toward the door. "I'll come to see you later after you are settled."

"Look at all these small cereal boxes!" Paul Henry exclaimed as he opened another package. "Each box would barely fill a plate."

Annetta reminded Paul Henry that Clara lives alone and doesn't need as much. "She only needs a little box each morning."

"Don't disappoint him," Lena said. "He was probably planning to eat with her after seeing the marshmallows and candy."

Hannah Mae, staring at the little boxes, said, "I wonder how these would taste." Pointing to another box, she said, "These are good. Grandmother had some one time, but Mother said they cost too much."

Lydia Ann was having fun scrambling through the paper and boxes on the floor. Hannah Mae named the things as Clara opened them: a plastic pail with soap, sponges, and bath tissue. As Clara saw the names of all those who gave her gifts, she realized that quite a few people had sent gifts but weren't able to come to the party.

"What do you have, Paul Henry?" Annetta asked after he heard him excitedly say, "Look."

"Oh, I was just looking. There are three bowls with lids and they're full of things."

"What kind of things?"

"Everything," he said. "Shoestrings, toothpaste, matches, safety pins, paper clips, Jello, a pencil sharpener—oh well, you can look," he said, despairing from naming everything.

"Give me a bowl," Lena said. "I want to see, too."

"I guess they are all opened now," Paul Henry said with satisfaction.

"There is one over on the sink yet," Lena said.

Clara noticed the "Handle with Care" label. As she unwrapped another layer of packing, she finally came to a box. Paul Henry could hardly wait until she unwrapped it. It was a wooden picture of a cozy fireplace with the caption "Home, Sweet Home." Above, in glittering letters, it said, "Clara's Kitchen." But what did the numbers mean on the fireplace? Noticing the hands, Clara marveled in a whisper, "Oh, it's a clock!" Looking at Joanne, Clara said, "You made this?" knowing that Joanne often bought clock kits and put them on wooden scenes.

"Thank you so much, everyone," Clara said heartily, adding, "You planned this all behind my back!"

Chuckling, they said, "It wasn't easy. We were almost caught a few times."

"There was a shower for Annetta and me on Wednesday evening," Anna Lois said. "Lena had told me she was coming over because Verna and Dorcas were in the area. I didn't know why they were so thoughtful, making sure I could come, too. It was after our shower that they told us about the one they were having for you. They couldn't tell us before."

Chapter Twenty-Six

It was a warm September day. Caleb and Virginia had gone to a wedding in the Spring Hill District. Clara had done the laundry for Virginia in the morning and then started making the bread dough in between hanging out the last loads of wash.

The little ones had begged to eat dinner in Clara's kitchen, like they occasionally did when their parents went away, but the bread was ready to bake by dinner time. Clara promised the children there would be a surprise when the schoolchildren came home.

As Clara was folding the wash she saw Hannah Mae and Paul Henry walking in the lane, swinging their lunch pails.

"Aren't Mom and Dad home yet?" Paul Henry asked.

"No, they will likely be home for a late supper," Clara informed them.

"What's the surprise?" asked Hannah Mae. "Lena Jane said there's going to be a surprise."

"Go change your clothing first," Clara directed, as she hurriedly put the piles of wash away. Paul Henry took his wash upstairs; Hannah Mae put the towels away as she put her own pile of clothing on the stairs to take up later.

As the children all came in the kitchen, waiting, Clara took the ice pops out of the freezer that she had made a few days ago without the children's knowledge. This was cause for rejoicing. Lydia Anne's eyes shone in joy. As Clara was about to hand them out, she said, "Let's go outside and sit on the glider by the trees. Then I won't have to clean up if the ice pops drip."

The children bounded for the door. Lydia Ann started crying as if she was hurt.

"What happened?" Clara asked. Everyone looked innocent as tears streamed down Lydia Ann's cheeks. Again Clara asked, "What's wrong?"

Lydia Ann said, "Ice keim?" Clara showed her the pan of ice pops she still had in her hand. Lydia Ann's eyes started shining through her tears. The others were already out at the glider.

Taking Lydia Ann's hand and leading her out to the glider, Clara said, "We will eat the ice pops out here." Lydia Ann cheered and rejoiced as she saw the others waiting. It was a happy group of children who snacked on the orange and purple ice pops. Clara barely noticed the chattering and rejoicing. She only saw Lydia Ann licking her ice pop in pure joy, her tears dried up. *She saw that I was ready to hand out the ice pops, then thought I was denying them. She didn't understand that they were still getting the treat and she had to wait until she was outside. She assumed the joy was denied her.*

Clara's thoughts went deep. Was that how God felt with her at times when her heart ached and she shed tears of disappointment? When joys were denied her that she so longed after? When God knew there were joys, but not in the way she had thought? Clara thought, *Maybe if God gave me what I yearned after, maybe it would cause even more tears, like if I had given the children the ice pops in the kitchen. Likely they would have dripped and I would have nagged at them or complained and spoiled their fun. Here they can enjoy them even more. Maybe at times God feels so much mercy and pity toward my tears, as I felt toward Lydia Ann. When I shed tears because I thought the joys were denied me, He had better things in view for me. What does the Bible say? . . . for ye that are evil and still know to give good gifts to your children, so much more know I, too, give good gifts to you.*

Clara thought of the words:

> *For by and by the mist will lift*
> *And darkness turn to day,*
> *Then looking back we'll praise His Name*
> *Who led us all the way.*

The mist had lifted. Lydia Ann's tears had all dried and joy showed on her face. She understands now.

Clara thought of the song she once heard Anna Lois sing that had brought the flow of tears, relieving the tension.

> *Renew my will from day to day,*
> *Blend it with Thine and take away*
> *All now that makes it hard to say*
> *Thy will be done.*

Clara thought of the words Raymond occasionally referred to in his sermons, "The bud may have a bitter taste, but sweet will be the flower." It could refer to so many different things.

In the evening, after Caleb and Virginia were home and Clara returned to her kitchen, she sat at her sewing machine, working on the twenty-five slips she needed to finish by the end of the week. She remembered again how Lydia Ann's disappointment had soon turned to joy.

Hearing the sound of happy children playing in the kitchen above, Clara thought of the time Norma encouraged her to use the things in her hope chest now, even though she had been secretly yearning after dreams of a home with a husband and children. She was too stunned for tears that day; it was a hard jolt to her. Sometime later she came across a poem that described her innermost feelings better than she could say it. She had copied the poem and hung it in her kitchen where she could read it daily to remind her of the need to bloom even though she wasn't planted in the fairest garden.

The Violet

> *Down in a green and shady bed*
> *A modest violet grew.*
> *It's stalk was bent, it hung its head*
> *As if to hide from view.*

And yet it was a lovely flower
With colors bright and fair.
It might have graced a rosy bower
Instead of hiding there.

And yet it was content to bloom
With modest tints arrayed
And there differ its sweet perfume
Within the silent shade.

Then let me to this valley go
This pretty flower to see
That I may also learn to grow
In sweet humility.

*   *   *

The barn chores had been done once again. Neighbor Harry's son Neil was helping to do the chores that Paul Henry and Clara couldn't do, like climbing the silo to get silage down. Paul Henry could climb up the silo, but he hardly had enough muscle to get enough silage down for seventy steers. and Clara was afraid of heights over twenty feet.

As Clara read a bedtime story to the children and put them to bed, she reminded Paul Henry that he may as well go to bed, too, saying that if his mom and dad did come home tonight, it would be late. They had gone to Missouri for an ordination and thought they would not be home until morning.

The next morning there was still no sign of Caleb and Virginia. The children were eagerly looking forward to seeing the van drive in the lane. They did the chores again; Neil had gotten enough silage down for the morning feeding.

It was time for Paul Henry and Hannah Mae to leave for school. Clara could see that Paul Henry was disappointed that he had to leave before his parents came home. He had gotten up early and willingly helped with the chores, even doing some extra things.

Clara felt his disappointment. Hannah Mae didn't say much except that she hardly remembered how Lena Jane looked anymore.

The dreary, damp November morning made Clara feel drab, too. The trees had shed most of their leaves and all the earth looked forsaken. After doing the breakfast dishes, Clara took Lydia Ann and the little boys along out to feed the chickens. She also checked the pig stable. The children enjoyed playing with the cats in the barn, trying to get them to sit on the bales of hay with them.

The air felt so damp and all seemed so bleak as Clara looked down the road. No van was in sight. *What could be keeping them?* Troubled thoughts were entering her mind. Leaving the chicken house, Clara heard a bird clearly singing a merry song. Looking around, she tried to see the bird. *Maybe in one of those tall trees. Oh, yes, now I see it.* It was a lowly sparrow singing such a rich gay tune to a quiet dreary world. What inspired the sparrow to be so happy this morning?

Coming toward the house, Clara saw the children playing in the dead leaves along the fence. She watched for a moment as they played, but it was chilly sitting idle, so she got the rake and decided to rake some of the leaves that had piled in the flower beds. Some had not blown away last week when they had a windy day. As she raked, Clara heard another bird singing lustily. It reminded her of a poem, something about hearing a sweet song of a bird singing alone among dead trees. She would have to look up that poem.

When the children were getting cold and tired of being out-side and Lydia Ann needed attention, Clara took them inside. When they settled into playing Clara got her poem books, which included quite a collection by now. As she paged through them, trying to find this particular poem, she couldn't find it anywhere.

Clara was surprised when she realized it was nearing dinner time and Caleb and Virginia had still not returned home. She decided to make a big kettle of chicken corn soup, using canned chicken. *That way, there will be something I can quickly heat whenever they come home. It will be a sufficient meal.*

After dinner, she again searched her poem books. Though she didn't find the one she was looking for, she found many other inspiring ones. Lydia Ann had fallen asleep on Clara's lap, so she laid her in her bed. Clara, who had also dozed, later saw that both boys had fallen asleep, too, one on the sofa and the other one on the rocking chair. *Guess the damp, cool air made us all tired.*

When the schoolchildren came bounding in the door, Paul Henry's face fell as he looked around the quiet kitchen. "Isn't Dad home yet?" he asked.

"No. I'm wondering if they decided to stay longer for something," Clara answered.

"Do you think we'll need to ask Neil to come again, or shall I try to get enough silage down?" Paul Henry asked in a challenging voice.

"We'll wait and see."

"May we eat supper in your kitchen?" Hannah Mae asked.

Clara decided to grant them that joy, rather than seeing them watch and wait and become more disappointed. After they did a few chores, they had an enjoyable suppertime. Clara used her small kettles and small bowls, serving some goodies the children weren't used to having for supper.

Lingering at the table, Clara watched the children. The little boys had the marble roller that Clara had bought at a sale. Lydia Ann was playing with the tin tea set that Clara had had when she was a girl. The cups and saucers were still in good condition. Hannah Mae was saying she wanted to wash the kettles and new plates and the glasses that had birds on. Paul Henry was curled up on the loveseat with a book he hadn't read yet. He was a good reader. Clara hadn't realized he would be able to read that book.

Suddenly the door opened upon the relaxed scene and Caleb stood there smiling. It was like a fire drill. Paul Henry sprang up from the love seat, book in hand, asking where they had been so long. Lydia Ann, outstretched hands clutching a few pieces of the tea set, also came running. John Wayne asked for Mother and Lena Jane.

Finding the kitchen empty, Virginia came downstairs, too. Lena Jane rushed through the door with a bag. Together, the children chimed, "Is there something for me?" The children had learned to look forward to seeing the little gifts brought home by the child who went along. Virginia had begun to tell well-meaning friends that if they wanted to give something, they needed to remember the ones at home, too. The children's excitement rose high as they sorted through handkerchiefs, a notebook or pad, a pen, and a coloring book. Lydia Ann was clutching a little bag with a zipper as Earl David unwrapped a piece of chewing gum.

"Did you have supper?" Clara asked.

Virginia shook her head as Caleb added, "We didn't have any dinner either, except for the drink, pretzels, and apples we had packed."

Clara jumped up, thinking fast. "Just stay here. I made chicken noodle soup at noon in case you'd come. I'll heat it. There's still enough of other things, too."

While the soup was heating and while they ate, they talked about their trip. Caleb commented on the privilege of coming home and finding the children at home and relaxed. "Six months ago I would have had to go and pick up the children at several different homes and do the chores later."

Virginia said, "And I would have their suitcases to unpack and hardly know what was dirty and what was clean. Often I would find a sock missing and not realize Hannah's covering was missing until Sunday morning."

Caleb and Virginia asked Clara if she was worried when they hadn't arrived last evening or this morning. Clara admitted she was concerned this morning, and Paul Henry was quite disappointed. Caleb said, "We would have been more concerned if the children had been scattered in various homes and we hadn't returned as planned."

Looking at Caleb, Virginia said, "I was thinking of that, too," explaining to Clara that one time they came home a day later than first planned. When Caleb went to pick up Hannah Mae and John Wayne at Leroy's house, there was no one there and they didn't even leave a note. Noticing Leroy out working in the field, Caleb talked to him. Leroy said that his wife had a dentist appointment in the afternoon so they took the children to Alsons. "We had told them we'd be home late morning," Caleb said. "It was always hard on us and also hard for the children to fully trust us. It seemed they were fearful at times. I hope we never take you for granted and take advantage of you. Remind us if we do."

"I don't like it that we came home later than we thought, but there wasn't much I could do. At the ordination we planned to stop at the Honeywell settlement and sleep there so we would feel rested when we got home. When we got there, the message was out that we were coming. I guess other travelers had stopped, too, and had planned church services for this forenoon.

"I trusted things were well at home. Some people were disappointed that we left right after church. My cousin had prepared dinner for us, but that would have made us a few hours later yet."

In the evening as Clara went to bed, she remembered some thoughtless remarks she had made earlier about the young minister who had been at Benjamin's funeral. Later, he was in the area and went home without having special church services. At Raymond's ordination, he left before dinner and she couldn't even ask for a copy of the poem he had recited. Things looked so different when she viewed them from the other side. Yes, when the mist is lifted and one can see more clearly, things look different.

> *For by and by the mist will lift*
> *And darkness turn to day,*
> *And looking back we'll praise His Name*
> *Who led us all the way.*

It made Clara feel small and unworthy when Caleb honored her, since she enjoyed this job so much more than working in the store. It seemed that through the children she gleaned so many spiritual insights. She would have never thought of helping Caleb and Virginia if Caleb hadn't offered. Even when she considered it and accepted it as a leading, she remembered the jolt it brought to her when her sister Norma suggested she use the things in her hope chest. Unknowingly, she had still been waiting for some dream of life to be fulfilled and was going to help at Calebs in the meantime. Did those dreams now fade away?

225

Caleb had said this need was for the present time. If she could already see what God has for the future, she wouldn't be able to help them now. The future isn't revealed yet. The mist was still over the future years.

The afflictions didn't seem so hard anymore. At times she still had to fight a yearning, but she wasn't beckoning the temptation so it didn't conceive. There was no one who tempted her but the yearnings were still there.

Clara remembered the Sunday about a month ago when she was with Anna Lois and Annetta for dinner. She had enjoyed the day and, as they visited, she had learned some interesting facts and some things that plagued her mind. When she came home to her little house, the thoughts churned in her mind. There were two families leaving who had been visiting with Caleb and Virginia.

As Clara ate her supper, she thought of sharing some of the things she had heard with Virginia. Sharing would help digest the news and maybe Virginia could share some of the things she had learned from their visitors. Just as she might go upstairs and talk to Virginia, she heard they were eating their supper. Instead Clara started writing a letter to Alice, but she would so much rather talk to someone.

Clara finally left the letter lay and went upstairs. The kitchen was deserted but she saw Virginia and Caleb in the barnyard. Paul Henry was pulling Lydia Ann and the two little boys in the wagon. Hannah Mae and Lydia Jane were going out the field lane with Caleb, waiting for Virginia to catch up.

The field lane went way out back past the bush and along the meadow leading to the back fields. They were going on a leisurely walk, likely enjoying the late autumn scenery. Caleb and Virginia were likely sharing the conversations of the afternoon.

Just thinking about it caused Clara's eyes to mist, but she mustn't think about it. "For by and by the mist will lift and darkness turn to day, when we shall see what the afflictions work for us an eternal weight of glory." Another song began going through her mind: "Tell me not of heavy crosses or of burdens hard to bear." What did those words mean anyway? Two weeks ago Caleb and

Virginia held a singing for the young folks and they sang that song. The words were so encouraging and comforting, as satisfying as a sermon. Some of the songs Clara had sung at singings that she hadn't realized the meaning were now becoming so satisfying. She lit the lamp and got the songbook out of the bookcase headboard in her bed. The shelf was a handy place to keep songbooks, the Bible, and her poem books.

Finding the page, she read:

I'm dwelling on the mountain
Where the golden sunlight gleams;
O'er a land whose wondrous beauty
Far exceeds my fondest dreams.
Where the air is pure celestial
Laden with the breath of flowers.
They are blooming by the fountain
'Neath the never-fading bowers.

I can see far down the mountain
Where I wandered weary years,
Often hindered in my journey
By the ghosts of doubts and fears.
Broken vows and disappointments
Thickly sprinkled all the way,
But the spirit led unerring
To the land I hold today.

I'm drinking at the fountain
Where I ever would abide,
For I tasted life's pure river
And my soul is satisfied.
There's no thirsting for life's pleasures
Nor adorning rich and gay
For I've found a richer treasure,
One that fadeth not away.

Here were the words Clara was looking for:

Tell me not of heavy crosses
Nor of burdens hard to bear,
For I found this great salvation
Makes each burden light appear.
And I love to follow Jesus,
Gladly counting all but dross;
Worldly honors all forsaking
For the glory of the cross.

Oh, the cross had wondrous glory,
Oft I proved this to be true;
When I'm in the way so narrow
I can see a pathway through.
Oh, how sweetly Jesus whispers,
"Take the cross; thou needst not fear.
For I've tried the way before thee
And the glory lingers near."

It was like an inspiring sermon. Clara had failed so much. She thought of the "ghosts" and doubts that had hindered her in her teen years and of adorning herself rich and gay, broken vows and disappointments thickly sprinkled her way. But it had cleared the way. The mist had lifted; the Spirit led unerring.

I can see a pathway through. Vainly I would have turned off many times if the Spirit had not led unerring to the land I hold today. The song doesn't say we won't have crosses, but it says, "Tell me not of heavy crosses nor of burdens hard to bear. For I've found this great salvation makes each burden light appear." Yes, when we see what the afflictions work for us, the burdens will appear light.

About nine years ago Clara was eagerly waiting for her seventeenth birthday. What would the next years bring?

Oh, how sweetly Jesus whispers,
"Take the cross; thou needst not fear.

For I've tried the way before thee
And the glory lingers near. "

Yes, the mist will lift one day at a time. The poems and the song said about the same message in different words:

There's so much no I cannot see;
My eye is still too dim,
But come what may I still can trust
And leave it all to Him.
Looking back, we'll praise His Name
Who led us all the way.

I may not understand, but I still can trust, for He has tried the way before me and the glory lingers near.

Clara thought of the poem she had in her kitchen about the violet growing unnoticed in the ditch.

And yet it was a lovely flower
With colors bright and fair.
It may have graced a rosy bower
Instead of hiding there.

And yet it was content to bloom
With modest tints arrayed;
And there differ its sweet perfume
Within the silent shade.

Then let me to this valley go
This pretty flower to see
That I may also learn to grow
In sweet humility.

"And there differ its sweet perfume." *Caleb and Virginia made it sound as if that's what I was doing. They appreciated it so much.* But she had to keep fighting to not be tempted to bloom

229

in the rose gardens. *I'll just be a violet in the valley.* "For by and by the mist will lift—and looking back I'll praise His Name."

When she was drifting off to sleep, a German song came to Clara's mind:

> *Vas mich auf deiser velt betrüt*
> *Das vird ein Kurtd zeit.*

What a comforting balm if she could always remember that when things trouble her and disappoint her. *Things that grieve me on this earth are only for a short time because we are here only a short time.*

But the things that my soul loves and which satisfy stay on in eternity. Like 2 Corinthians says, looking on the things which are not seen.

Chapter Twenty-Seven

Clara flung the bed sheet across the clothesline and spread it out evenly, pinning on the clothespins. The chill of the nippy March weather caused a steam to rise from the warm, wet sheet. As she hung up another sheet which connected to the diapers she had hung out with the other load, Clara felt the diapers were a little stiff. *Must be cold enough to freeze the wash, but it won't stay frozen the way the west wind is making the wash flap,* Clara mused as she went back to the wash house.

It wasn't the usual laundry day, but a few of the children had had the flu, which created more dirty wash. Virginia suggested doing some of the laundry today so there wouldn't be an overload on Friday. The towels and light-colored children's clothing needed to wash a little longer. It didn't take long to hang up the sheets, so Clara went into the house for a moment to see how Virginia was coming along with the applesauce.

As she opened the door, Clara saw a pan of apples on the table. One kettle was cooking on the stove and Virginia was at the other end of the kitchen caring for baby Ion Keith who didn't sound very happy.

"Clara, would you stir the apples on the stove, since you're here? I was hoping to get the baby to sleep, but it's not working out. Maybe we just won't get many apples done today."

"I have only three more loads of wash to do," Clara replied as she stirred the apples.

The little boys were playing with their wooden barn and animals; Lydia Ann was likely taking a nap. It was good to see Earl David feeling well enough to play again. *Hopefully in a few days, Ion Keith's blurred eyes will become sunny and happy again*, Clara thought as she returned to the wash house and began feeding the wash through the wringer.

Clara then thought about tomorrow—the long-awaited day was finally here. As the children would say, "We have to sleep one more time." Clara smiled to herself.

She pinned the small dresses and nightgowns and a few towels on the line which began flapping right away. She looked at the blue sky with white clouds, hoping this clear, cold weather would kill the flu bug.

Continuing to pin the wash to the clothesline, Clara gazed across the landscape, trying to grasp the fact that tomorrow would be Erma's wedding day. She will be united to Evan, the young man whose wife had passed away a few years ago, and Clara was asked to be a table waiter. Weddings were more special now since she didn't get invited to as many anymore.

She had just heard that Erma and Evan might be dating. Then they were published to be married! What an uproar it caused in their circle of friends. *Whatever did they talk about before this took place?* Clara wondered to herself. At least Erma would still be in the district, even if the older circle of friends would be losing her. She was somewhat older than Clara; most of the girls were. A few others had joined their circle since they were beginning to feel out of place with the younger folks.

Clara thought back to the Sunday she had been with Anna Lois when the whole gang was there, and they had been discussing about Evan possibly seeing one of them. Clara was trying to remember what Erma had said, but then she remembered that Erma had not been with them that Sunday. She had been away, but they thought maybe she would come anyway. When a few boys went past in a buggy, they began kidding that perhaps it was Evan.

Clara was so caught up in her thoughts that she hardly realized that the washing was done. Mechanically she was letting the water out of the washing machine and cleaning up the floor.

Coming back into the kitchen, Clara noticed the baby in his high chair, a few toys on the tray. He was complaining and Virginia was putting apples through the food mill while Caleb sat at the table cutting up apples.

Clara, noticing that there were no apples on the stove, got a dish pan, dumped some apples in it, and started cutting them up. Virginia sighed when Ion Keith threw his toys down and started crying. Caleb tried to comfort him to no avail.

Wiping her hands on her apron, Virginia said, "Well, maybe he's ready to sleep now. I'll try it again." As she was getting the squirming baby out of the high chair and picking up the toys underfoot, the tray crashed to the floor.

Above the din of the crash, Clara thought she heard the door. Or had she just imagined it? Seeing Caleb turn his head toward the door, she knew he had heard something, too. Sure enough, the door was opening.

Before Caleb got to the door, a lone man walked in carrying a small satchel. Caleb stopped in his tracks.

Shutting the door, the man looked at Caleb with a grin that seemed to say, "Surely you remember me."

Stroking his hair and with a catch in his voice, Caleb said, "Ammon Weaver?" With a hearty welcome, the two men met halfway and greeted each other with the holy kiss. Clara heard Virginia give a sigh of relief. Maybe she was fearing that a van load of visitors had arrived.

Even the baby quieted a bit as he looked at the stranger. As the man shook hands with Virginia he was answering Caleb's questions. "How are you traveling? Are you by yourself?"

"I came by bus," he replied.

"And you walked from town?"

"I started walking, thinking I would go to Martin Eberly's and he could bring me over; however, a native farmer picked me up and brought me right to your lane."

Virginia took the baby into the bedroom.

The visitor stood for a moment talking until Caleb remembered the apples he was cutting up. "Is this an apple peeling party?" Ammon asked.

"We don't even have to peel them. We're just cutting and coring them," Caleb responded, adding, "I volunteered to help. The women had some interruptions so I tried my hand."

"And you were hired right away," Ammon guessed as he rolled up his sleeves and looked around to see where he could help.

Clara remembered the apples Virginia had been putting through the mill and, picking up the pans of apples she and Caleb had been cutting, she noticed that Caleb's pan was full. Adding a little water, she put them on the stove.

The men continued visiting, hardly aware that they were cutting up apples. Ammon said, "I thought that likely I could go along with you to the wedding tomorrow."

"Wedding?" Caleb questioned blankly, looking at Ammon.

Ammon, looking dumbfounded, laid his knife down on the table. "Don't tell me I have the wrong week," he said, hopelessly. Then, as if speaking to himself, he said, "No, I made plans with Leonard to go home with him. I know Evan's wedding is tomorrow." He popped another apple in his mouth.

Caleb's face then lit up as he remembered. "Oh, yes. Is the wedding tomorrow? We aren't going."

Ammon looked at him as if he doubted what Caleb had just said.

Caleb explained, saying, "Allen has that wedding. He is Erma's uncle."

Ammon was thoughtful for a moment. Caleb, almost reading his mind, said, "You can take our team."

Virginia came out of the bedroom without the baby. Hopefully he was finally sleeping.

"Where does Erma live?" Ammon asked. "Or isn't the wedding at her place?" he inquired further.

Caleb nodded his head as Virginia reminded Caleb that Clara was going to the wedding. "That's why we're trying to get all the work done today."

Turning to Clara, Virginia said, "You could go along. How were you planning to get there?"

Looking toward Virginia, Clara responded, "I was planning to go with Annetta and Lena."

"Well, now they won't have to drive over here," Caleb said. "I'll send Paul Henry over to tell Annetta when he comes home from school."

Clara's heart dropped to her feet as Ammon and Caleb continued to talk and cut up apples. As Ammon popped another apple in his mouth, Caleb asked, "Have you, by any chance, not had dinner yet?"

"I guess I didn't, now that I think about it," Ammon replied matter-of-factly. Looking at the clock, he said, "It's all right. The apples will hold me over till suppertime."

The door flung open and the schoolchildren entered. Soon they brought out the pretzel can from the pantry—a regular routine since Paul Henry was always hungry when he came home from school.

Caleb went over to the desk and wrote a note, asking Paul Henry to take it over to Annetta's house. Paul Henry stuffed pretzels into his coat pocket and was off as Virginia called after him, "Don't stay long! It will soon be suppertime."

Clara kept glancing at Ammon. He reminded her of—who was she trying to think of? As she continued to ponder, something was coming back to her. Seeing his blue eyes, she wondered, *Did Virgil age so much since I last saw him? Surely his eyes wouldn't fade in color. They were blue but not that blue. No, Caleb called him Ammon. But his hair line and blue eyes resemble Virgil.*

The men continued to visit.

Virginia and Clara continued to can the applesauce. When Caleb asked for more apples, Virginia replied gratefully, "That's all of them."

"Already?" Caleb sounded surprised. "I thought you had a lot of apples to do."

"It would have been a lot if Clara and I had to do them all without help," Virginia reminded him.

The men moved to the other end of the kitchen, still talking. Caleb asked questions about the sawmill and of mutual acquaintances from years ago. Clara realized by now that he was one of Caleb's friends who had been with the young folks with Caleb. She wondered if perhaps he was a widower. He seemed to know Evan quite well.

When the last batch of apples was ready to be put through the mill, Virginia suggested, "I suppose the wash is dry by now," and she went to bring it in. By the time she came back inside, the men were in the barn starting the chores.

Virginia suggested they have an early supper since Ammon had had no dinner.

"What kind of baked things can we have for supper?" Virginia asked as she folded the wash while Clara was getting supper on the table.

"We have some chocolate cake yet," Clara reminded her.

"I know, but it's not fresh anymore and it didn't have a nice texture to begin with."

Supper was ready and they were waiting for Paul Henry to come back. Finally Caleb suggested they start eating. As the children were gathering around the table, Paul Henry came in, puffing and trying to catch his breath. Seeing the others at the table, he quickly took off his coat.

Looking at his son, Caleb asked, "Where have you been so long?"

"I only stayed a little while," he said taking his place at the table, still out of breath. "Why couldn't I take my bike?"

"Why didn't you?" Caleb asked. "Did you walk over there?" Caleb asked unbelievingly.

"I walked when I got tired from running. I thought you didn't want me to take my bike. You said I should run over," Paul Henry finished innocently.

Caleb looked at his son for a moment as if deep in thought. Virginia reminded Caleb that everyone was at the table and they bowed their heads for silent prayer.

By the look on Caleb's face, Clara could tell that he was thinking of a spiritual application about the trust of a child doing what he was told to do. Caleb often used lessons in his sermons that he learned from his children, comparing their trust to the way we should put our trust in God.

Ammon commented on how good the homemade bread tasted with apple butter. Virginia had thought they had a poor supper for a guest—potatoes, peas, and noodles cooked in leftover beef broth. She also served homemade bologna in case someone wanted a sandwich instead of apple-butter bread.

"I can tell this is homemade soup. It doesn't taste like soup out of a can. Homemade things are just better." He also commented on the homemade bologna.

Clara and Virginia made eye contact when Ammon said, "And the cake tastes like good homemade cake. It has body to it. The cake mixes are so light; there's nothing to them."

"And we would probably enjoy store-bought bread and cake once in awhile for a change, thinking they were so soft," Caleb admitted. "So you haven't found a cook yet?"

"No," Ammon drawled, slowly lifting his eyes to meet Caleb's as he chewed on a toothpick. "Sister Ina has a whole house full of girls. She doesn't have any boys and the oldest girl will soon be finished with school. Ina comes over at times and brings food along, but since Dad isn't here anymore, she doesn't come as often."

"Your dad's not here?" Caleb interrupted.

"It's been almost a year since he passed away."

"Did we hear about that?" Caleb asked Virginia.

"I don't believe we did, unless we didn't realize who he was. Was he sick for a long time?" Virginia asked.

"No. He wasn't feeling well for a few days. He didn't have much pain, but he was uncomfortable. I wanted to call the doctor but he refused. One night he got worse and we had to go to the hospital. He died before surgery. They think his intestines were blocked or twisted.

"And what can I say when Ina comes? She nags at me, saying 'Why don't you take this wall out? It would make the kitchen lighter and nicer.' She thinks I should get rid of the old rocker because the arm is cracked and loose. But it's more comfortable than the rocking chairs they're making these days. She nags about my tea towels and pot holders, saying I don't wash them often enough. After she's been there and puts things away, I can't find them.

"I don't suppose her girls would be much help to me. You knew that my brother Karl lives in Illinois. He never liked working at the sawmill. My sister Ethel wasn't well for a long time and often needed hired help. She's better now, but she has small children. Lorraine lives in Kentucky so I do my best.

"Karl keeps urging me to Illinois, telling about a house nearby where I could live. But I can't leave the sheep to roam the hillside that Dad has raised. I can't bring myself to gather them up and ship them to the stockyards. The dog that was always on Dad's heels, helping to manage, laid around awhile after Dad died. Now he finally gave up and accepted me, trustingly running along with me and taking me on the same well-beaten paths that Dad took around the buildings in the meadow.

"It doesn't seem right to get rid of the chickens, especially the bantams, that are always scratching around and crowing in the morning. All the animals seem to be a link in keeping memories of Dad alive. The bantams wait around for any food I can't eat. They get fed pretty well. I'm not as good a cook as Dad was; I occasionally throw things out that aren't edible, or if I make too much."

"I guess Evan found out it's best that man doesn't live alone," Caleb summed it up in a serious tone. Ammon steered the conversation in a different direction and they continued to visit.

When the dishes were done and the laundry all put away, Clara returned to her own kitchen, thoughts continuing to swirl around in her mind. She had been looking forward to going to the wedding, but going with this strange man? *What will people say? Caleb never asked me if I was agreed; he just sent Paul Henry over with the message saying I have another way to go to the wedding.*

In the morning, as Clara was combing her hair and getting ready for the wedding, she continued to think, *What will the people say when they see us arrive? Hopefully we'll arrive early before many people are there.*

Suddenly her kitchen door opened, disturbing her thoughts. As Caleb stepped in, Clara saw an expression on his face that she could not define. "Is he ready to leave?" Clara questioned.

"No," Caleb answered slowly, "he's washing the carriage and I'm ready to harness Jewel." Hesitating a bit, Caleb said, "I know you know the way to Erma's house, but Ammon will likely travel a different route. He likes to drive on Hill Top Road when he's in the area. It will be a little out of the way, but you can take Salem Road to Cross Corners, then take Lake Front Road."

"Lake Front Road?" Clara questioned. "That would be over too far."

"It's not so far above Erma's road. It's closer than taking the Indian path to Cross Corners."

Clara thought for awhile, then nodded her head. Caleb went out the door. *Hill Top Road*, she thought to herself. *If we have to go up that long hill, we'd better get started.* Clara's patience was wearing thin by the time they were ready to leave.

Ammon seemed surprised when Clara came out to the carriage. "You weren't around this morning. I thought I would have to pick you up somewhere."

Clara explained that she had her own quarters in the basement and helped Caleb and Virginia when they needed her.

"Are you Virginia's sister?" Ammon asked. Clara nodded her head. As they exchanged bits of conversation, Clara learned that Ammon was Evan's cousin. She still wondered if he was a widower, since he was invited to Evan's wedding. However, as she remembered Ammon and Caleb's conversation, she thought maybe he was an older single boy.

At first, Ammon carried the conversation; but then he seemed to be in deep thought, staring ahead, silently driving along. As they approached the long hill, Jewel started slower and began walking. Finally it seemed that Ammon roused out of his thoughts, as if coming out of a trance. "Here's where the girls were walking up the hill, trying to lighten the load for the horse pulling the spring wagon."

Clara looked at him blankly. Guessing by her puzzled look, Ammon said, "Caleb never told you?

"When I was younger, there were some girls from our area of Ohio who were visiting in this area. Coming up this hill in a spring wagon, a few girls got out and walked up the hill. Walking ahead of the spring wagon, they came up the hill and turned in this lane," Ammon continued to explain as he guided the horse off the road onto a narrow, grassy lane, saying he wanted to let the horse rest a bit.

Continuing to reminisce, Ammon said, "To a passerby this land looks like any other lane, and many never notice that the lane winds back to the woods. It's the place where my life changed forever.

"The girls—Wilma from this area and Emmaline from Ohio—just walked a short distance to rest while they waited for the others to come up the hill. Emmaline was walking ahead and didn't notice that Wilma had stopped to tie her shoe. Hearing a crash, Wilma thought that the spring wagon was hit. After a few seconds all was quiet.

"When Wilma looked she saw a tree sprawled on the ground. Not seeing Emmaline, she walked over to the tree. Emmaline looked up and said, 'A branch hit me and knocked me down.' After that Emmaline didn't respond anymore and was taken to the hospital.

"I had been seeing Emmaline for about two years. When I was notified that she was in the hospital, I went to see her, but she still had not regained consciousness. Since she was stirring, I thought she'd wake up soon and stayed all night. The doctors didn't think her skull was fractured and believed she'd wake up. Her parents arrived the next morning. I talked to her before I left. She opened her eyes a little, but they didn't focus. The last thing she said to me was, 'I'll meet you at the golden shore.'

"Soon after I left, she began having difficulty breathing and died within two hours. A blood clot had passed to her lungs."

Pointing, Ammon said, "It was the other half of that tree." Looking to where Ammon was pointing, Clara said, "You mean where the new growth is appearing on the side?" There was a thick twig now growing there.

"Ah—yes, I hadn't noticed. Is that growing in the same tree or is it just a tree growing nearby?" Ammon asked.

"It looks like the same kind of buds that are pushing." As Ammon guided the horse to turn around, Clara looked closer and said, "Yes, it's growing out of the same trunk."

Ammon was silent as he guided the horse back onto the road and continued on as Clara directed him on Salem Road leading to Cross Corners. He hadn't said much since they left the spot.

Clara, still trying to grasp everything, said, "I seem to remember hearing that story when I was younger, but I didn't realize it happened in this community."

"Well, the funeral wasn't in this area."

Clara asked further, "Was it a windy day like yesterday?"

Ammon shook his head. "That was the strange part. It was a very calm day with only a slight breeze. And the tree wasn't weak or old. Half of the tree just gave way—one of God's mysterious ways," he added.

As she looked at Ammon's face again, Clara asked, "Do you have a younger brother Virgil?"

"No, I don't. Karl is the only brother I have. I have several sisters. Why?" he wondered.

"You remind me of a boy named Virgil who I met at a wedding. Now I remember. I think his last name was Stauffer and Caleb said your last name is Weaver."

"I do have a cousin Virgil Stauffer. How do you know him?" he asked, becoming interested. "Your name isn't Minerva," he said looking at her. Then he answered himself, "No, you can't be."

"No, I'm Clara. I don't really know Virgil. I saw him at a wedding several years ago. He seemed like a decent boy, not following the popular styles. He left his light shine and was friendly. I respected him."

Ammon nodded and said, "If everyone saw the good in him, he would not have had so many afflictions in life. He dated a girl named Minerva who didn't understand or respect his morals. She thought he was self-righteous and got others to believe that, too. His name was ruined and their friendship ended. It left a scar on his life.

"I was thinking I would see him today, but he is my cousin on the Kilmer side. I'm a cousin to Virgil and Evan, but Virgil and Evan are not cousins. Do you understand?"

Without really listening, Clara heard what Ammon was saying and pictured the scene at cousin Andrew's wedding. She recalled the conversation she had heard while the girls were hunting their wraps. As she remembered that she wasn't able to determine Virgil's expression behind those blue eyes, it was now becoming clear. *Maybe his eyes revealed a joy of seeing someone who wouldn't mock him for his morals.*

When Ammon and Clara arrived at the wedding, Clara made a hasty escape from the carriage as everyone looked to see who was arriving. At least her group of girls were in the house.

"Here she comes," the table waiters cheered as Clara came to the basement. "We almost thought you weren't coming, but Annetta assured us you had a way to come."

Some of the girls closer in age to Erma and close friends like Annetta and Lena were ushers. Anna Lois and Vera were gift receivers, and Frances (Erma's cousin) and Jane were witnesses on Erma's side.

During the services most of the table waiters found chairs in the room next to the kitchen. They sat on the chairs that were lined up along the side, partly facing the other guests who faced toward the front of the room facing the kitchen. Clara became aware that Ammon was seated in the second row in the front toward the other end of the room near the window.

Since this was a second marriage for Evan, the message was a little different than the usual wedding message. Lloyd mentioned the ones in the Bible who asked Jesus about the man that married a woman and the man died. The woman married his brother and he died and so on until all seven brothers had married her. They wondered, in eternity, whose wife would she be, but Jesus reminded them that in the resurrection there is no marriage, nor male and female. We will all be like the angels. Marriage is just for this life.

During Allen's message, he referred to life as a tree, saying, "If there is a young tree and half of it dies, we graft a new twig so the tree can continue to grow. There is still life in the tree. But if it's an old tree and half falls away, the other half is aged too and we don't graft a new twig to it. It would be no gain to graft a young twig, for the other part of the tree would soon lose strength and wither off."

Clara thought of the tree she had seen on the way to the wedding. Though one-half had been lost, there was a new branch growing out its side. She raised her eyes for a moment in the direction where Ammon sat. Meeting his glance, they both looked quickly away.

While Clara filled the water glasses at the table in the living room, she noticed two boys at the table who were having an intense conversation while eating. They were hardly aware of the others around them. Looking again, she noticed that one of them was Ammon. Who was the other one? When he looked directly at Ammon she saw those very blue eyes. It was Virgil! How could it be? Ammon had said he was his cousin but was not a cousin to Evan.

When Clara refilled the pudding dish and put it back on the table, Ammon looked up and gave her a smile, seeing Clara raise her eyebrows questioningly as she looked over toward Virgil. Ammon nodded his head slightly. Virgil noticed Ammon looking at Clara with a knowing look. Virgil made eye contact with Clara for a brief moment as Ammon wiped his hand over his forehead as if to say, "I'll explain later."

Meeting Virgil's glance made Clara squirm. She turned away and yet, from the corner of her eye, she saw Ammon talking to Virgil after motioning slightly in her direction as if explaining something to Virgil. When she reached the end of the table, she noticed they were both looking her way. She headed for the basement.

Late in the afternoon the married people and some of the others were leaving. Clara went to the wash house to get a jar of cream to whip for the supper dessert, while some of the girls were starting to stretch out the table. When she came back into the kitchen, Ammon asked her, "Are you ready to leave?"

"You mean now? I—I am invited to help with the supper table yet," Clara stammered.

"Oh!" he said, his expression changing. He took a deep breath. Apparently the thought had never occurred to him. Finally, he said, "Do you think you'd be able to find another way home, since I have to get Caleb's team back? My driver will be picking me up there in about an hour and a half. I'm not invited for supper," he added.

"I'm sure I can go home with the girls I was planning to come with."

Just then two boys wanted to go out the door and Clara went on her way. It was time to get supper on the table. Clara was a bit disappointed. She had been looking forward to hearing from Ammon as to why Virgil was at the wedding.

Sometime after supper Clara met Erma and asked her if that was Virgil Stauffer. "I thought Ammon said he's not related to Evan."

Erma looked at her a moment, not understanding why Clara was talking about Ammon and Virgil.

"Yes, Virgil is here. He is my cousin and also an acquaintance of Evan's," Erma explained.

It would have been interesting to hear Ammon talk about his surprise in seeing Virgil at the wedding after all. But Ammon had left her life as quickly and unexpectedly as he had entered.

During the few weeks following the wedding, Clara sewed nightgowns for the store. Hardly aware that she was sewing, she sometimes found herself just staring out over the sewing machine, not able to concentrate on what she was doing. Picking up a nightgown, she saw the sleeve was sewn inside out and had to be ripped open.

Some nights Clara lay awake for a long time thinking, wondering why things had taken place as they had: Ammon coming so unexpectedly, going with him to the wedding, and being introduced to Ammon's past sorrows. *Why did God lead us together? What was the purpose?* At any given moment her thoughts dwelled on the tree that Ammon had showed her, and the fact that he didn't notice the new growth that was taking place on the tree. She remembered how Ammon became silent as he grasped what was happening to the tree.

Ammon's thoughts had been deep. Then the bishop was led to explain this very thing in the wedding sermon. Clara shuddered when she remembered again how she had looked up when Allen had mentioned it and Ammon had done the same. She also squirmed as she remembered how stunned she was when she saw Virgil and how she looked at Ammon for an explanation. At times Clara deeply wondered what God had constructed under the mist.

Some days the temptations pressed sorely. Clara wondered why God had denied her speaking with Ammon again, cutting off the ride home. Then she realized that if it would have been granted her, likely the temptations would have pressed even harder. Every once in awhile she had to rip open a seam; she couldn't concentrate on sewing. She even found herself singing, "By and by the mist will lift . . ."

Chapter Twenty-Eight

On a November day as she hung out the wash after Calebs left for an ordination in Mississippi, Clara pondered over the words from the Bible that had once been such an admonishment and comfort to her and now had proved their power and truth again. "God will not suffer you to be tempted above that ye are able to bear, but will make a way to escape that you can bear." God had not failed her; He had again made a way of escape.

The news had shattered the community when word leaked out that Ammon was dating Lena. Clara's eyes misted a bit at the giving up of the dreams she had been entertaining too much. She felt happy for Lena, who was older than she was and nearer Ammon's age. Lena had so faithfully cared for her mother during the years she had Alzheimer's. Her mother died about eight months ago, leaving Lena alone in her grief. Now God was sending her a strong helpmate.

Likely Lena would someday go to the house and see the sheep on the hillside and watch the bantams roam around the place. She would cook Ammon cakes that have body rather than the store-bought spongy ones, and she would bake bread and cook apple butter to put on it. Lena would be missed in the circle of girls, but they would rejoice with her. She had been faithful in her lowly lot and now would be entrusted with greater things.

The mist had lifted; the view had become clear. Ammon needed to be aware of the new growth to the tree to help him see the need of his own grafting. *How vain I would be to enter on ways that God has not chosen for me if He wouldn't interfere.* Erma's wedding had brought Lena and Ammon together. How different things look after the mist is lifted.

Clara tried to fight the thoughts that continued to tempt her. If Lena and Ammon marry, their circle of friends would be brought together again, and it would bring Virgil, since he is a cousin to Ammon. She must not think about it. "Each victory will help you some other to win," the song reminded her.

As the February sun shone in the window, sharing some warmth, Clara gathered up more doughnuts and laid them in the hot lard. She was making doughnuts for Virginia, and Virginia suggested she do it in her own kitchen, which is safer than having small children around hot lard.

Clara watched as the bubbles gathered around the cold doughnuts and sizzled, causing the doughnuts to expand. Life was bringing so many changes. She thought of the words, "And watch the fleeting changes of life's uncertain ways," while she flipped the doughnuts over on the other side.

Lena and Ammon were published to be married in a few weeks, but their minds were immune to that. They just had time to get used to the idea when the news leaked out that Vera was dating Virgil!

Clara watched the bubbles rush up to the new batch of doughnuts in the hot lard, sizzling and forming bubbles. After the doughnuts were raised, the bubbles dissolved into the lard. This reminded her of the dreams of life and temptations that are trying to come rushing in life, then vanishing after the purpose of them is fulfilled. They grow and sizzle out after they have worked for the exceeding and eternal weight of glory.

As Clara got a bowl out of the cupboard to sugar the doughnuts, she saw the poem about the violet.

. . . And yet it was a lovely flower
With colors bright and fair
It might have graced a rosy bower
Instead of hiding there.

And yet it was content to bloom
With modest tints arrayed
And there differ its sweet perfume
Within the silent shade.

If only she could be more like the violet, content to bloom with modest tints arrayed and here differ its sweet perfume in her little world.

. . .That I may also learn to grow
In sweet humility.

While watching her friends being transplanted in the rose gardens. Then Clara heard herself singing:

For by and by the mist will lift
And darkness turn to day,
And looking back we'll praise His Name
Who led us all the way.

Yes, when the mist lifts we understand and praise His name. When the mist of Jordan lifts, then can I better praise Him to let me grow within the silent shade. Maybe in the rose garden the sun would press down hard at times. Yes, the mist will lift by and by.

Later in the day, after school Paul Henry stopped in and dropped her mail on the table. A joy filled her heart when she saw her circle letter had come containing letters from other older single girls throughout other communities and states as well from this area.

She wouldn't read them all now. Lydia Ann had asked her to redress her doll. While Lydia Ann was getting the clothing together, Clara quickly searched for Bertha's letter. Her letters always contained refreshing phrases for her thirsty soul, renewing her faith.

As she read the letter, Clara smiled at how Bertha's disappointing days turned into a blessing. That sounded just like Bertha. Coming to the end of the letter, she read the poem:

> *Is this the right way home, oh, Lord?*
> *The clouds are dark and still.*
> *The stony road is sharp and hard;*
> *Each step brings some new ill.*
> *I thought the road would brighter grow*
> *And the sun with warmth glow*
> *And joyous songs from free hearts flow—*
> *Is this the right way home?*
> *Yes, child, this very path I trod*
> *The clouds were dark for me.*
> *The stony road was sharp and hard,*
> *No sight but faith could see*
> *That at the end, the sun shines bright*
> *Forever where there is no night*
> *And glad hearts rest from earth's fierce fight,*
> *It is the right way home.*

As she read the line, "No sight but faith could see," tears of sympathy and understanding filled her eyes and spilled over when she read, "and glad hearts rest from earth's fierce fight." She would have to copy that in her notebook. Maybe some day she'd want to share it with someone.

Sensing that Lydia Ann had returned, Clara looked up and saw her dark brown eyes staring at her own tear-filled eyes. In innocence, she asked, "Where does it hurt?"

Clara smiled at the child's concern and answered, "My heart just hurts a little."

Lydia Ann dropped her doll and doll clothes on the floor and showed Clara where she hurt her leg yesterday in the barn after she crawled into a cow pen. Her mother had put a bandage on it.

"I didn't even cry," Lydia Ann said looking at Clara.

Clara picked up the doll and clothing and asked which dress she wanted on the doll.

The earth would be a dull place if it contained no small children, Clara thought, and she realized how much more she valued the contents of her faith chest than that of the things she used to treasure and dream about in her hope chest.

After the doll was dressed, Lydia Ann was off upstairs to join the rest of the family. Clara rose and went to the sewing machine to work on some nightgowns that were on order. Her eyes caught sight of the poem she had hung by the sewing machine—the poem that she had hunted—and read it:

> *I heard a bird at break of day,*
> *Sing from the autumn trees,*
> *A song so musical and calm,*
> *So full of certainties.*
>
> *No man, I think, could listen long,*
> *Except upon his knees;*
> *Yet, this was but a simple bird,*
> *Alone among dead trees.*

Clara was suddenly refreshed in spirit that she also could praises to God, even if alone among the dead trees. *I can rejoice that the mist will lift, when I can better see the purpose of blooming in the valley; hidden from the view of the well-beaten path leading to the rose garden of marriage.*